A Wee M[...]

"Peggy Winn brings a bit of Scotland home to her Scottish-themed shop in Vermont, but this time it's more than she bargained for in this enjoyable debut. A great start to a new series!"
—Sheila Connolly, *New York Times* bestselling author of the County Cork Mysteries

"The very first paragraph of *A Wee Murder in My Shop* hooked me. . . . It is the town of Hamelin, Vermont, however, that charms its way into the readers' hearts. . . . A fun start to the ScotShop Mystery series." —Fresh Fiction

"Fran Stewart has done something so incredibly right with this new series. She whisked me away to the land of Scotland right from the beginning, and the magic of Scotland carried through, even when Peggy returned . . . to Hamelin. . . . A strong start to what is going to be a fabulous series. She's created very memorable characters, full of charm and mischief, and readers will be fondly recalling this adventure long after they turn the last page. If you haven't picked up this first book in the ScotShop Mysteries yet, go grab a copy today, because it is going to be one series you don't want to miss!" —Cozy Mystery Book Reviews

"Scotland, a seven-hundred-year-old ghost, a hunky police officer, and [the] murder of a cheating boyfriend. What's not to like in the new ScotShop Mystery series?"
—Lesa's Book Critiques

"An interesting concept that you might expect in a time-travel romance, only it is a cozy mystery—which provides a completely different flair." —Mysteries and My Musings

Berkley Prime Crime titles by Fran Stewart

A WEE MURDER IN MY SHOP
A WEE DOSE OF DEATH

A Wee Dose
of Death

Fran Stewart

BERKLEY PRIME CRIME, NEW YORK

An imprint of Penguin Random House LLC
375 Hudson Street, New York, New York 10014

A WEE DOSE OF DEATH

A Berkley Prime Crime Book / published by arrangement with the author

Copyright © 2016 by Fran Stewart.
Penguin supports copyright. Copyright fuels creativity, encourages diverse voices,
promotes free speech, and creates a vibrant culture. Thank you for buying an authorized
edition of this book and for complying with copyright laws by not reproducing, scanning, or
distributing any part of it in any form without permission. You are supporting writers and
allowing Penguin to continue to publish books for every reader.

BERKLEY® PRIME CRIME and the PRIME CRIME design are trademarks
of Penguin Random House LLC.
For more information, visit penguin.com.

ISBN: 978-0-425-27032-5

PUBLISHING HISTORY
Berkley Prime Crime mass-market edition / January 2016

PRINTED IN THE UNITED STATES OF AMERICA

10 9 8 7 6 5 4 3 2 1

Cover art by Jesse Reisch.
Cover design by Diana Kolsky.
Interior text design by Kelly Lipovich.

This is a work of fiction. Names, characters, places, and incidents either are the product of
the author's imagination or are used fictitiously, and any resemblance to actual persons,
living or dead, business establishments, events, or locales is entirely coincidental.

If you purchased this book without a cover, you should be aware that this book is stolen
property. It was reported as "unsold and destroyed" to the publisher, and neither the author
nor the publisher has received any payment for this "stripped book."

Penguin
Random
House

*This book is lovingly dedicated to my sister Diana,
who believes in me and my ghosts.*

Acknowledgments

I owe a huge debt of gratitude to the group of artists who invited me to go along with them to Folly Beach, SC, for an entire week of painting—or, in my case, of writing. They went off to paint each day, leaving me alone, in a windswept house overlooking the ocean. The shape of Wee Dose formed itself to the backdrop of seabirds calling and waves rolling in.

Then my friend Peggy Dixon offered me the use of her mountain cabin. That was where I wrapped up the story amid towering North Georgia pines. Having a mama bear and two cubs living in the area helped with inspiration. So did the ride on the mule.

Sharron Grovner, a woman who works at the Reynolds Mansion on Sapelo Island, suggested the Univex and invented a story line unique to her, in which she had Karaline give a ride to a stranger (NOT recommended) who just happened to be an out-of-work pastry chef. I told her that with such a vivid imagination, she should be writing books herself.

Erica Jensen, my Middle English researcher, finds lovely words for Dirk.

Someone at Kittredge Foodservice Equipment & Supplies in Williston, Vermont (I'm sorry I didn't get his name), confirmed that it would take an SUV to haul an SRM-20. Then he passed me on to Bob Beattie, who assured me that Chester could get away with wearing red suspenders. I relocated Kittredge's warehouse/showroom from Williston to Winooski for the purposes of the plotline. When I lived in Vermont years ago, I learned that the Abenaki word *Ouinousqui* (as spelled by early French explorers) meant *wild onions*, which grew plentifully along the "Onion River."

Michele McMahon, a nurse who works with the Emergency Preparedness departments of three Georgia counties, said a ten-hour operation was more believable than the four-hour one I'd originally written, considering the extent of gunshot damage. She also admitted that cold ghostly healing hands would be a big help, and we grossed out everybody else at the table as we talked about perforated intestines and nicked diaphragms.

David Funderburk, biology teacher extraordinaire, shared stories of his years teaching biology to students of all ages and grades and gave me the silver nitrate story.

Jesse Reisch illustrated the cover of *A Wee Murder in My Shop*, the first ScotShop Mystery, and put a Scottie dog on the cover—something I hadn't even considered—so, of course, I had to go back and write in a dog for the Sinclairs—and, in this book, Scamp for the ScotShop.

Scamp evolved from only a vague idea to a real pooch after I contacted Rhea Spence, president of the Scottish Terrier Club of Greater Atlanta, who invited me to a dog show. There I met Judi Helton. Both these women added greatly to my knowledge of Scotties and educated me on the value of maintaining distinct breeds.

Kari Hill of Charthill Scottish Terriers was showing several of her dogs that day, and spent a great deal of time explaining, sharing, bragging about, and just generally loving her dogs with me. She showed me their teeth, let me pat their waterproof coats, explained their history, let me feel their heart-shaped rib cages, and showed me how stable their broad rear ends are when they "play patty-cake." She's the one who suggested that Scamp might like to sit in the display window. "Give him an ottoman, would you? He'd like something soft to sit on."

Edwin Lowe gave me the term "GBBD."

Finally, I must thank my agent, John Talbot, who found me and coached me through the process of being traditionally published; Michelle Vega, my editor at Berkley Prime Crime, who recognizes deadwood, sees what needs to be expanded, and still manages to treat me with utmost gentleness; and all the fantastic professionals at Berkley Prime Crime, who turn my manuscripts into works of art.

From my house beside a creek
on the other side of Hog Mountain, GA,
Fran Stewart
April 2015

1

The Joy of a Wee Cabin

Marcus Wantstring wasn't looking for a place to die. He was looking for a quiet place in the snow-covered mountains of Vermont to get his thoughts together so he and Denby wouldn't look like deadbeats. He didn't want anyone to think less of Denby, now that Denby couldn't defend himself.

He propped his cross-country skis outside next to the overly tall door and looked around the small cabin. The perfect place for his purposes. He was glad an early blizzard was on the way. There usually wasn't this much snow in October. Snow would keep other people away. He had a deadline. *Deadline*, he thought, and the emphasis was on "dead." He shook his head—too much drama.

He had another problem, too. It niggled at the back of his consciousness. One of Denby's most promising graduate students—John Nhat Copley. Denby had found a printout of a sparse e-mail balled up in the trash. Something about identity theft. It sounded like a big plan, but surely nothing could come of it. Copley may have been brilliant, but he was stupid as a paramecium to leave the printout behind. Denby, of course, had brought the e-mail to Marcus for a brainstorming session. Marcus hadn't questioned why Denby was going through the trash. Denby had always seemed to have his own way of doing things.

They'd had no way of knowing whether Copley had infected any of the other students with his stupidity, but nobody else seemed to be acting any differently. Denby tried to track down the e-mail's sender, but the account had been closed down. Still, just in case, the two professors had collaborated, then e-mailed Copley, asking him to explain himself. They drafted another letter, an official one, banning Copley from the department, but decided not to send that one. Innocent until proven guilty. But Copley never replied to the e-mail. He disappeared, seemingly overnight.

Marcus chuckled to himself. Maybe Copley had been writing an espionage thriller, and the supposed e-mail was part of the manuscript. This wasn't the time to worry about it. He had his own priorities. But why had the boy taken off?

He slung his backpack onto the sturdy central table and pulled a thick green binder from it, along with a water-purification kit, an aluminum pot stuffed with numerous packets of food, and a box of utility-grade candles. He moved the binder to one of the two chairs and removed the food packages from the cooking pot. He unhooked his hiking boots and pulled out an extra pair of socks. He ran his finger across the wildly improbable pattern of brilliant variegated yarn. His wife had knitted them for him as a Halloween joke years ago—before . . . before everything happened—and they'd turned out to be his favorites, maybe not for wearing to work, although he'd done so on occasion when the weather was cold enough. And, of course, every October thirty-first for sure. He loved the things she knit for him. Sweaters, socks, scarves. He always felt like he was wrapping her love around him when he wore them.

She'd started calling him Mark soon after her surgery. Although he was Marcus to everyone else, Mark was a special connection between himself and the woman he loved with all his heart, even after all these years together. He paused, thinking fondly of how she'd slept through his gentle good-bye kiss that morning well before dawn. He was a lucky man. His lips drew up in a smile, one that was surprisingly soft on so angular a face.

He didn't know his luck was about to run out.

2

The Joy of a Cozy Fire

People who don't like winter simply should not move to Vermont, as far as I'm concerned. Visit in the summer or fall, by all means, and buy lots of souvenirs here in Hamelin. Buy an extra number of them in my store, the ScotShop— preferably expensive items like full dress kilts, or even lots of little items, like tartan ties or reproductions of the Loch Ness Monster. Buy one for every single relative back home. But either live somewhere else, or quit your infernal bellyaching. Ten degrees Fahrenheit is the way winter works in the Green Mountains. Get over it. Or get yourself a good wood-burning stove and four or five sets of thermal underwear. Silk long johns and sock liners. Good woolen hats and gloves. Or GORE-TEX if you want to be fancy.

Of course, I didn't say any of this to Emily. Thank goodness this was a phone call. I couldn't have hidden my irritation face-to-face.

"Mark left me all alone again, Peggy," she whined, her

voice almost echoing, as if she were in a barrel. "It's bad enough that he works in Burlington all the time and we only come here on weekends, but now he gets a week off, and does he stay here? No. He took off before dawn on his skis and didn't even say good-bye. Here I am freezing cold in this godforsaken house."

She even sounded cold, and I could swear I heard her teeth chatter; but I wasn't going to feel sorry for her. Their house was one of those new energy-efficient ones outside of town. Probably had R-150 insulation all around—or whatever number meant a lot of warmth. I moved a little closer to my woodstove. "Just make yourself some hot chocolate," I advised. "That'll warm anybody up."

"But he left me alone, Peggy. Why does he do that?"

I'd seen Emily's husband only once. Tall and lanky beside his short, pudgy wife, the two of them like the ancient cartoon characters Mutt and Jeff, walking up Hickory Lane, past my house. As far as I could see, he hadn't said a word the entire time I watched them. She'd talked nonstop, of course. I heard some time ago that the loneliest people were the ones who were unsuitably married. Not that I had any way of knowing from personal experience.

"Emily!" I interrupted her flow. "You might enjoy cross-country skiing if you'd give it a try." Not that I believed for a moment she ever would. "With the Appalachian Trail not half a mile from your house, think of the gorgeous scenery. But you have to go outside if you want to enjoy it."

"You sound just like Mark. He taught me to ski when we were first married, but I didn't like it. I never could get the hang of it, and he just wouldn't understand."

I rolled my eyes at Dirk Farquharson, the fourteenth-century ghost I'd acquired on a trip to Scotland this past summer, who stood looking out my living room bay window.

I pointed to his left. "Whoops," I said into the phone. "Have to run, Emily. There's the door."

"You go answer it, Peg," she told me. "I'll wait."

"No. I'll probably be a while. I'll catch up with you later." I disconnected and heaved a sigh.

"Ye were nae quite honest with Mistress Emily. There is naebody come a-calling at the door."

My fourteenth-century Scottish conscience. Even though I could almost see through him, even though he'd been dead 653 years, he still had opinions that were hard to shake. "I didn't say there was anybody standing outside. All I said was, *There's the door.* And"—I pointed again—"there it is." It seemed perfectly logical to me. "If she wanted to think someone was knocking on it, that's her problem."

He made that low-pitched, grumbly Scottish sound of disapproval.

"Don't growl at me," I said, even though I rather liked hearing it. It emanated from his massive chest. I tried to keep my eyes from scanning the length of him, but lost the battle. He was so tall, so black-haired, so gentle, so fierce, so . . . Scottish.

"Ye should nae tell untruths."

So stubborn, too. "This is the way things are in the twenty-first century, as I've told you numerous times. I don't like getting trapped on the phone. Anyway, what's it to you?"

He gave me a long, level look from under those thick straight brows of his. "I didna ask to come here," he said. "I didna desire to leave my home."

"Yeah, well—"

"I dinna like some of what I see here. Now."

"I may not like it, either, but there's nothing I can do about it."

"Nay. Ye are nae right about that. Ye *could* do something. Ye could stop telling untruths."

"Would you rather have me tell her she's boring me out of my gourd?"

"What would be a *gord*?"

"Never mind that. You just need to loosen up a little and accept things the way they are." I tried not to sound supercilious, but from the look on Dirk's face, I didn't seem to have accomplished it. Poor Dirk. I was grumpy about Emily and I was taking it out on my ghost.

"Mistress Emily seems lonely to me."

He was probably right. She'd walked into the ScotShop about four months ago and spent an hour complaining. It was a slow day, so I couldn't begrudge her the time, but it struck me as a little bit weird that she found so much fault with everything. Wasn't there any joy anywhere in her life? Dirk had, of course, felt free to eavesdrop with impunity, since he was invisible to her. Naturally I hadn't been able to reply to any of his comments while she was within earshot.

Since then she'd taken to calling me on my days off, and I usually felt too sorry for her to send her to voice mail.

"Her husband's looking to retire down here," I said. "That's why they bought the house."

"What would be this *retyre*? I asked ye once before, but ye didna answer me."

The words Dirk didn't know would fill a dictionary. Of course, I didn't understand a lot of the words he used—he'd died in Scotland when people were still speaking Middle English, like Chaucer. I'd decided there was some sort of transcendental translation agency at work for most of our speech, but we still had a few words to learn. Sometimes I could figure out what he meant just through the context: *Ye needna whinge so* meant he wanted me to stop complaining. Well, right now I wanted *him* to quit grumbling. "'Retire' means to quit working and take it easy."

He squinted. Two lines appeared between his heavy eyebrows. If he wasn't careful, those lines would etch themselves into his face. No, wait. He was a ghost. He'd never get any more wrinkles than those crinkly laugh lines he already had around his eyes. Nothing had changed for him since 1359, the year he died. Except that he and the shawl he was attached to had been transported to twenty-first-century America, a country that hadn't even existed when he was alive. Well, the land existed, and people were here; but America wasn't even an idea in any Scottish head 653 years ago.

Retire. I could almost see his brain still shuffling the idea around. Back in the fourteenth century when he was alive, maybe nobody ever retired. If they survived infancy and childhood, then they worked all their lives, got old, and died. Or at least that was what I thought had probably happened. I was truly going to have to bone up on my history. Chaucer's *Canterbury Tales* was about all I'd known of the time back then, until I bought an old shawl and met Macbeath Donlevy Freusach Finlay Macearachar Macpheidiran of Clan Farquharson. You can see why I opted to call him Dirk.

3

Settling In

Marcus Wantstring glanced at his green three-ring binder. Thank goodness he'd found it; otherwise this whole trip would have been a waste of time. He hadn't known where it was at first, and the early-morning dark was getting considerably lighter by the time he remembered he'd left it in the car. So he'd stuffed it in his backpack on top of a brand-new bag of Tootsie Rolls. Well, it had been *almost* brand-new. Marcus patted the rolled candies in a zippered pocket on his pants leg. A Tootsie Roll was a good reward for having left so quietly, locking the garage side door behind him, so he hadn't woken his sleeping wife.

He reached for the binder and flipped through it idly, reading a sentence here, a paragraph there. He jotted a five-pointed star in the margin on page 153. He'd have to do something about that section. Without any particular reason he could identify, he remembered that next week was his wife's birthday, and her sister had planned to fly up from D.C. as a surprise. With this storm, there was a chance nobody would be flying anywhere. He ought to call her and select an alternate date, just in case. He turned back to the first page and jotted today's date in his distinctive green ink. *Call Josie Calais again (when I get cell service)*, he wrote, wondering as he did so why he was bothering to write himself a note. He wasn't likely to forget something as important as his wife's birthday surprise.

He left his camping ax where it was for the moment, stuck through a loop on the side of the backpack. He spread his sleeping bag out on the lower level of the rustic bunk bed built into a corner. Might as well get comfortable since he'd be here three days at the very least, maybe four.

He left enough food for one meal on the table and put the rest of the packages on the wooden platform of the top bunk. He was tall enough that he didn't have to strain to check for rodent droppings. Only a few, and they looked pretty dry; they were old enough that he might not have to worry about mice nibbling through the packaging.

Idly, he pulled out one of the half dozen Tootsie Rolls still left in his pants pocket. Nothing like a Tootsie Roll to sharpen mental focus. He unwrapped it and stuffed the wrapper back in his pocket along with the two others he'd already placed there. *Bring it in with you, take it out with you*: the motto of any good camper.

He rounded the table to sit on the second chair—the green binder was on the one closest to the door—and bent to remove his cross-country skiing shoes and replace them with his crazy socks and his hiking boots.

The blizzard inundating the East Coast didn't bother him. Vermont always made it through blizzards without even noticing them, but this storm would have the eastern half of the country shut down. Except for Vermont. He needed solitude?

Well, he sure was going to get it. Nobody would be out plea-sure skiing on this snowy Sunday.

Emily stood next to the phone for several minutes, glued, as it were, to the spot. She didn't want to be a complainer. She always hated herself when she did that. But she just couldn't seem to stop herself from nitpicking about every-thing and everybody. Especially about Mark. There was something that bubbled out from somewhere inside her, making her criticize her husband, complain about him. Bad-mouth him. Like a little chained monster in her that clawed its way up her throat—her throat. Emily felt like she was choking, and she eased a finger into the collar of her turtle-neck. She pulled the fabric away from the front of her neck. As she did so, she felt the faint ridge of the scar.

These spasms never lasted for long, but when they hit like this, she didn't know what to do except to loosen the stretchy fabric, stand still, and wait for her body to slow down. The monster inside her was what made her do it, the choking, the complaining. It made her grouse at everyone. She was always harping at Mark. She couldn't stop herself. It wasn't his fault, but something inside her—that monster—believed that if she had never gotten married in the first place, if she'd fol-lowed her dream without interruption, somehow she wouldn't have had to go through . . . what she'd had to go through.

She'd read in some self-help book her sister Josie had given her about how the *deepest self*—that was what it was called—knew the truth at a visceral level, even if one didn't want to acknowledge it. Or admit it. Well, it was all very well and good to theorize up one side and down the other, but living with . . . a monster inside her, there was no way to get past that fact. She wasn't even sure she knew whether she had a *deeper self.* It had been so long since she'd believed in anything.

Once her throat stopped the spasms, she straightened the magazines and newspapers on the coffee table, wishing again that she had tidied the house in Burlington before they'd left this time. Sandra would see it, and Sandra was a good enough friend not to care, but Emily would have felt better if she'd taken just a few minutes to wash the dishes. She hadn't, because Mark had been in such a hurry to leave. She didn't understand him. She hadn't understood him for years. And, of course, she'd forgotten to water the plants, but she'd called Sandra and asked her to stop in and take care of that. She would *never* have asked Sandra to wash the dishes she'd forgotten about. Never.

4

Pop Goes the Weasel

Mac Campbell had always been graceful on skis, much more so than when he walked on solid ground. Every gliding step he took today, though, seemed to fuel his anger. He had never been one to be particularly aware of his body, except when he admired his physique in the privacy of his own house, so he didn't pay any attention to the way his muscles tightened with every negative thought. He'd been mad at that woman for months, and he still felt irked as hell about all the crap around Mason Kilmarty's death in Peggy Winn's Scot-Shop store last summer. Mac was CHIEF of the Hamelin, Vermont, police force. In his mind, the capital letters were automatic. Yet that upstart Peggy was the one who'd discovered Mason's murderer.

He'd never admit it to anyone, and he hardly admitted it even to himself, but he, Chief Mac Campbell, hadn't had a clue. Not a single clue, while that half-baked twit of a female had overpowered the perp. *Perp.* Mac liked words like that.

Sounded so—so *cop*. Twenty years he'd policed in Hamelin, with him in the top position for eleven of those years. Good thing the previous chief had croaked, and there was Mac, the best—well, the only—candidate to fill his shoes.

Irritation made Mac ski faster. Heading uphill like this, it was easier the faster he went. Slow down too much on cross-country skis and you'll tend to slide backward. He was making good time, though.

He hadn't skied or even hiked this particular trail in three or four years. There were others he enjoyed more, especially the Fife; it was quiet, even though that trail had four or five houses on it. In the summer, the Fife skirted far behind the houses; in winter, they were closed up tight.

Nothing ever changed in Hamelin, so he was sure there wasn't any new construction out here. This trail, the Perth, had only the one cabin. Just one room and an outhouse. There was an old wood-burning stove, too. Maybe he'd come back this summer and stay a few days.

For today, he planned to ski right on past it. That way, he should get to the top of the Perth trail in another two hours. He'd eat the sandwiches and one of the energy bars he'd packed and then head back toward Hamelin. Maybe take the other fork on the way down just for some variety.

Trouble was, Hamelin was too quiet. Mostly speeding tickets, an occasional burglary, penny-ante stuff. Only a few murders, usually by stupid dolts just asking to get caught. No scope for real policing.

Mac's idea of real policing involved car chases, shoot-outs, hostage situations, and a little karate thrown in for good measure. Not that he practiced the kata very often. Still, he knew how to do Swallow Pivoting on a Beach and Extract from a Castle with the best of them. Or were those Kung Fu moves? Couldn't keep the names straight. He'd taken lessons here and there over the years—karate, jujitsu, tae kwon do, kung fu. There were a couple of dojos in the nearby town of Arkane. It was easy to mix up all those names. He raised his ski poles into a double sweeping block. If Peggy hadn't gotten there first, he could have taken out that son of a gun with a few well-placed—

In that moment of inattention, he didn't notice that the ski tracks he followed veered two or three feet to the left of a slight mound. Mac went straight, and his right ski caught on something. *Probably a snow-buried branch*, Mac had time to think. Mac had skied cross-country all his life. Since he was five. He should have been able to recover quickly, but he'd been so focused on his anger over Peggy Winn, and so off balance with his poles in the air, he'd taken just a moment too long to react. He was down, spraddle-legged, before he could even squawk. He felt the front half of his ski immobilized by the branch. The front edge of his ski shoe was locked into place on his ski. The inside of his right leg slammed against something hard.

The *pop* of breaking bone—and the excruciating pain— told him something was wrong. Very wrong.

Earlier in the week, Wantstring had tried to ignore his students' collective sigh of relief when he canceled the next two graduate seminar classes that met on Saturdays and Mondays. He couldn't blame them. They needed more time on their papers. He'd felt his own sigh of relief over those cancellations. His research assistants would handle the undergraduate classes until he returned.

He pulled two USB thumb drives from one of his multiple pockets and tucked one of them under the rolled-up flannel shirt he used as a pillow. He wedged a second one in between two logs halfway down the woodpile. Enough wood inside for a week at least, and twice that amount outside under the wide overhang of the roof. The cabin had been well designed for a Vermont winter, even one like this, with heavy October snows.

He distributed a few other small items here and there around the cabin. Time to get the fire built so he could melt snow for washing. He patted his shirt pocket and felt his green ballpoint pens and the box of waterproof matches. What more did he need?

He thought for a moment and retrieved two of the energy bars he'd stowed on the top bunk. He put them on the simple square table next to his lunch. Nothing like an energy bar snack for later, to get his brain revved up in an hour or two when he was bound to get stuck on a difficult paragraph. Thinking about the bars reminded him—he retrieved his cell phone from the windowsill and checked those bars. No service. That was just as well. Nobody would have any reason to call. He'd made it clear that he was going to be unavailable for an entire week. The phone charge wouldn't have lasted more than a few days at best. He powered it off with a deep sense of satisfaction.

Once all his supplies were arranged to his liking, he stepped away from the cabin to gather a pot of snow to melt for wash water. With his filter system, he could use the snowmelt for drinking water, too.

He had an itchy feeling, like somebody might be watching him, but one quick glance around the clearing and at the trees beyond reassured him that he was alone. Completely alone.

5

When the Store Is Closed

I pulled my old plaid shawl tighter around my shoulders. I couldn't help being grateful for having bought it in that mysterious shop in Pitlochry, one of my favorite towns in Scotland. That had been four months ago. Little had I known the shawl came with its own baggage—this almost transparent, incredibly rugged ghost, complete with full-sleeved home-spun shirt, a Farquharson tartan kilt—the old-fashioned kind made of nine yards of handwoven and hand-felted fabric. He had to pleat it each morning, lie down on it, roll it around his . . . I was getting distracted here. Anyway, he didn't have to do all that anymore, now that he was dead.

I took two more well-aged maple logs from the stack in the corner and added them to my beautiful bright red Defiant FlexBurn wood-burning stove. Flames leapt up as I closed the door. I moved the damper lever back to keep the heat from overpowering the living room. Through the heavy glass insert, the thick bed of coals glimmered brightly, casting a

reddish glow over the dark living room. Even with the cur-
tains wide-open, the cloudy afternoon light seemed to be
growing dimmer. There'd be more snow by midafternoon;
they were predicting at least another twenty inches overnight,
on top of the two feet that had fallen last night. Probably not
a full-out blizzard, but it might be close to one. Nobody would
be going anywhere tomorrow.

Fine with me. I wasn't opening my store, the ScotShop, a
piece of old Scotland, today. There weren't any tour buses
scheduled, and—this time of year, at least, once the autumn
leaves were off the trees—the tour buses were about the only
thing to liven up the downtown area, especially on a Sunday,
and the ScotShop was always closed on Mondays. The blizzard
that had stopped most of the eastern cities in their tracks was
just one more regular old winter day here in Hamelin. By
Tuesday, they'd have the roads cleared and we'd have an influx
of tourists, although the regular tour buses from Boston might
not be able to make it. The store was ready. Last Friday, I'd
received a long-awaited order of kilts, tartan ties, ghillie
brogues, and *sgian-dubhs*. Gilda, my shop assistant, who was
finally back from her sixteen-week sojourn in the alcohol rehab
center, had helped me log most of it in and get it on the shelves.
Sam and Shoe—they were my twin cousins and employees
as well—had pitched in. Many hands make light work. My
mother always used to tell me that. Still did, as a matter of
fact. Like an eerie echo, my ghost had told me the same thing
as he'd watched the four of us unpacking, pricing, and display-
ing the new merchandise.

Once last summer, he'd told me how sorry he was that he
couldn't help. Ghosts can't pick things up. Can't eat. Can't sleep.
Can't even . . . Well, never mind that.

"Don't worry about it, Dirk," I'd told him when there was
nobody around to hear me talking to him. Nobody else could

see or hear him—nobody except my dear friend Karaline Logg, who owned the Logg Cabin, the wonderful restaurant across a small courtyard from the ScotShop. It was open for breakfast and lunch only—and Karaline made a very good living offering the state's best maple pancakes, to name only one of her specialties.

Karaline had picked up my shawl one day and found out that she could see my ghost, although other people—well, one other person: Harper—had held it to no effect. No effect, that was, other than a speeding up of my heart as I wondered how I was going to explain Dirk, who appeared to be a permanent part of my household, to Harper, whom I would have loved to have as a permanent part of the same place. Only Harper hadn't seen or heard anything out of the ordinary.

I wasn't really sure why I was the one who'd bought the old, old tartan shawl, one that had been handed down from great-grandmother to great-granddaughter through thirty or thirty-five generations. The perfectly ordinary-looking woman who'd sold it to me in Pitlochry when I went to Scotland on a buying trip had mentioned that she had no daughters or grand-daughters to pass it on to, so the shawl would have to go to her sister's line. But if that was the case, why had she sold it to me? And why hadn't I been able to find the store again when I went back the very next day?

It was all a mystery to me. Peigi, Dirk's long-dead lady-love, had woven the shawl—in the fourteenth century, if you can believe something as crazy as that.

There were days I thought I'd just made this all up, like a waking dream, but then I'd turn around to find Dirk talking quietly to Shorty. My cat could see him. Spiders were attracted to him. So was Tessa, my brother's service dog, although Tessa had learned early on not to try to lick Dirk's face or his fingers. Animals—or people—who touched him accidentally ended up with a disconcerting pins-and-needles feeling, and if they made the mistake of colliding with him, it could leave them disoriented or, even worse, flat on the floor, for quite some time.

But I'd learned all of this slowly, over the past four months. The basic truth was that, somehow or other, the shawl had found its way to me, a twenty-first-century woman with a penchant for all things Scottish. This 653-years-dead Scot came along with it. If I folded the shawl and set it aside, Dirk disappeared. Where he went I didn't know, and he didn't, either. He'd tried to describe it, but spoken language just didn't come close.

All I had to do to get him back was to place the shawl around my shoulders, and there he was, as dependable as the door.

I'd found his presence particularly comforting—after the initial shock, that was—but this closeness was beginning to wear. I felt like I was back in college again with a clinging roommate. It wouldn't have been so bad having a hunk like him around, except that he found a lot to criticize about my life and the way I chose to live it.

His particular beef lately had been the fact that I wasn't married. "We don't have to get married in the twenty-first century," I'd explained over and over again.

"Ye dinna have a man," he'd observed—last August, I think it was. It was one of those bright, brilliant days. I'd taken him for a walk along the shores of Lake Ness, just north of Hamelin. We'd sat down on a grassy bank, and he lay back with his arm under his head while I picked dandelions and made a yellow chain, splitting half of each stem carefully and threading the next flower through it.

There was a whole congregation of little spiders in the grass around him. I didn't know whether other ghosts attracted spiders—not having met any other ghosts—but Dirk certainly did.

"Ye need a man to protect ye," he said.

"I don't need protection."

He'd narrowed his eyes at me, but rather than belabor the point, he struck out with another fourteenth-century argument. "And what about bairns?"

"Bairns? You mean children?" I knew darn well what a bairn was; I just didn't want to deal with my conflicting feelings about child raising right then. I was only thirty. There was still time. Trouble was I had to find the right man.

Harper.

I tried to cancel that thought. Nothing had happened between us. Nothing except an increased pulse on my part.

"Aye. Ye dinna have a man, and ye dinna have bairns who will care for ye when ye've lost half your teeth and can eat naught but gruel."

"Gruel? Yuck!" I joined one end of the dandelion chain to the other and placed the resulting crown atop my head. "I'll have you know I have investments to pay for my old age, and what makes you think I'm going to let my teeth decay? I have a very good dentist, and I get my teeth cleaned twice a year."

I hadn't explained either my financial situation or modern dentistry to Dirk—at least I didn't think I had.

"Dih-kay? What would that be?"

"It means 'rot.'" I'd read enough to know how many people lost their teeth back then. "Decay is what happens to teeth when people don't use toothbrushes."

Toothbrushes he understood. In fact, he'd told me once that he'd been taught to use a sturdy willow twig with a smashed end to clean his teeth. An extraordinary fourteenth-century toothbrush. His teeth were certainly white, as white as the daisies intermingled with the dandelions in the field around us.

"The snow, 'tis falling."

I looked up, surprised to find myself in my living room.

There was no crown of yellow dandelions, no daisies, no spiders, no lake beside me, and the August sunshine had turned into cloudy mid-October. Dirk, outlined against the gray light of the bay window, seemed particularly pensive. He spread his arms wide and stretched. How can muscles get tight if you're a ghost?

6

A Bone to Pick

Back inside the cabin, Marcus set the snow-filled pot on the empty woodstove. Nothing fancy about this one. In fact, it was little better than the old potbellied stoves had been a hundred years ago. But it was more than adequate for heating this one room.

He looked inside the utilitarian monstrosity. Good. It had been cleaned out, and the last person there had been smart enough to leave a thick layer of ash in the bottom. He shut the door with a sense of satisfaction. The only problem was that the guy hadn't left any kindling. There was a hefty stack of thick logs piled in one corner of the room, but there wasn't anything small enough to catch fire easily.

Cross-country skiing always warmed a person up, but he could feel the cold beginning to seep in. He pulled his favorite soft brown scarf out of the rain hood pocket on his parka, where he had stowed it early that morning. He adjusted it around his neck, making sure the ends didn't hang below his jacket. No need to snag it on a wayward branch. He went to the backpack, unhooked his small ax—just the right size for small logs or kindling—and stepped through the door. The outside pile of firewood, under the overhang of the roof, looked dry and dependable, but there wasn't any kindling there, either. He'd rounded the side of the cabin earlier and checked on it before he parked his skis and came inside.

He and his wife had found the cabin the previous summer. They'd gone hiking up this trail for a picnic shortly after they bought a retirement home just outside the little town of Hamelin, Vermont. Later, they'd thrown a magnificent party, inviting all his colleagues, the graduate students, and neighbors from Burlington. He and his wife had been surprised at how many people showed up. Two of the other professors had looked into buying property in the area, too. His wife had been nervous before the party, but she'd relaxed once the crowd gravitated to the kitchen of the new house. That was where parties—the good parties—always ended up. It was supposed to be an early-afternoon affair: stop by, eat some, talk some, and leave in time for everybody to drive back to Burlington before dark. But somehow or other a group of them ended up hiking the trail, toting graham crackers and chocolate and, of course, marshmallows for s'mores, which they'd toasted over a fire in the clearing. Later, they'd hiked higher up the mountain so they could take the other path—the steep one, the treacherous one—back to town. Stupid thing to do, but nobody had fallen. He glanced out the window. No sign of the fire ring now, not under all that snow. Nothing in the clearing, nothing in the surrounding woods. Just him and his work.

He wondered occasionally if they should have kept quiet about the purchase. No sense in having his colleagues think he was on his way out. But he'd deliberately never said the word "retiring." He'd called it a vacation home. He was still a couple of years away from mandatory retirement—and he'd had plenty to say about *that* policy—but he'd finally decided retiring wouldn't slow him down. He might not have access to the university's lab after he retired, but he still had his mind. Last year, an article about him in *Science Magazine* had declared that his mind was incisive. He liked that. *Incisive.* Like a surgical tool.

Mac lay there with snow drifting gently onto his face, stunned by the agony that tore through him. Of all the stupid things that might have happened, this took the prize. Nobody knew where he was. Even if someone had seen him, he went out skiing so often, nobody would think anything about it. He didn't have to be back at the station until Thursday. A little vacation, he'd told them, although he'd planned to return home before nightfall and spend the next three days watching TV. Nobody would miss him. He knew these woods. He'd never been lost. He'd never been hurt. At least not until now.

He was less than an hour outside Hamelin, but the trail he was on—the Perth trail—wasn't a very popular one. It had a killer steep gradient once you got beyond that little cabin halfway up the trail. But surely someone crazy enough to ski the Perth would come along soon. Maybe the people who'd made the cross-country tracks he'd been following would turn around and come back this way. There were two of them. That much he could tell from the tracks. One of them must have been lagging behind the other, because one set was always on top.

Mac raised his head enough to peer back down the trail through a haze of pain, hoping against hope that someone might be skiing up the trail behind him. He dimly realized that his tracks had pretty much obliterated those he'd been following. It looked like only one—at most two—people had skied here.

Mac might have congratulated himself on his tracking skills, but jolts of pain prevented any positive thoughts. His right leg. This wasn't good. It felt like a badly torn muscle at the top of his leg, but the waves of fire coursing up from the vicinity of his shin were what had him really worried.

He did a quick survey of the rest of him. Head, fine. Arms, check. Heart, still beating. Left leg, workable. How could he have fallen so badly? He'd been thinking about the double sweeping block, and maybe his mind might possibly have wandered, but that wasn't the problem. No, the problem was Peggy Winn. If she'd behaved the way a civilian was supposed to behave and let the police apprehend the killer last summer, then Mac wouldn't have been distracted while he was skiing and he never would have fallen.

The other problem was those people ahead of him—they hadn't tested the path well enough. They shouldn't have led him into such a trap. What was a big rock doing in the middle of a ski trail? Those people ahead of him should have moved it. How could anyone get in a good day's skiing with idiots like that in front of him?

He'd fallen onto his left side. He pushed himself up an inch at a time, every slight movement an exercise in agony, until he could slip off his backpack. Despite the pain, he hauled the pack forward and flipped open one of the side pockets. Empty. Mac swore vehemently. He always put his cell phone in there. Without much hope, he searched the other pockets.

He had enough food and cigarettes for two days, even though he'd planned to be home by nightfall. It always paid to pack extra. He had two bottles of water. He had waterproof matches, so he could melt snow for drinking. He didn't have a sleeping bag, but he'd brought a compact emergency tent, more to conserve heat and protect from the wind than anything else. Here, deep in the woods, he wouldn't have to worry about wind. The rock escarpment rising on the right-hand side of the trail might be a good place to hunker against, if he could get there. He could cover himself with the tent, but without a sleeping bag, he might lose his toes to frostbite before morning if he couldn't keep them moving.

And he most definitely could not. Even *thinking* about moving his toes incited the flaming agony running up his leg.

Ahead, at the top of a small rise, the trees thinned a bit. He must be close to that vacant cabin. Maybe those two people skiing ahead of him had gone there. If so, they'd have a fire. That was better than an emergency tent any day. He could get warm. And they could call for help. Everybody carried cell phones. He yelled for help, but the snow and the surrounding trees seemed to absorb the sound. He heard a faint reverberation as his voice bounced back at him from the high rock cliff. He doubted anyone would hear him unless he could get closer to the cabin.

Even if nobody was there, he could start a fire and maybe he could send some sort of smoke signal. He'd have to think about that one. The fire was the most important thing. It was cold enough now, maybe ten or fifteen degrees, but temps were supposed to plunge to subzero before morning. By then, he had to be out of here. The snow—forecasters said it was a blizzard moving in—would be no fun to deal with.

Before he could move, though, he needed a splint of some sort to immobilize his leg. The only thing even vaguely straight and solid was a ski. He pulled two fat Ace bandages out of his pack. He'd almost removed them from his pack before he left. Now he was mighty glad he hadn't. Groaning with the effort, he removed his left ski and set to work on getting off the right one. The more it hurt, the angrier he got. The angrier he was, the less he seemed to feel the pain.

Still, the grinding of sharp bone on the muscle tissue inside his leg came close to making him pass out. When he finally finished, his leg was bound to the ski, from his thigh all the way down as close to his ankle as he could reach. There was no way he could crawl with his leg sticking out straight like that. He'd have to pull himself along on his left side. This was going to be a long day.

7

Cutting Up Kindling

Marcus Wantstring had less than a week to finish this. Wrap up all the loose ends. Tweak the rough spots. Revise the computer file.

The blizzard would keep casual skiers away for at least the next three days. He glanced up at the cloud cover. That blizzard had better hurry. There was only a foot or two of snow on the ground so far. Not nearly enough to keep him dependably isolated. Still, he was sure he wouldn't be interrupted.

He had no idea who owned this cabin, but found justification for using it in the tidy hand-lettered laminated sign tacked beside the door:

feel free to stay for a day or two
clean up after yourself
leave firewood for the next person

Whoever wrote the sign should have said, *Leave some kindling, too*, he thought. He needed more than a day or two, but he doubted the owner, whoever that was, would object to even a week's stay here in the beginning stages of a blizzard. From everything he'd heard around town, the Perth wasn't a frequently used trail, not like the other ones, so there was a good chance nobody would come anywhere near the cabin. There hadn't been any ski tracks ahead of his on the way up here.

He needed solitude in a situation like this. His wife, dear as she was, could not stop talking for more than ten minutes at a time. Luckily, although she enjoyed picnics in the summer, she wasn't one to ski.

He and Denby had stumbled onto this—what should he call it? This project?—entirely by accident. Eight years so far. Eight pretty good years. He couldn't drop the ball now. Not with Denby gone. He had to keep up his end. He had to complete the contract, but there was no way he could finish it at home. Not with his wife popping in and out of his office. And not at school. Not with all those people around. Even with his office door locked, people would wonder what was taking him so long in there. This would be the last one. He couldn't keep going without Denby. He didn't even want to try.

"I recall many winters in Scotland," Dirk told me, "when the snow was so thick we were hard put by to keep ourselves alive. The cellar below our house was dug deep, back into the hill."

The hill, as he called it, was the impressive Ben y Vrackie, now something of a tourist destination north of Pitlochry. I'd first seen Dirk there when I took a walk up that particular mountain to a grassy meadow. He'd initially mistaken me for his ladylove. Once we got that straightened out, it took him a while to resign himself to being dead.

He said something else, but I'd missed his train of thought. "Into the hill," I said. "Like a cave?"

His eyebrows lowered. "Ye werena listening, yet again. But aye, 'twas cavelike. One winter, when I was but a lad, we lost many of our goats. We spent months in the cave."

"What did you eat?"

He gave me a quizzical look. "The bounty of the summer garden, of course."

"Oh," I said. "Of course."

"Neeps, mostly. Carrots. Cabbage. Onions. Nothing else lasted so well."

Neeps? Yuck. I knew that was what they called turnips. How on earth could anybody last a whole winter on turnips and cabbage? Still, it would sure be better than starving to death. If I had to depend on my own garden, I'd never make it. Other than a hill of zucchini, an area full of radishes, three tomato bushes, and the big asparagus patch that had been here for generations, my idea of gardening was asters, dahlias, dill, milkweed, sunflowers, daisies—and the dozens of other plants bumblebees and butterflies needed in order to thrive. I'd tried growing carrots one summer, but they ended up unbelievably crooked—guess I should have pulled more rocks out of the stony Vermont soil.

". . . are they doing, foreby?"

I came back with a start. "Who? What?"

He nodded out the window, and I joined him, accidentally grazing his elbow and feeling that increasingly familiar sense of cool water flowing across my arm.

He stood a little straighter, so I knew he'd felt me touch him.

Outside, on the two feet of snow accumulated on the front lawns throughout Hamelin, a bevy of X-C skiers glided along the narrow parallel paths they'd been carving into the top few inches of snow cover in this our first big snow of the season.

"Practically everyone in town skis," I told Dirk. "Either downhill or cross-country, or both."

"Skees." He tried out the word. "What would be *down-ill*?"

"Down hill." I emphasized the two syllables. "It's not like what *they're* doing." I gestured out the window. "In downhill skiing, you go really fast down the side of a mountain."

"For why?"

Good question. "For the thrill of it, I guess. I'm too chicken to try Alpine—downhill—skiing. I've seen too many people with broken bones. I prefer the X-C way."

"What would be an eksy weigh?"

"Huh? Oh. They're initials. X. C. That means cross-country. Sometimes it's called Nordic skiing. Cross-country is the kind they're doing out there."

"Do ye ever break your bones in eksy skeeing?"

"Nah. It's pretty sedate—at least it is the way I do it. Nothing ever happens to people on cross-country skis. Unless they're stupid enough to ski alone and get lost in the mountains."

Except for the wrap-up, which he hadn't decided on yet, Marcus had everything on USB flash drives. Denby had firmly believed in backing up everything more than once, and he'd taught Marcus to do the same.

He took a deep breath and picked up one dead branch from the snow-free area under the overhang of a thick beech tree. He ought to pay attention if he was going to gather enough kindling, but his mind kept drifting as he mulled over possible scenarios.

He'd never been able to work things like this out on the computer. He needed a hard copy, something he could flip through, jotting ideas in the margins. Denby wanted it the other way around, all of it on the computer. Marcus had argued with him. "We can't use the system here at work. What if somebody stumbles onto it?"

"Passwords," Denby purred. "Unbreakable passwords."

"No such thing," Marcus had insisted.

"Don't worry." Denby even smiled. "I've got it covered."

Marcus hadn't liked it, but so far the system seemed to have worked.

Denby took odd moments during what little free time he had at work to add a bit here, a bit there. Marcus couldn't do that. He'd printed out this latest version from his laptop at home, and it was a good thing he had. As he'd left his office at the University of Vermont on Friday—was today really only Sunday?—one of his graduate assistants had complained of a computer glitch. It seemed to have eaten a large number of documents. He'd shown Marcus the directory. Denby's whole password-protected folder was gone, as were several folders of older reports and data from failed experiments. "No great loss," Dr. Wantstring had assured the student. "I have a printout of everything I need."

He had his backups, too. That was what thumb drives were for.

He lopped off another dead branch that hung from a few threads of wood. Live wood was no good for kindling, but with the snow piled up the way it was, most of the fallen branches were covered completely, unless they were tucked under a thick pine. Thank goodness the forest constantly renewed itself, with trees that grew where older ones had died.

He looked around the clearing. This whole area was a well-managed woodlot. The trees weren't crowded by any means, but they were close enough to offer protection to one another from windstorms and the like.

He paused, leaned the ax against the tree trunk, and placed

his right hand, made into a fist, against the center of his spine at waist level. He arched his back against the pressure. He never used to get stiff like this. He held the pose for a couple of seconds and listened to the birds. Behind him, across the small clearing, a blue jay—he was pretty sure that was what it was—began to scold something, probably a squirrel bedeviling the bird. He would have turned to look at it, to see what the bird was upset about, but his back needed about five more seconds to ease out those muscles.

For a moment, he thought he heard a voice. A man's voice. Someone calling for help? He glanced around him, back across the clearing, which seemed to be where the voice originated, but the sound wasn't repeated. He thought he saw a movement under a copse at the top of the small rise on the far side of the clearing, but then that noisy blue jay burst from the trees, squawking. That was what he'd heard. Not a voice. An irritated bird.

He forgot about the jay when he noticed a fallen tree a few yards farther on. It looked like it had been dead at least a year. There was a deep, blackened scar along the upper side of the fallen trunk, leading Marcus to assume that a lightning strike had caused the tree's demise. The way of nature. He set to work on the upper branches with gusto. Long-dead wood burned easily as long as it hadn't been in contact with the ground. He'd leave extra kindling for the next poor soul who came along.

Dr. Wantstring picked up the pile of kindling he'd harvested. He'd break it—or chop it if he had to; some of these branches were fairly thick—once he got inside. He turned at a sound behind him. The figure skiing toward him over the clearing was the last person he'd expected to see. "What are you doing here?"

"I felt like skiing. I just came for the day. The mountain is beautiful early in a storm like this."

"How did you know I was here?"

"I didn't. Coincidence, I guess. Don't let me slow you down."

Wantstring didn't believe in coincidences. Not usually. The last thing he wanted—or needed—was an interruption like this. Still, his inborn good manners, the result of a mother who'd insisted, made him school his thoughts. "Did you have a good trek up the path?"

"As good as it could be. I followed a set of tracks. Maybe they were yours? It was good to have tracks to follow."

"Right." Wantstring cringed inwardly at how abrupt he sounded, but he truly did not want anyone around. "Here, let me get this kindling inside. I'll get a fire going and you can warm up for a bit. Do you want to have lunch before you leave?" He emphasized "leave"; he didn't intend to be rude, but he also didn't want to encourage anyone to stay. "Did you bring food?"

"I have a couple of sandwiches."

"Good. Park your skis and come on in." He brushed the blade of his ax against his pant leg to remove the dusting of snow from the metal. "Once the cabin warms, we can talk while we eat. I don't want to keep you too long. You'll need to get back to town before the snow gets too deep. Don't head farther up the mountain." He extended the ax toward the steep mountainside behind him. "The trail gets really steep. Only the best skiers should try it. You'll need to go back the way you came."

"I know."

Inside, Dr. Wantstring stamped the excess snow from his boots, leaned the ax against the wall beside the door, and crossed the floor, pulling the scarf from around his neck as he went. He draped it over the back of the chair. "Make yourself at home." He dropped the kindling beside the stove and casually lifted his manuscript from the chair that held his scarf.

"I'll just make a little more room." He stepped to the woodpile, wondering about the law of probability. Why now? Why here? Was this truly a coincidence? Maybe he was being overly careful, but if one person could consider an oncoming blizzard a great time to ski, another one might, too.

"Need any help?"

"No. Of course not. You just go ahead and park yourself on that chair." Using his body to shield the action, he tucked the manuscript behind the piled-up wood in the corner. He picked up a log, rummaged in the pocket of his flannel shirt for matches, and knelt beside the stove. "This won't take any time at all."

In the end, Dr. Marcus Wantstring was right. It did not take any time at all. The ax made it go much faster.

8

The Joy of a Wee Run

The second ski was too good for Mac to leave it lying beside the trail. With his rotten luck, somebody would come along and steal it. He took his bearings. Nearby, to the left of the trail, two skinny white birches formed almost a semicircle as they bent toward each other across one of the lower branches of a thick-girthed sugar maple. Between that and the rock cliff, he'd be able to find this spot easily once he was back on his feet. Grunting with the effort, he shoved the leftover ski beneath the light, fluffy snow. There. Safe. He added one of his ski poles to the stash but kept the other one with him.

The backpack weighed three tons as he struggled to get it on. He couldn't leave it. He'd need the water and food. It might take those people in the cabin a while to get help up here. With his luck, they'd be the kind of people who were never prepared for anything. You sure couldn't trust anyone these days.

The cabin couldn't be that much farther ahead. His body

was still warm from the effort of skiing and the ordeal of getting his broken leg splinted, but he knew the heat would begin to leach out—had already begun to, in fact. There'd be a fire. Surely the people who'd skied ahead of him would have started a fire there.

He laid his head down on his gloved hands to catch his breath. Just a minute to rest. Maybe two minutes. Then he'd get started.

A long while later Mac raised his head and stared with bleary eyes at the snow sifting onto him. Had he fallen asleep? Something had woken him, some sound, but he couldn't place it. At the top of the hill in front of him, he saw a blur of movement, something dark. He had the crazy—no, it was insane—thought that maybe it had been a person disappearing behind the crest. He called for help, but his voice came out more like a croak than a yell. Whoever it was couldn't have heard him. He could have sworn he'd seen a knitted cap sinking out of sight. That was impossible. Whoever it was, if it had been a person, would have stopped to help.

Mac's eyes gradually cleared and he looked around him. He'd obviously been asleep. There was another inch of snow. For now, all he heard was silence.

It wasn't far, but getting to the top of the incline seemed to take hours. He peered over the rise and spotted the small cabin in the clearing. One set of skis stood propped up to the right of the door. He called out, but nobody appeared. There wasn't any smoke from the chimney, so maybe one of the two guys whose trail he'd been following was out collecting firewood.

Mac took a deep breath, noticing the almost buried tracks of the second skier who had moved off the trail a few yards to the right. Probably wanted to take a quick pee against one of those trees. Those tracks rejoined the first set of tracks partway down the incline. Mac could clearly see the outhouse on the far side of the clearing. Couldn't the guy have waited that long?

He shouted, but nobody came to the open door. He was probably hard of hearing. Mac was having trouble getting enough breath. Damn. This would be over soon, though. Once the guy in the cabin called for help, Mac would be okay.

The backpack weighed four tons now. Even though it took him two tries to make it only one foot farther along the path, at least from here it would be downhill, and he wasn't talking about skiing. He wanted a fire. He wanted shelter. He wanted help. And they were all just a hundred feet away. A hundred agonizing feet.

I turned from the window. "This snow looks too good to pass up." I picked up a skein of neon pink yarn as I passed the table at the bottom of the stairs. "I'm going skiing."

"I will go wi' ye."

I turned on the bottom stair and looked him over. His sleeves were rolled up above his elbows. He had hand-knit stockings that came almost up to his—I had to admit it—gorgeous knees, but he probably didn't have anything on under his kilt. I stopped that thought before it could progress. "Stay here. You're not dressed for it."

He tilted his head to one side. His mouth was open. "Surely ye jest."

I slapped the newel post. "I'm not kidding, Dirk. It's probably five below out there."

"Below what?"

"Didn't you have temperatures back then?"

"*Temprachoors*? What would they be?"

"You know. Fahrenheit. Or did you use Celsius?"

Dirk looked at me like he thought I'd lost my mind.

I spoke slowly, as if he were five years old. "How on earth did you know how cold it was outside?"

The kilt pin holding his plaid over his shoulder—it was made of antler—moved as he took a deep breath. "The snow was one indication. If 'twas melting, the day was becoming warmer. If 'twas like this"—he turned to look out the window—"we'd have a wee fire. Even a wean could tell 'twas cold."

"Well, there's a big difference between just above freezing and five below."

He turned back to face the window. "I dinna understand this *five below*."

"That means it's really cold. If you go outside now, you'll freeze."

"Nae. I willna. I canna feel the cold. I canna feel anything." His voice faded away.

I shifted my feet on the bottom stair. "Stay here, Dirk. I'll just go a little way up one of the trails. Maybe the Perth. It's an easy one, the bottom part of it. Be back in a jiffy."

"I will go wi' ye. Ye said it could be dangerous if one *skeeded* alone."

"Skied. And only if they're lost in the mountains, and you can't get lost on the Perth."

He crossed his arms. "I am coming wi' ye."

Stubborn Scot, I thought. "This snow is too fluffy, and you don't have skis. How do you know you won't sink in?"

"We will discover that soon enow, would ye not say?"

I threw up my hands. It would serve him right if he fell in and got stuck. "I have to change clothes."

"I will wait for ye. Dinna take long, for ye wouldna want

to be caught out of doors in the dark." He turned his obstinate face back to the window.

No, I *wouldna* want to be skiing after dark, but I also *didna* like him telling me what any halfway intelligent adult would already know. Grrr.

It took too much energy to keep calling out. The door of the cabin stood tantalizingly open. It looked like one or two steps up, but he could make that. He'd come this far. At least he could get inside, off this cold ground. Hopefully, whoever was staying here would be back soon and they could get a fire going.

By the time he hauled himself up the steps—the snow fell so freely in the clearing they were practically buried by now—he was close to exhaustion. The thought that if he didn't keep going he'd freeze to death kept him motivated. That and the possibility that whoever was using the cabin might not come back for hours, so it was up to him to save himself.

"Anybody home?" That sounded stupid. Of course there wasn't; they would have heard him long ago. They must have taken snowshoes out to walk around. He inched forward another foot or so, enough to see into the square room.

The man sprawled on his back beside the cold woodstove wore bright orange-, red-, and yellow-striped socks. The man's pant legs were stuffed into the socks. Any good skier knew that technique to keep cold air from flowing up inside your pant legs. But this man would never ski again. He was quite obviously dead. Mac had seen enough dead bodies to be sure, even if it hadn't been for the state of the guy's skull and the ax beside the body. For a moment, Mac forgot his own situation and tried to pull himself to his feet. The pain swamped him, and he collapsed in agony. It was a long time before he managed to shrug out of his backpack and a longer time yet before he could make it across the floor to check the guy's pockets.

No wallet, although patting the guy's pockets wasn't the easiest task considering the state of Mac's fingers. No cell phone. No driver's license tucked into the top of his heavy orange socks, the way some skiers did. The only things Mac found in the guy's pockets were three empty Tootsie Roll wrappers in his pants and two ballpoint pens in his shirt. Green, no less. Who carried green pens, for God's sake? Who was this guy? Why did somebody have it in for him?

A niggling thought crept up the back of his spine, lodged in a primitive part of Mac's brain stem, and wouldn't go away. Mac never felt fear. He was big. He was strong. What was there to be afraid of? He was the chief of police. But what would happen if a bear wandered in, following the smell of blood, the scent of dead meat? Most of the bears would be hibernating by now, but there were always a few, usually the cranky males, who wandered the forest until well after the first snowfall. The dead guy didn't smell too bad yet; Max could tell he'd been killed only recently. The blood on the floor hadn't frozen yet, and the blood that had soaked into the collar of the guy's brown plaid flannel shirt was still a bright red. But the smell would build if Mac didn't get help soon. The bear would come. Mac could have kicked himself for not bringing his rifle along.

He made it across the floor in record time, considering the state of his leg and the awkwardness of the ski splint. He closed the door and wedged one of the two chairs in the room under the knob. No bear was getting in here while Mac had breath.

Still, what if it wasn't a bear trying to get in? What would happen if the ax wielder came back? Even if the wedged chair held, there were four windows.

Even if the ax was still inside the cabin, Mac had to admit to himself—he'd never admit it to anyone else—that in his present condition he couldn't fight off a kitten, much less a murderous maniac. Not with his leg the way it was.

Mac's gut clenched. The police chief of Hamelin was scared.

9

Crisp Enough to Freeze

The air was crisp enough to freeze the little hairs inside my nose, so it had to be colder than ten degrees. Anything warmer than that, and your nose hairs don't freeze. Just one of those handy little Vermont truisms. So maybe the old Scots didn't need thermometers. Dirk was right, doggone him.

I grabbed my skis from the shed out back and, while Dirk pestered me with questions, I took a moment to scrape them lightly and buff on a layer of blue wax. Most everybody in town prepared their skis like this well before the first big snow-fall was predicted.

I usually did, too, but with the big kilt shipment we'd had to process Friday and Saturday, I hadn't taken the time. It wouldn't take long to whip my skis into shape, though.

People new to the art of cross-country skiing usually bought tons of paraphernalia that we old-timers didn't bother with. An old-timer in skiing is anyone who's been on skis their whole life, whether that life is five years or, as in my case, thirty.

Sporting goods stores like to sell new skiers fancy little pouches filled with four or five different colors of ski wax for different snow conditions—purple, red, blue, green, and yellow for gliding and another set of colors formulated for kicking off. The klister waxes are like glue. I guess you use those to keep from sliding off the side of an icy mountain. Sure can't go fast with sticky gunk on your skis.

Then there were scrapers, spreaders, corks, warming irons, rilling tools, special brushes made of some sort of exotic bristle; the increasingly expensive list seemed to multiply every year as more people took up the sport and more companies saw the possibility of a big profit margin. Maybe professional long-distance racing skiers needed some of those things, but most of the rest of us just threw on a basic coat of blue wax at the beginning of the season and headed out once the first snow fell.

I loved gliding across a fresh snowfall. I pointed myself out of town toward the forest. Dirk stayed close to my side. After all, this was his first snowfall in more than six hundred years. I doubted that was a factor, though, as to why he stuck so close. "Stuck" was the operative word. He couldn't stray more than a yard or two from the shawl as long as we were outside my house. There was some sort of exception to the ghostly rule, though. In my house and in the ScotShop he could roam around to his heart's content, but anywhere else he was restricted unless he was carrying the shawl. Maybe I should have let him carry it, but there was a piece of me that wondered if he might run away with it if he had the chance. Of course, where would he go?

I could have let him hold it. Was it mean of me to hang on to it? I didn't need its warmth while I was moving. That was one of the beauties of cross-country. The very act of moving on skis allows the legs and arms, fingers and toes—and every other part of the body—to flex and bend, thereby keeping the muscles warm. But if I slowed down or stopped while I was up on the Perth, I'd need the shawl.

"Is this all the speed we will be going?"

"Why? You want to run?"

Beside me, Dirk let out a long, sustained, "Ahhhhh. I havena run anywhere for . . ."

"Since you died?" I lengthened my stride and picked up the pace until I fairly flew.

Dirk kept up with me with no apparent effort. He didn't have to deal with friction. *Or stumbling blocks*, I thought as I veered to the left to avoid a snow shovel someone had left lying at the end of their driveway. He seemed so energized, so . . . bouncy almost; I had the feeling he wanted to run for hours.

I slowed down, backtracked, and stood the snow shovel upright in a snowbank so the owners could find it, even if two more feet of snow fell before they came out to shovel again.

"That was most kind of ye, Mistress Peggy." Dirk sounded diplomatic—something I wasn't used to, coming as it did from him. "Now, though," he went on, "might we run again?"

As we reached the edge of the forest, where the path began to ascend, I slowed down a bit and glanced at his feet. There weren't any footprints. I guessed that made sense—after all, he couldn't open doors, couldn't really touch anything—but it was still a bit of a surprise. "What does it feel like, Dirk? Walking on top of the snow, I mean."

"Och, it feels a bit like drinking too much ale and not knowing where my feet are."

"Did you do that a lot?"

He threw an indignant look my way. "Nae, certes. But young men will try. I suppose they still do?"

I thought about my twin brother's occasional summer

forays into bars in Arkane, the next town up the road—there weren't any bars in Hamelin. And no telling what he'd done when he was off at college. He couldn't have been too wild, though, since he'd graduated summa cum laude. Then he fell off the framework around a dinosaur skeleton he was repairing and shattered his back.

". . . ye listening?"

"Huh? Oh. Yeah. Young men. They *do* still drink, and nowadays with cars in the equation, it's a much more serious problem."

"And why would that be?"

"Because when they're drunk they don't have the reflexes or the judgment to drive safely. A lot of people are killed every year by drunk drivers of all ages—not just young men, although statistics say they're the worst."

"Does he live nearby?"

"Who?"

"Master Stuhstissticks."

I say "huh?" a lot around Dirk. I said it again before I figured out what he was talking about. "Sta-tis-tics." I emphasized each syllable. "They're—"

But I didn't get to explain. The fir tree I'd just glided under had way too heavy a burden of snow. I must have brushed my head against one of the lower branches, and the whole load dumped on top of me.

By the time Dirk stopped laughing, which took considerably longer than it should have, I'd brushed myself off and gotten most of the snow out of my jacket. "Should we not turn back now?" he asked between very un-ghostly snorts.

"No. I want to go farther. I haven't been up here on the Perth in a couple of years."

"What would be this *pirth* ye speak of?"

"All the trails around here are named for towns or shires

in Scotland. This trail is the Perth." I twisted my upper body
to the left and pointed with my ski pole. "The one on that
hill over there on the far side of town is the Inverness trail.
The Dunbarton and Fife trails are behind us, on the opposite
side of Lake Ness, and the—"

He raised a hand to quiet me. We had dozens of named
trails coursing up the mountains from this valley. Obviously
he didn't want to hear about all of them.

"There's a cute little cabin in a clearing up ahead. It might
be fun to go that far."

Dirk cast a dubious eye at the sky—or what we could see
of it through the snow-laden braches of the trees surrounding
us. "Are ye sure o' the path?"

"We're not going to get lost, if that's what you're worried
about." I twisted to gaze back over my right shoulder and
pointed with the other of my ski poles. "Look. You can see
Hamelin from here through the break in the trees. We're not
that far out of town." I pulled the pink yarn out of my jacket
pocket. It's surprising how well wool compresses. "I'll tie
yarn on trees as we go," I said, matching my actions to my
words. "That way we won't get lost even if the path gets totally
snowed in." I always carried yarn with me when I skied—as
much a habit as fastening my seat belt in the car. "At worst,
we can always just head downhill and we'll be sure to run
into Lake Ness—it's not frozen yet, so we can't miss it. Then
we turn left, and we get to Hamelin. Anyway"—I pointed to
the parallel dents that marked the snow ahead of us—"a
couple of other skiers have already come this way. Maybe
we'll meet up with them."

"Mayhap, but then I'll not be able to say anything."

"It's never stopped you yet." Carrying on a conversation
while nobody else could hear Dirk asking for explanations of
twenty-first-century words and customs had been something

of a challenge in the months since I'd . . . acquired . . . him last summer. "You never seem to shut up when I ask you to."

He gave me one of those affronted looks, which was rather daunting coming from such a big ghost, but I turned away from him and from the tree I'd just yarned, and skied on.

Quite a few pink-beribboned trees later, we came to one of my favorite spots on the Perth trail, and I glided to a stop. A wall of solid rock rose a good twenty or thirty feet to our right, with winter-withered ferns clinging to cracks in the granite. Come spring, they'd green up and look like a veritable nursery. "Look at that cliff." I stopped and pointed to my right, and Dirk raised an eyebrow. I could almost hear him thinking, *Ye think I canna see it?*

"I love this place."

"I can see why ye maun."

"I come up here to picnic sometimes."

"What would be a *nick*?"

"Huh?"

"A nick. Ye said ye come here for to pick them. Is it a wee flower?"

"Picnic. One word." I spelled it for him. The explanation took considerably longer.

The snow was trampled a couple of yards to the left of the path. When I finished with the English lesson, I nodded toward the mess. "Looks like at least one of the skiers in front of us had a problem."

"He fell?"

The answer was so obvious, I didn't reply.

"Mayhap he tripped on this rock."

Dirk stood with one foot hiked up on top of a good-sized rock. Behind him—through him—I could see a rather large fallen branch. How could anybody not have seen those? "Sometimes rocks break away from the cliff face. Usually they fall straight down, but this one must have bounced to come this far. How could anybody have missed seeing such an obstacle?"

"Mayhap he was looking at yon lovely cliff instead of watching his skees."

I studied the trampled snow. "It can't have happened too long ago or the snow would have filled in more, even with as little snow as is getting through the trees."

"Quite the tracker, are ye?"

"You would be, too, if you'd grown up around here."

"I learnt enough tracking when I was a lad; although"—he pointed to the narrow parallel lines we'd been following—"I never tracked wee beasties with great long footprints like that."

I moved off the path to my left. I could feel a good-sized branch under my skis. Thank goodness my skis hadn't snagged on it. I glanced down and saw just a hint of smooth brown through the covering of snow. I yarned a branch on the slender birch ahead of me, thinking all the time how silly it was to leave yarn *here*, since I knew this place so well. The trunk leaned across a branch of an enormous sugar maple, and I thought about Robert Frost's poem "Birches." Had some boy, or girl for that matter, been swinging from this birch to that one nearby and back again, gradually bending the trunks as the trees grew? "Birches grow in Scotland, don't they?"

"Aye. Many."

"Do children ever climb them and bend them down like this?" I gestured to the trees.

"Aye. Of course. Then, once they are bent, the goats like to climb them."

"You're teasing, right?"

He looked incredulous. "Do ye not know that goats climb slanting tree trunks?"

"Can't say that was part of my education. Not too many goats around Hamelin."

I headed up the trail, and he kept pace, shaking his head in exasperation. "What kind of world has this become, where the most common knowledge is lost?"

I plowed to a stop and glared at him. "I'm supposed to feel bad about a lack of goat lore?"

"Ye needna beceorest so."

"I'll baykerayst if I want to." *Whatever that is. It's probably related to whingeing.* "I may not know about goats, but you don't know about spreadsheets. Or mass transportation." *So there.*

He narrowed his eyes at me.

I found myself shivering and picked up my pace. The skiers ahead of us must have started dragging something—a load of firewood, maybe? The tidy parallel ski tracks had been obliterated by something wide. If I had to guess, I'd say they'd pulled a canvas tarp behind them. That cabin was fairly close, over the rise ahead of us. If they were there, I'd ask them what they'd done to make such a mess of the trail. I sure hoped a good fire was warming the interior. If not, I was going to start one.

10

Whoops!

Mac Campbell wasn't ready to die—not from a broken leg, not from starvation, and not from freezing to death—but he gave serious thought to how small a chance he would have of staving off a murderous attacker in his present shape. He could never be accused of having too active an imagination, but the danger he saw himself in stoked the imaginative flames way more than he found comfortable. He massaged his fingers. Get a fire started. That was what he needed to do. There was kindling, some of it sticking out from underneath the body, but enough off to one side. A convenient stack of woodstove-sized logs filled a corner of the room.

For some time, Mac didn't worry about the body. He worried about how to drag himself around it so he could reach the woodpile. Why hadn't they put the woodpile next to the door? That would have made more sense. Then he worried about how to coax a log off the pile without collapsing the whole shebang onto himself. Luckily, he'd dragged one of his ski poles along

with him. He heaved himself back to the door where he'd left
the pole, cursing under his breath—it took too much energy to
swear out loud. Eventually he just threw the pole ahead of him
and floundered back to his objective. He had to get a fire started.
Had to. He couldn't feel his toes. The only thing he could feel
for sure was that he had to relieve himself. He had no idea how
to handle that problem.

Why'd they stack this woodpile so high? The basket web-
bing around the point of the ski pole finally caught on a small
branch stub. He'd have a fire going in no time. All he needed
was one stupid log to set atop the kindling. He'd worry about
log number two later. He yanked hard, and the left-hand end
of the stack seemed to come apart. One log glanced off his
shoulder; one landed on his outstretched fingers. Mac didn't
care if a murderer was close enough to hear him; he swore
with a vengeance, all the pent-up anger, pain, and fear of the
last several hours pouring out in a tsunami of invective.

The serene winter silence shattered as a round of oaths blasted
from the cabin across the clearing, not a hundred feet away. I
backed up a step—hard to do on cross-country skis—and
almost fell. I recognized that gravelly smoker's voice. For some
reason our illustrious police chief, Mac Campbell, was hell-
bent on cussing out the firewood.

Even with that cabin door shut tight, I could hear Mac
easily. The cabin—nothing more than a shack, really—had
no insulation. The walls were one plank thick, and the windows had been put in there before double-glazing was ever
invented. Nothing fancy about the place at all.

Dirk started forward, but I motioned him back. I needn't
have bothered. For one thing, he couldn't see my gesture since
he was in front of me. And for another thing, when he got about

three yards in front of me he pulled up short, as if a big bungee cord had reached the end of its limit and hauled him back toward me. "Don't go any farther," I said unnecessarily.

"I canna, lest ye go as weel."

"I'm not going to. That's Mac Campbell in there, swearing like a sailor. I don't want to meet up with him if he's in this kind of mood."

"Mayhap he is hurt."

"Mac? Not a chance. If he has enough energy to cuss that loudly, he doesn't need us around."

There was no smoke from the chimney, but I heard a distinct clang as Mac—or somebody—banged the woodstove closed. There's no other sound in the world like the clunk of a woodstove door.

I inspected the scene, noting details about the cabin and its environs. "He's alone."

"How would ye know that?"

I motioned toward the dark brown wall beside the closed front door. "There's only one pair of skis there." All the more reason to avoid him. He'd have only me to vent on.

It looked like an army had been here, though; the track of the tarpaulin—or whatever they'd used—was still faintly visible in a wide path even under the heavy new flakes. Still, there had been only Mac's and one other person's tracks up the trail.

Dirk must have been thinking along the same lines. "Where is the ither person, the one who made the second set o' skee tracks?"

"Either the other guy's out collecting kindling or he and Mac weren't together in the first place. The other skier might have just skirted the cabin and gone on ahead. There's a path around back of the cabin he might have taken. It's pretty steep, so you have to be a good skier to manage it. It goes farther up the mountain and then a branch veers off back toward town."

"If 'tis difficult to skee that part of the trail, then would ye not say a skeeing person would have to be well accomplished to go there?"

"What do you mean?"

"Someone who falls on the path"—he gestured down the slope behind us—"wouldna be likely to approach a challenging trail, aye?"

"So, you're saying that if Mac's in the cabin, he must be the one who fell back there?" Dirk nodded, but I wasn't convinced. "Mac's too good a skier for that. He wouldn't have fallen."

"Then where would be the ither man who made the second set of wee tracks?"

"I don't know. There are some sharp drop-offs up there, and in this much snow, it wouldn't be wise for anyone to take that part of the trail, especially not somebody who's no good on skis." I waved my hand vaguely to indicate the hillside behind the outhouse. "He probably took the trail back to town."

The sounds emanating from the cabin had died to a low rumble.

Dirk spread his right arm in the direction of the cabin. "Do ye not agree 'twould be courteous for us to—"

"No. Absolutely not." I lowered my voice, just on the off-hand chance that Mac might hear me and come out to investigate. "I'm not going anywhere near that man if I can avoid it. I don't intend him any harm, but I'm certainly not going to let him ruin my trek with his sarcasm." I raised my feet up onto my tiptoes—or as close as I could get to it—several times to keep the circulation going. It *was* getting distinctly colder.

"Look." Dirk pointed to a faint trickle of smoke rising from the old fieldstone chimney. "Now he has a wee fire lit, he will be less likely to swear at ye. Let us go inside. I can see ye shivering like a newborn kid."

In answer, I raised my right leg and ski as high as I could,

straight out before me until the square back edge of the ski
rested on the ground in front of me. I twisted my leg and the
ski clockwise, leaving the back in contact with the ground,
and set my foot down, facing back behind me, leaving my
legs in a ballet-like position, the right one pointing vaguely
west, back toward the way we'd come, and the other heading
sort of east. It was quite a trick, but it was also the only way
to turn around quickly on cross-country skis. Then I shifted
my weight to my right leg, leaned slightly on my right ski pole
to get my balance, and lifted my left foot straight up so I could
cross the front of my left ski over the back of the right one
and bring it around so they both faced back toward Hamelin.
It was a complicated maneuver, and I couldn't tell you how
many times I'd fallen trying to perfect it when I was a kid.
Now it was like second nature. "I'm outta here. He's got a fire
going. Mac's a big boy. He can take care of himself."

"We havena been verra neighborly."

"Mac is not a neighbor. Mac is a . . ."

Dirk cleared his ghostly throat, and I didn't finish my
sentence.

On the way back down the mountain I collected pink yarn
markers as I went. It's wonderful the way you generate heat
when you're skiing cross-country. And when you're arguing
with a stubborn ghost.

Even a good night's sleep—mine, not his; ghosts don't sleep—
didn't stop him. Monday morning he kept at it. "Ye shouldna
ha' left Master Campbell when he was swearing like a sail
man."

"First of all, it's a sailor, not a sail man. Secondly, don't call
him a master. He's not a master of anything except his ego.
And thirdly, I had no intention of going in there."

"He may ha' been hurt."

"He wasn't hurt. Not if he had enough energy to cuss out a pile of firewood."

"Ye dinna ken that for certes."

"Dirk! Quit telling me what to do."

"My name isna Dirk. Why d'ye insist on calling me that when my name is Macbeath Donlevy Freusach Finlay—"

I cut him off before the last two names. "I know darn well what your name is. Macbeth? Nobody uses that name nowadays. And I can't say all those others fast enough. Anyway, I get them mixed up."

"Ye wouldna if ye paid attention."

"Oh, go sit down and wait for me to get ready."

"And ye say I tell ye what to do. Now who is giving instructions?" With every indication of affronted dignity, he walked over to my wingback chair.

"That's *my* chair. Why do you always have to sit in it?"

Without missing a beat, Dirk—or whatever his name was—strode to the woodstove and wouldna—I mean would not—turn around to face me.

Good. Now I could finish getting ready. I reached for my boots but got sidetracked straightening all the shoes piled beside my front door. How could anyone have so many shoes? The shawl kept hanging down in my way, so I crumpled it up, set it on the little table there in my entryway, and brought order to the chaos in a few minutes of concentrated effort.

When I finished, I slipped on the right pair of boots and turned around.

No ghost.

I looked at the shawl crumpled on the table. I thought you had to *fold* it for him to go away.

A tiny spider balanced on the edge of it. It shook one of its little front legs at me, like a minister in a pulpit saying, *Shame on you*.

Emily answered on the first ring.

"Em? This is Sandra. I'm sorry to call you so early, but I have bad news."

Emily recoiled from the phone. Bad news? She didn't like bad news.

"Are you there? Emily?"

"Yes. I'm here."

"Somebody broke into your house."

"Broke in? What do you mean?"

"Your kitchen is okay, but the living room—the couch cushions are all askew. And in Mark's office off the den? It looks like the books on the bookcase have been moved around, and I know Mark's laptop was right in the middle of his desk yesterday afternoon when I came in to water the plants the way you asked me to. And it's not there now. I looked around and I can't find it anywhere. Do you want me to call the police now or do you want to come home first?"

"No!" Emily looked at the clock. Was it really only 8:20? She felt like she'd been up for half a day. "No, don't call them. The kitchen is a mess. I didn't straighten up before I left."

"Emily Wantstring, that's ridiculous."

"Just wait. Once Mark gets home from his little ski trip, we'll drive up there together."

"There's a whole pane of glass broken on the back door. It's freezing cold in here."

"Oh, dear. Can you tape a hand towel over it?"

Sandra chuckled. "No, Emily, I can't. I'll clean up the broken glass and get Ron to put up a piece of plywood. That should hold it, but you really need to come up and be sure nothing else is gone."

Emily moved the notepad she kept next to the phone over about an inch and lined it up with the edge of the table. "All right. I'll drive up there tomorrow."

"Today, Emmy. You have to come today, before more snow hits tomorrow. Driving will be safer."

"Oh, fiddlesticks. All right."

They said their good-byes. Emily hoped against hope that Mark would get back. She didn't like driving alone. But she knew he wouldn't. He'd told her three days at least. She ran her hands up and down her arms, trying to make the cold go away. Hot chocolate would cure a lot of this, she thought. She'd whip some up and put it in a thermos to take with her.

11

SRM20

The ScotShop was closed on Mondays, but Gilda and I had decided to spend a few hours stocking the shelves, taking advantage of a day without customers. We were making good progress, when Karaline pounded on the door. I could tell something important was going on by the look on her face, and I unlocked the door as fast as I could.

She rushed in. Well, considering that she'd had a ruptured appendix two months ago, she was moving as fast as she could. "My second Univex died!"

"I'm sorry to hear that, K. What the heck is a Univex? Do we need to hold a funeral?"

She stuck out her tongue at me, so I knew it couldn't have been too much of a disaster.

"It's a big commercial mixer. Made by Univex. The Tuesday morning breakfast crowd tomorrow is going to expect buckets of rolls, and they always go through dozens of loaves of fresh bread. There's no way I can handle that much volume with only one Univex."

"So, what are you going to do?"

"You and I are driving to Kittredge. That's the food service supply store where I get all my equipment. It's in Burlington. Well, it's in Winooski, but that's next door to Burlington, just across the river."

"What makes you think I can take the time to go that far?"

She looked pointedly around at the closed store. "There's supposed to be a heavy snow moving in overnight, so we need to go now."

Heavy snow was great for the ski slopes, but sometimes didn't work well for tourist towns. Thank goodness it wasn't usually like this in October.

"I called the store. The woman I spoke with said they had only one SRM20 in stock. They've ordered more, but with another storm in the forecast, there's no telling when they'll get here. That means we need to leave now. Now!"

"All right, don't get your britches twisted." I'd borrowed that phrase from Moira, our Southern-born police dispatcher. I thought it expressed the thought very succinctly. "You weren't planning on driving, were you?"

"Of course. We have to take my SUV."

"You've been out of the hospital how long?"

"Six weeks. That's long enough. I feel great."

I stared at her.

"Okay, okay. I feel fairly good."

"I still don't think you should drive."

"Okay. You can drive for me."

She was right. I could. Karaline and I had keys to each other's cars. And houses. "Why don't you stay here?"

"No way."

I threw up my hands in exasperation. "All right, but I have to go home first. I left my purse there. Why don't we take my car?"

"You've obviously never seen a Univex SRM20. We'll take my SUV, and we'll just barely be able to cram the box in the back. The woman told me exactly how big the box was, and I measured my car to be sure it would fit. Let's just go."

"I want my purse. I can't drive without my license."

"Okay. Jump in my car and we'll swing by your place on the way out of town."

I neglected to remind her that my house was in one direction and the road to Burlington was in the opposite direction. Karaline was too upset for logic. "Go ahead and lock up, Gilda. We can finish the shelves tomorrow morning while it's still slow."

"That's okay. I'm on a roll. I'll keep going for a couple of hours."

A few more hours I'd have to pay her for. At overtime rates. Oh well, the store was thriving. I followed Karaline out of the ScotShop.

Shorty sat just inside the front door. It looked like he'd been lying on the shawl—it was kind of squashed—but I tried to keep my eyes averted. Maybe Karaline wouldn't notice it. He wove around my ankles meowing. I pulled off my gloves and bent to stroke his silky back. Karaline walked past the two of us and looked around. "Where's Dirk? He's usually waiting."

I tried desperately not to look at the table where I'd put the shawl, but Karaline must have seen my eyes veer that way. That, and the fact that Shorty jumped back up on the table, settling onto the blue and green plaid.

"You didn't! What did you do this time?"

"What do you mean, what did *I* do? How about what he did?" And then I remembered that he hadn't done anything. I'd crumpled up the shawl by mistake. Still, if I hadn't, he would have been telling me what to do and how to do it or what not to do and how to avoid doing it. It was just as well he was off wherever he went. "Let's leave him in there. We haven't had any girl talk in a long time, and he's too bossy."

She nodded, but took her sweet time doing it. "I have to use the facilities."

I pointed toward the powder room on the main floor. "You know where it is. I'll use the one upstairs." We'd both learned over the years never to head out onto snowy roads without emptying our bladders. No telling how long you might be stuck behind a wreck or slowed down by a tourist who didn't know how to drive on snow. "I ought to feed Shorty, too, just in case it takes longer than we planned."

She hung her parka on a hook behind the door and headed for the bathroom. "Well, hurry. This won't take me a minute."

I threw my coat across the wingback chair, picked up Shorty, and headed upstairs. I intended to put on a heavier sweater whether Karaline was in a hurry or not. She could jolly well wait.

Emily was not a fast driver even in the summer, but in the winter, she felt compelled to crawl as slowly as possible. The road wound through the mountains. Whoever had plotted the trail originally must have been planning for bicycles—or, more likely, for horses—not for cars. When Mark drove it, she enjoyed watching the scenery unfold, but now, driving it herself, she wished she'd hired someone to come along with her.

If she were honest with herself—and she was trying to

be—she had to admit that she didn't have any friends close enough to chat with: nobody who would be willing to make this trip with her, either as driver or passenger. Sandra might, but she was on the wrong end of the road. And even Sandra didn't like to linger too long over a cup of coffee. Emily's sister might have, if her sister hadn't moved to Washington D.C.

What's wrong with me? Emily wondered. Deep down, she knew the answer.

She crept around the next few hairpin turns, her thoughts tunneling deeper with each change of direction.

My sister loves me, she thought. *Mark loves me.* She was sure of that. But something more than her voice had died when the cancer hit. Emily loved Mark, but afterward . . . after she . . . It was like nothing existed for her. She was in a cold place. And she had pushed Mark away, not let him comfort her. Instead, she had chattered, chattered all day long. No wonder Josie moved away. And poor Mark. What a good man. Maybe she could change somehow. Maybe she could make it up to him.

There had been times she should have been able to relax a bit, like that party they'd had when they first bought the house in Hamelin. The easy conversation in the kitchen felt forced to her; the laughter-filled hike up the mountain trail, except she wasn't laughing with the others; the campfire in the clearing. She grimaced. She hadn't even enjoyed the s'mores.

The back end of the car slipped a little on an icy patch and Emily's stomach turned. Even though she recovered quickly, she felt shaken. Icy roads were a fact of life in Vermont, something she'd learned to deal with years ago. Why had this one little fishtail bothered her so much? At the next scenic overview she pulled off the road and turned off the engine. She clasped her gloved hands at the top of the steering wheel, bent her head onto her hands, and thought, long and hard, about her way of dealing with life. The scenery may have been spectacular, but Emily Wantstring never noticed it.

I took a quick glance sideways at Karaline. Her parka looked bulkier than usual. Maybe that was what was making her hunch up so much. Or maybe it was her appendectomy scar. "Are you feeling okay?"

"I'm fine. Keep driving."

I sure hoped her heater would kick in soon. We'd been driving—and talking—for at least half an hour. Of course, most of the heat was probably gathering back there in her capacious back bay.

Karaline smiled.

"What are you grinning about?"

She pushed a wayward hair off her face, not an easy feat when you were wearing heavy mittens. "I was just thinking about Halloween."

"Why? Are you doing something special this year? You'd better hurry; it's already the fifteenth. Are you planning to turn the Logg Cabin into a haunted house? If so, I want to be in on it."

"Not hardly. No, I was thinking about an old college prof of mine. He had these crazy Halloween socks."

I downshifted as we began a steep descent. Once the car was well under control, I expected her to explain, but she just kept grinning to herself, so I prompted her. "Socks?"

"They were heavy, like what you'd wear hiking or skiing, but they were bright, almost neon. Orange and red stripes, with some yellow thrown in here and there."

"Like from variegated yarn? Were they hand knit?"

"I dunno. They just looked like Halloween."

"Were there little goblins or skeletons knitted into the pattern?"

"No, just the stripes."

"Not even a ghost?" As soon as I said it, I snapped my mouth shut. Maybe she wouldn't notice.

No such luck.

I gripped the steering wheel as I straightened out of one of the hairpin turns.

"Speaking of ghosts, you really shouldn't have rolled up Dirk like that, you know. It's not fair to him."

"I couldn't help it. It was a mistake."

She wouldn't turn to look at me, but I could see her mittened hands flex in her lap. "How do you wrap up a ghost by mistake?"

"My shoes were all messed up, and I was trying . . . Oh, never mind! It's not going to hurt him. He'll still be perfectly fine when I unwrap him this evening. Or tomorrow." I hoped I sounded as indignant as I felt. I hoped I didn't sound as defensive as I thought I might. It *had* been a mistake after all.

"Can you pull in and stop up there?"

"Sure. Why?"

"I have a cramp. Have to stand up for a bit."

I turned left into a scenic overview and parked next to a tour bus. Dozens of tourists snapped pictures of the sweeping panorama. I had to admit the valley stretching out below the mountains was stunning. But I wasn't in the mood for scenery. Why weren't all those potential customers at my ScotShop buying lots of goodies to take home with them? Maybe I should get out and pass around some store brochures. The fact that the store was closed on Mondays was irrelevant.

Karaline stepped out of the car. "This parka's too hot." She took it off, opened the zippered compartment that held a rainproof hood, and pulled out—

"Karaline, you didn't!"

"Yes, I did. You can't stay mad at him forever." She put her parka back on. "You have to admit, it's kind of fun having a ghost around."

"You're not the one who has to live with him twenty-four/seven. You'd get tired of having him tell you how much better it was in the fourteenth century all the time."

"So, just give me the shawl for good. I'd be happy to have him."

My mouth must have dropped open or something, because she laughed at me. "Admit it! You'd miss him if he were gone permanently." She opened my shawl—*my* shawl—and placed it around her shoulders. Dirk appeared right next to the SUV, glorious—I had to admit—in his Farquharson kilt. He was so tall I could see only his broad chest and a few inches of his black hair drifting over his wide shoulders. His hair shifted gently in an otherworldly breeze. A breeze from the fourteenth century. I turned my face resolutely forward.

He bent to look in Karaline's open door. "Ye could wish me well-come if ye would."

Karaline opened the back door and he slipped in. "I thank ye, Mistress Karaline."

"My pleasure."

I could swear she smirked as she took her seat.

"So," I said, "how was never-never land?"

"How long—"

"It was—" I started, but he kept talking, leaning between the seats, his head turned toward her, away from me.

"—have I been gone, Mistress Karaline?"

I wanted to glare at both of them, but there were tourists swarming all over the parking lot, so I didn't dare look away in case I backed into one.

"She wrapped you up this morning."

"It was an accident. Sit back," I told him. "Your seat belt isn't fastened."

Karaline guffawed so loudly I couldn't hear Dirk's next few comments. That was probably just as well.

As we pulled beyond the tour bus, I saw a familiar car. "I don't believe this."

"What?"

I pointed. "Look at who's hunched over her steering wheel."

"Ye maun stop so we might help Mistress Emily. It would appear she is crying."

"He's right. Pull up next to her."

12

The Joy of a Scenic Drive

Emily started when someone tapped on the car window, but then she saw it was Karaline, Mark's former student, the tall young woman who owned the restaurant where she and Mark had eaten that one time. Why only once? They should have gone back there. She wiped at her tears and unlocked her door.

"Do you need help, Mrs. Wantstring?" Karaline leaned down to peer inside the car, her eyes reflecting worry.

"No, dear. I'm just having . . . I'm just . . . Mark went skiing and . . ." Emily rested one of her hands on her winter coat, right over her heart. "Everything is wrong, and I don't know what to do." She couldn't stop herself. All her fears poured out in disjointed sentences. Karaline knelt in the snow beside the open door and laid a hand on Emily's knee. That felt so comforting, Emily wished she could prolong the contact somehow. Maybe if she talked just a little while longer?

*   *   *

I turned away from the sight of Emily's tearstained face.
The break-in, the need for her to inventory the house, and
the fact that Mark had left her alone. She didn't seem to need
to come up for air.

"Ye dinna want to leave her here alone on the side of this
wee hill," Dirk said with a certain air of finality.

"It's tempting," I muttered. "And it's a mountain, not a hill."

"It is naught but a hill to someone born as I was in the
Highlands."

Emily raised her head. "What did you say?"

"Nothing." I gave Karaline a *get us out of this* stare.

"I know what we can do." She stood—a little shakily, I
thought. Her stitches must be bothering her—and brushed
snow from her knees and the hem of her parka. "We'll follow
you to your house to be sure you make it okay."

Emily sounded incredibly grateful. Dirk smirked. I felt
like a heel.

"I have another idea." Karaline sounded entirely too bright,
and she wouldn't look me in the eyes. "Peggy can ride with
you, Emily. In fact, she can drive your car for you so you won't
have to worry about this twisty mountain road."

"I would say 'tis an excellent idea, Mistress Karaline."

I glared at Dirk. "'Tis not."

"That's right." Karaline spoke loudly, probably to hide
the fact that I was talking yet again to a ghost Emily couldn't
see. "Peg's a good driver, and you two can have a lovely chat
all the way to Winooski."

"You can't drive that far in your condition. It's one thing
to bop around town, but all the way to Winooski? Think of
your stitches."

"Those stitches are completely healed. Anyway, we're

almost out of the mountains, and from there it's a straight shot up to Burlington."

"I don't want you out of my sight," I said. "I don't know where Kittredge is. And what if you get another cramp?"

Karaline gave in with surprisingly good grace. "If I get a cramp, I'll pull over." What was she up to? "Give me your address, Mrs. Wantstring. I'll pop it in my GPS, and we'll go there first. I'll lead the way."

"That wasn't what I had in mind."

"I know." She jotted down Emily's address and headed for her car. "See you in Burlington."

"Right," I said, and tried not to sound venomous.

To top it all off, Karaline opened the door to her SUV and Dirk hopped in and slid over to the passenger seat. He wasn't coming with me? What kind of ghost would do a thing like that? Was he mad at me? Of course, she had the shawl. And I was the one who'd crumpled him up. It may have been an accident, but he'd still been sent to a place where he didn't want to be.

I made sure Emily had her seat belt fastened and followed Karaline—the traitor—out of the scenic overview.

What a lovely young woman, Emily thought. *If Mark and I had ever had a daughter . . .* She let that thought drift away and tried to keep from studying Peggy's profile. *How kind of her to do the driving this way. I ought to invite the two of them in for coffee when we get to Burlington, but I really do* not *want them to see my house if it's messed up.* She considered just serving them in the living room, but women tended to be drawn to kitchens, didn't they?

"I hope they didn't destroy any of my china. I think Sandra would have noticed if they had. All she could tell was the missing laptop." Emily paused for a quick breath. "Mark said it was just a spare. I don't know why he needed it. He never took it to work with him."

For the first ten miles I endured a recounting of what I'd already heard. I finally tuned out. I wondered if she'd ever told any of this to Harper. Harper. I let that thought linger, and Emily's voice faded into mere background noise.

As happy as I was to think about him, I had a feeling something was going on. Why hadn't he called in all this time? I didn't even know for sure where he was. *South America* covered a lot of territory. Well, if he ever came back, I'd ask him.

The next few miles went by rather quickly, taken up as they were by my thoughts of just what might happen if Harper and I ever got a chance to be alone together. We'd never quite gotten anywhere. I'd thought, soon after I met Harper, that we might have had a chance, and there had been that one time he'd kissed my cheek, but then he'd left, and it seemed like our relationship—if you could call it that—had come up against the proverbial brick wall. Of course, then it occurred to me that Dirk would be prowling around making comments and probably getting rather incensed if Harper and I were supposedly alone. For some reason, it felt good to think of having two men competing for me—even if one of them didn't know about the other one, and that other one just happened to be dead.

Emily ground her narrative to a halt, and I took in a deep breath. The road straightened out for a short while, and I could feel myself relaxing. "You and Dr. Wantstring have been married for more than thirty years, right?"

"Thirty-seven to be exact."

"Wow. Do you have any children?" I couldn't remember if she'd ever mentioned any.

"Two sons. No daughters." She paused. There was something in her voice, but I couldn't identify it. Maybe Emily had always wanted a little girl.

"Do they live close by?" What a stupid question. If they did, they'd be here helping her, instead of making me drive all the way.

"One's in Oklahoma. The other lives in Iowa."

"Oh. Do you have grandchildren?"

I shouldn't have looked over at her. The pain on her face was blatant.

"No," she said.

"Do you get a chance to see your sister very often?" Now, why did I ask that? Senators couldn't just go roaming around the country, visiting relatives anytime they wanted to. Or, come to think of it, maybe they could.

"No," she repeated, but this time there seemed to be a hard edge to her voice.

"I'm sorry, Emily. I didn't mean to pry." Casting about for something to say, I asked, "How long did Mark plan to be gone?" Beside me—silence.

Eventually we moved out of the mountains. People who live out West think the Rockies, Sierras, and Tetons are the only respectable mountain ranges, but our Green Mountains are tall enough, thank you. And they're far older than those upstart Rockies. Or the Scottish Highlands.

Once we were in the valley, I felt my shoulders loosen. It was another five miles before she started talking again. Once she started, though, she didn't slow down.

13

Endurance Test

I didn't lose Karaline, although with Emily's nonstop chatting it was a miracle I didn't. I couldn't hear myself think. I was sorry—truly sorry—that her house had been broken into, but I was ready to throttle her by the time we reached Burlington.

It didn't take us long to get to Emily's house. I followed Karaline onto one tree-lined street and then another, and pulled up before a modest one-story white house. It looked somewhat lost, surrounded as it was on both sides and across the street by three- and four-story edifices. I was willing to bet those would cost a small fortune to heat. Two enormous maples in the front yard were bare now, of course, but I could tell they'd join their leafy hands above us come full summer.

She must have called ahead, because someone waved out of an upper window of the house next door. "Oh, good! Look," Emily said. Her voice lifted, and I could hear the relief. "Sandra must have gotten back from her meeting early. She said she wasn't sure she'd make it on time. I'm so glad she's here. She's my neighbor, the one who discovered the break-in. She always waters our plants for us when we're gone. They've been here for years and years."

Even though I felt sorry for the poor woman, I was already dreading the trek back to Hamelin. Luckily, that turned out to be wasted worry.

Emily leaned against the open car door. "I think I'll stay for a few days."

Dirk and Karaline sauntered up next to us. "This is a lovely house, Mrs. Wantstring."

Dirk looked around as if trying to locate the chickens that any family must need. He still didn't quite understand the concept of grocery stores. Why had I never taken him to one?

Cancel that question. I knew darn well why I'd never shown him the inside of a grocery store. I didn't think I could cope with all the impossible-to-answer questions. Maybe I *should* take Karaline up on her offer, I thought. Not to take him permanently—I had to admit I wouldn't like that at all—but just to borrow him once in a while, like when she was on her way to shop for food.

I tuned back in, just in time to hear Karaline say, "It's really close to UVM."

Emily nodded. "Yes. Mark always walks to work." I had the feeling she wasn't engaged in the conversation. "Do you want to come in and have some coffee before you go?"

That was one of those tricky questions, wasn't it—the kind that seems to be saying one thing but actually means something else altogether? She'd emphasized *before you go*, as if that were the most important part of the question. Or did she really want us to come in with her? Before I could answer, her neighbor came out of the house next door and down the walk. We endured introductions, said a quick good-bye, and got the heck out of Dodge City.

Dirk accompanied us into the Kittredge showroom and Karaline handed me the shawl. While she talked with some guy at the front counter—he wore red suspenders—I spent the next few minutes drifting around between the displays trying to explain to Dirk, as quietly as possible, that I'd never seen equipment like this before. Finally, I just made up answers. "That thing grinds up grapefruit," I whispered. He'd seen me eat grapefruit often enough and was still in awe at how I could take for granted something as precious as a citrus fruit. I went on to the next display unit. It held a variety of implements I'd never seen before. I picked one at random. "This thing," I said in a whisper, "is for cutting waffles apart after they're cooked."

"I didna ken Mistress Karaline served whaffels at her wee restaurant."

"She doesn't. That's why you'll never see one of these things at the Logg Cabin."

"This is verra interesting. Why d'ye suppose the writing on the wee box says *dough scraper*?"

Phooey on him for looking at the boxes below the display. Not to be daunted I said, "Because waffles are made from a kind of dough, and you scrape them off the waffle iron."

Fortunately, Karaline chose that moment to call out, "Hey, you two, come on over here. We've got a problem."

The man behind the counter looked startled. "You two? What two?"

Karaline put her hand over her mouth. "I mean . . . my . . . uh . . . my friend is a twin, and I tend to think of her and her brother at the same time."

He nodded, still looking rather bewildered, but I could see him draw the conclusion that, *Customers are always right—no matter how nuts they seem to be.*

I sidled up next to her and waited for him to turn his back to reach for paper coming off a printer. "Great save," I whispered. "So, you think of my brother all the time whenever you're around me?"

"Master Drew likes ye rather much," Dirk observed, and Karaline's blush spread from her toes to the roots of her dark hair.

At least, I assumed it started at her toes, since it had gained so much power by the time it reached her neck. Kind of like a tidal wave. Too bad he was working on the West Coast for a month. Some museum had a dinosaur they needed advice on. I'd told him to stay off the frame. Poor Drew. His credit card info was stolen three weeks before he left for California, and he'd had a horrible time trying to get it straightened out in time for his trip. Identity theft was such a pervasive threat. And you never knew when you'd be hit. Maybe I needed to set up one of those text alert systems that sent me a notice each day as to what my balance was.

I pulled myself back to the immediate moment. "What's the problem?"

"They sold the SRM20, the only one they had."

The man cleared his throat. "If you'd put down a deposit and asked us to hold it for you . . ." He sounded truly apologetic. Dirk went behind the counter to inspect the man's suspenders. He seemed fascinated by them.

I felt sorry for him—the man, not Dirk. "When can you get another one in?"

"That's the trouble," Karaline said. "With the storm blanketing the East Coast, their warehouse is shut down."

"So," I asked again, "how long?"

The manager, who sported a name tag that read, *Chester Kerr, Manager*, was contrite but unwavering. "If we get a truck here any sooner, I can call you, but it looks like it will be Tuesday at the earliest."

"That's not bad," I said, although I hated the thought of driving back here tomorrow. "Maybe we can get a motel room overnight."

"What would be a *moh tell room*?"

Karaline made a rude sound, and I couldn't tell whether she was reacting to Dirk or to the manager. "He's talking *next* Tuesday, a week from tomorrow."

"Oh. Are you sure?"

"All the phone lines in our distribution center are down."

"What about e-mail?"

He shook his head. "The power is out. I tell you, nothing is moving anywhere."

Karaline rolled her shoulders back. "If I pay for it now, will you hold it for me when it gets here?"

"Of course."

After she paid, she motioned as if she were leading a cavalry charge. "Come on, you two. We might as well go. See you next week, Chester."

His eyes crinkled in worry and I could see his lips form a question. *Two?*

Well, we made it up Colchester Avenue and left onto East, but then Karaline turned right on Carrigan instead of heading straight toward Main Street. "Where are you going, K?" But I guessed I already knew. We were on the UVM campus.

She pulled into a parking place. "Let's stop by the microbiology lab." She held the door open for Dirk to exit. "As long as I'm here, I'd love to see the labs." I hurried to catch up with her and Dirk.

"What if they won't let us in?"

She shrugged. "Don't worry. They will. I belong here." She twisted her mouth. "At least, I used to."

She took the stairs two at a time, obviously familiar with the place. I guessed things hadn't changed much since she'd been a student here. The hall was immaculately clean and rather sterile-looking. We rounded several corners and stopped before a closed door.

Dirk passed us and inspected a metal plaque. "This wee sign says Marcus Wantstring, M-D-P-H-D." He spelled the letters one at a time. "What would these wee letters mean?"

"Medical doctor, doctor of philosophy," I said.

"Would he be Mistress Emily's husband?"

"Uh-huh," Karaline said.

"Can I help you?" I jumped at the voice behind me and turned to see a young man in a lab coat. A shock of white-blond hair, serious dark gray eyes, and a firm mouth. Two out of those three seemed to indicate we'd better answer quickly or he'd call security.

Dirk circled around to the young man's left. The blade of his dagger glinted in the light from a nearby window. Karaline stepped in front of me. "I was a grad student here about ten years ago. I was in town and thought I'd stop by to see the old place." She inclined her head toward the door. "Too bad Dr. W isn't here.

He pressed his lips together so firmly they went almost white. "Yeah. He's on vacation for a week."

The young man held out his hand. "I'm PD. Actually, my name's Conrad Turney. PD's my nickname."

"Are you one of W's graduate assistants?"

"Sure am."

She introduced me, then looked toward Dirk as if she'd thought about introducing him as well. I saw her clamp her jaw tight against the incipient laugh as she caught herself. Instead she said, "Peggy is a good friend of Dr. W's wife."

Before I could object to that designation, Conrad looked at me in some confusion. "Isn't Mrs. Wantstring too old?" He looked like he thought friendship with anyone over forty must be impossible.

"Ye shouldna speak so of Mistress Emily."

I agreed with Dirk. "She's the same age as Dr. Wantstring."

He cocked one eyebrow, as if to say, *Yeah? Isn't that what I said?*

Karaline interrupted. "So who's the other grad assist? If you're PD, the other one ought to be—Q?"

"Nope."

"PD for 'police department,' so FD for 'fire department'?"

"Wrong. I'll give you a hint. PD stands for 'polka dot.'"

Karaline thought for a moment. "Stripe?"

"You got it, and"—he looked at his watch—"she should be here right about—now."

I looked around at the empty hall. Conrad—PD—pointed back toward the hallway we'd come from as a young woman practically staggering under an armload of heavy books rounded the corner. "She should have been polka dot instead of me, cause she's always on the dot."

"And you're usually late." She sounded good-natured about it, though.

"She has to count her bugs in exactly two minutes. She comes in on the weekends, even if she doesn't have a Saturday class."

"I'm here on Sundays, too."

I happened to be looking at PD, and he narrowed his eyes slightly. Maybe he wasn't as dependable and didn't like being reminded of the fact?

She didn't slow her pace at all. She passed us and might have nodded her head as a hello, but with that pile of books right up to her chin it was hard to tell. She disappeared into a room two doors down from where we stood, and I turned back to look at Conrad again. Polka Dot seemed like such a silly nickname for a guy.

"We almost called her Rabbit, because she's so good at being invisible."

From the room two doors down came the comment, "And we would have called you Skunk, 'cause you stink."

Enough of this nickname stuff, I thought.

"So," Karaline said, "anything good going on in the lab?"

"Which one? We've got so many projects going on, Stripe and I can't keep up with them. Most of them are from the last trip."

"What trip?"

"We went to the Amazon last summer. Found the most interesting bacteria. Let me show you. I can't take you into the lab, of course, but I have some photos in the . . ."

Karaline handed me the shawl, and the two of them headed down the hall, immersed in microbiology talk. I looked at Dirk and shrugged. "Looks like we've been abandoned."

"No wonder, if you're talking to the wall." Stripe appeared through the doorway and approached me. For some reason she sidestepped Dirk—almost as if she'd lost her balance for a second and had to veer a little to one side, although with those fancy tennis shoes she wore, I should think she had enough traction for an icy path, much less a sheltered corridor. With a ghost in it. She couldn't have seen him. It must have been the energy he put out. She stopped in front of me. "So, did PD ask you what you're doing here? We try to keep an eye out for strangers."

I explained, and she motioned toward the plaque on the door. "You must have known him well," she said.

"I don't know him at all. Karaline knows him. I only know his wife."

She raised her eyebrows. "The ditzy one?"

"Why do you call her that?"

"Oh, nothing much. It's just that she has something of a reputation around here."

I could imagine. I waited for her to go on, but she stayed silent.

My curiosity got the better of me. "What sort of a reputation?"

"Well, I hate to say anything against her, and maybe it's not her fault."

"What's not her fault?" Pulling answers from her was like trying to ride a bicycle through heavy mud. On the other hand, maybe it was just as well. I liked that Stripe didn't seem to want to say anything bad about Emily.

"The grad assists always help serve at the faculty dinners twice a year."

Not knowing where this was headed, I nodded.

"Last month she went flying out of the dinner for no reason at all and ran right into me. I had a tray full of plates. It was a real mess. She didn't even stop to apologize."

"Do you have any idea why she did it?"

In answer, she simply looked over at the closed door. "I'm not sure why he put up with her. It really looked like she was crazy."

"What would mean this *crayzee*?"

I'd forgotten about Dirk momentarily, and I jumped a bit,

but Stripe didn't seem to notice. What would they have called a crazy person in the era of Chaucer?

But then I thought of Emily's constant need to talk. Maybe she just had to connect and didn't know how. It sounded like Stripe was basing her opinion on just that one unfortunate event.

"She's not crazy. She has . . ." How could I say this without sounding stuffy? "She has some problems." Maybe Stripe would think she had a food allergy.

"Ye still havena explained *crayzee*, but 'tis good ye have spoken of Mistress Emily, since ye claim to know her so weel."

"Medical problems?"

How would I know? "Allergies," I said.

"I dinna ken what *allargees* are, but ye dinna sound quite as if ye are speaking on behalf of Mistress Emily."

He was right, doggone him. I *wasn't* on Emily's side in this, and I ought to be. "Mrs. Wantstring is very nice once you get to know her." And very talkative, but I didn't say that.

Stripe didn't look convinced. She kept studying the nameplate on Dr. W's door. "Where did all these spiderwebs come from?" She sounded indignant.

"No idea."

She reached out and whisked them away. I sure hoped the little spiders weren't caught in the middle.

Dirk moved farther down the hall and stood in the exact middle, halfway between any doors. I had a feeling the spiders would find him anyway. Maybe they materialized out of thin air.

I looked back at Stripe. "Can I ask what your real name is?"

"Just call me Stripe. It was a nickname from when I was a kid, and I'm used to it. Do you want me to show you where PD and your friend are?"

*   *   *

A few minutes later, as we turned yet another corner, and
headed for an inconspicuous door, I said, "I appreciate the
guidance."

"They have to give us maps when we first enroll, and
people still get lost sometimes."

"Did you get lost when you first came here?"

She slowed her step as we walked into the room. "Oh, yeah."
There must have been quite a story behind those two words.

". . . sounds worse than it is," PD was saying. "It's easy
to neutralize."

He and Karaline were hunched over a spread of what
looked like photographs of swirly amoeba-like creatures.
The vivid colors on some of the photos reminded me of juicy
oranges and tart lemons and bright green broccoli. My stomach growled. "I'm hungry. We didn't stop for lunch."

Karaline didn't move other than to comment, "You'd better
watch out, PD. She gets cranky when she hasn't been fed."

PD pushed aside the photo he'd been studying. "Good
idea. There's a soup place a block from here. I'll join you if
you don't mind." He didn't wait for an answer. "I'll be back
in half an hour. You handle things here, Stripe."

"Like heck I will. I'm hungry, too."

Stripe slung her lab coat over a hook and threw on a gorgeous parka. It looked thick enough to handle forty below zero
without a hitch. PD wound a soft light brown scarf around his
neck and added a Day-Glo orange parka. "I like for everybody
to see me coming," he said when he noticed Karaline's raised
eyebrows. Next to him, Stripe looked like a quiet mouse.

So there were five of us for lunch. Well, four of us. Dirk
didn't count because he couldn't eat anything.

Once I had a steaming bowl of potato leek soup in front

of me, I felt a little more sociable. PD, across the table from me, looked up from his clam chowder. "So, do you have any idea what Dr. Wantstring's been working on?"

I shook my head, but Karaline paused, her spoon halfway to her mouth. "Uh, no. No, not really."

He studied her for a moment. "That sounds like a yes to me. I'd be willing to bet you really do know something." He slurped a spoonful. "Ah, that hits the spot. So, what's he up to? What's he doing?"

Dirk strode around from between Karaline and me to loom over PD. "Whatever 'tis, ye shouldna tell him aught, Mistress Karaline." Dirk's hand hovered at his belt, close enough to draw his dagger on a moment's notice. The poor grad student didn't know what he might be in for if he didn't watch his step.

Karaline had just taken a mouthful of the thickest vegetable beef soup I'd ever seen, so I went to her rescue. "Why do you want to know?"

"No particular reason. It's just that he's been hiding things lately."

Karaline swallowed. "You mean squirreling stuff? Does he still do that?"

"Yeah, all the time, but that's not what I meant."

"What did you mean?"

"Well"—he stirred his chowder around—"you know how he's always so open about using his own projects to teach us? *You* wouldn't know, but"—he transferred his gaze to Karaline—"*you* would."

Karaline nodded.

"The last few months, ever since Dr. H died, he's been almost—what would you say, Stripe? Secretive? Is that the right word?" Stripe, intent on her bowl of tomato basil, paid no attention.

Karaline held up a hand. "Dr. H is dead?"

"Yeah, he died a few months ago." Undeterred, PD went on. "It's like he doesn't have time for us anymore, and then he cancels classes and takes off for a week."

Karaline found her voice. "This is your last year, right?"

"Yep."

"Then maybe he's just expecting you to show a little more initiative. Is your thesis anywhere near done?"

"Well, that's part of the problem. After we got back from the trip last year, I tried to change the focus of my paper, but Wantstring wouldn't let me."

Karaline pursed her lips.

"I know, I know. He's the prof; I'm the stupid student."

"I didn't say that. I tried the same thing on my thesis, and he told me I had to carry through, but he let R alter his topic."

"R?"

"R for Rice. I was K."

For Karaline, I thought.

"And I thought PD and Stripe were stupid names."

Dirk growled and Karaline punched PD's arm, but he refused to be stopped. "You still haven't answered my question. What's he so tied up in knots about?"

"Ye shouldna tell him anything."

Karaline glared at Dirk. "I know."

PD looked confused. "I know you know. That's why I'm asking."

"I don't know anything for sure. It's just that . . ."

I kicked her under the table, but she waved me away. "It's just that the last time I talked to him, he seemed worried about something."

"Dinna say another word! I mistrust this wee gomerel."

"Do you know what it was?" PD was certainly persistent.

"No," she said. "If I knew anything for sure, I'd offer to help him."

PD leaned forward over his chowder. "He sure won't let us help."

"Maybe he wants you to focus on your own work. What you showed me was pretty impressive."

Dirk raised his hands, palms upward, fingers spread.

"Don't ask me," I said.

"He told me about it before you two got there."

Stripe looked up at that. I could tell K meant before Dirk and I got there, but Stripe obviously thought K was talking about us two live people coming in from the hallway.

"Yeah, I guess it *is* impressive. I did good work, but it wasn't what I wanted to focus on."

For someone who was doing well, PD sounded incredibly surly.

"Well," Karaline said, "if you make any more break-throughs before I get back here next Tuesday, let me know."

"Sure. Why?"

"Peggy and I have to come back to Kittredge Equipment to pick up a replacement planetary mixer—it's called an SRM20—for my restaurant."

"You have a restaurant? What's it called?"

Stripe paid no attention to their conversation. She'd put down her spoon and was texting something. *I swear, we're all going to wear out our thumb muscles before we turn fifty.*

It seemed like all the way back to Hamelin, Dirk ignored me and spoke only to Karaline. I finally stopped listening and concentrated on driving. By the time we got home, it was too late to do much other than cook up some spaghetti. Then I propped open a couple of books for Dirk—he can't turn the pages—and went to bed early.

14

Second Time Around

Dirk was lucky, even though he was dead. He never had to worry about what to wear. I've known women who always set out an outfit before they go to bed at night, and then they just get up, put it on, and are all ready to face the day. The trouble was, by the time I got around to going to bed Monday night, I was too tired to face my closet. Who was I kidding? I *never* set out my clothes ahead of time.

When I finally made it downstairs Tuesday morning, I was wearing a bright white chemise over my dark blue silk long johns, a green overskirt, a navy bodice, and a Graham arisaidh—I never worried too much about dressing for my own clan because so many of my customers couldn't tell the difference. If anyone questioned me, I'd just say I was honoring the Graham clan today.

I found Dirk standing at my back door, looking out across the snow-blanketed lawn to the snow-laden trees beyond the fence. The storm that had sprung up overnight—sort of a side effect of the blizzard raging all the way down the northern Atlantic coast—had dumped another twelve or eighteen inches, and many of the more slender trees bent under the weight. I checked the outdoor thermometer that hung outside the kitchen window. Good. It was still cold enough the keep the snow from icing up and sticking to the branches. All we'd need would be a good breeze and the snow would blow off. I always hated it when branches broke under the weight of wet snow.

I adjusted the belt around my arisaidh, that wonderful invention of Scottish women in the Middle Ages, which served as an overdress in mild weather and as a coat when the weather was inclement. Inclement? Where had I come up with a word like that? Some of Dirk's old-fashioned speech must be rubbing off on me. I fiddled with the brooch that kept the top of the arisaidh from slipping off my shoulders.

In modern-day America, an arisaidh was a fairly pricey item. One of the advantages of owning the ScotShop was that I'd gotten all five of mine at cost. Sometimes it was awfully hard to decide which one to wear, though. I liked them all.

"Dirk?"

"Aye?"

"How many outfits did you have when you were alive?"

"Outfits? What would—"

I didn't let him finish the all-too-predictable question. "You know. Changes of clothing. Different things to wear."

He looked down at his kilt and ran his hand along the length of woven tartan fabric that made up the top part of his belted plaid. He raised one white-clad arm and then the other. "I have . . . I *had* a second shirt." He raised one foot and then the other. "And four pairs of knitted stockings. What others would I have needed?" The puzzlement in his voice was genuine.

"Nothing," I said. "I was just curious." Everything about

his life was . . . had been . . . simple and practical and easy. He couldn't remember how or why he died, though. I'd be willing to bet it was the Plague. The Fever—that was what they called it back then—hit Scotland in 1359, the year he died. He thought maybe that was what had killed Peigi, his ladylove—the one who'd woven the shawl he was attached to, hard as that was to believe.

His eyes always got all soft when he spoke of her. Even dead, he had a love life—sort of. And here I was alive with no boyfriend in sight. Harper, unfortunately, didn't count since he never gave me a thought. If he'd been interested, he wouldn't have stood me up. Three times.

At least I could leave Dirk stuck here in the house anytime I wanted to. So there.

"I'm heading to the Logg Cabin for breakfast this morning." I knew Karaline wouldn't be busy. This much snow overnight would cut down on the number of patrons. Tuesday morning was never a big tourist time anyway, at least at the ScotShop. There'd be a lot of locals at the Logg Cabin, but I knew she'd be able to take a few minutes. I pulled a twenty out of my purse and stuffed it in the tuck-away fold of my arisaidh. I put the purse back on a shelf behind the door. No sense carrying that heavy thing.

"I will go with ye." He headed toward the front door.

Before he could berate me with the fact that I had rolled him up yesterday, I said, "You stay here."

"I would enjoy seeing Mistress Karaline and speaking wi' her."

"She won't be able to talk to you. I can guarantee you the restaurant will be almost full."

"Mistress Karaline will want to see me even if she canna talk to me." He turned his back on me and looked out the window.

The trouble was, he was right. She'd be delighted to see him.

Okay, so I might be angry, but I was not a spiteful person. At least I didn't think I was.

"All right. If you insist." I stepped into my boots, slung the shawl around my shoulders, and pulled out a green down-filled Lands' End parka I hadn't worn in a while. I tried to pull it on, but the shawl was too thick—or the parka was too snug. I yanked off the shawl, folded it in half, and laid it aside. I donned the parka and some fuzzy green mittens. "Okay. Let's go."

There was no answer. Crapola on toast! I'd closed up the shawl. *Again.* I reached for it, but stopped myself when I remembered that Dirk got dizzy—and so did I, for that matter—when the transitions went too fast. We didn't understand the physical principles involved—who could?—but I'd learned the hard way that if he was folded up, I had to leave him there for a while so he could *reset* or something. I pulled my hand away slowly. Dirk was never going to forgive me. I tiptoed out of my house, even though I was fairly sure my ghost wouldn't—couldn't—hear me.

I called out my thanks to my elderly neighbor who had once again shoveled my drive for me, and headed for the Logg Cabin. All the way there I struggled with my conscience. I could have brought the shawl along with me. I could have just waited a few minutes and then opened it up again. I could have. But I'd left it . . . him . . . at home. On purpose. Maybe I wouldn't mention all this to Karaline.

I had a quiet breakfast, with no conversation to speak of. Karaline was swamped. It felt like everybody in town had decided to have breakfast at the same time. I thought about driving back home, but I didn't want to face the shawl. If I opened it, he'd be mad. If I didn't, I'd feel guilty.

I ate the last bites, paid, and headed for the ScotShop.

Gilda was there before me. "Shoe's in the back room," she said before I'd even shut the door behind me. That unique smell of old floors and new fabric usually brightened me as I walked into my store, but today it didn't do much to dispel the sense of . . . of loneliness.

I missed Harper. That was what was wrong. I did not miss Dirk. I didn't. I stuffed my gloves in my pockets and pulled out of my green parka. I straightened a tartan skirt that hung askew on the rack closest to the door and strode across the room to the cash register. I was absolutely not going to think about Dirk all day long.

"How's it going, Peggy?" Gilda reached for my parka. "The storeroom's so full, we can't reach the coat pegs anymore. I'll throw this over one of the boxes." She looked particularly bright this morning, with her blond corkscrew curls bobbing in all directions.

I looked her over carefully. Her eyes were clear, and her hands weren't shaking.

She drew herself up. "I haven't been drinking, if that's what you're worried about, and I went to my AA meeting last night."

"Why is everybody so defensive today?"

"You don't have to snap my head off." Ever since she'd gotten back from the rehab facility, she'd become what she called "assertive" and I called "obnoxious." Unfortunately, that brought Dirk to mind and my little mistake before breakfast. Crapola on another piece of toast. Was the whole day going to be like this?

It was.

First of all, Emily Wantstring showed up within minutes of opening, bringing in a gust of cold air when she opened the door. Thank goodness for the long johns I routinely wore under my long skirts in the winter.

"I changed my mind and drove home last night." She covered her mouth, but I could see an enormous yawn hiding back behind her hand.

"You shouldn't drive so late, Emily. It's not safe."

"I wanted to be here when Mark got back."

That made sense.

Just then, a flood of tourists poured in and Emily left. I appreciated the bus companies for dropping their passengers off right in front of the ScotShop—they tended to buy a lot either before or after they ate at Karaline's Logg Cabin Restaurant. But it did make for a hectic forty-five minutes or so with each busload. Two more busloads were scheduled, but one of them, based in Boston, called to cancel because of the weather. I tried to be gracious—after all, tour buses brought in the majority of my business. We rescheduled for the following week, but Susan, the woman who'd called, said she wasn't sure they'd be running again that soon.

"We'll just play it by ear and hope for the best." I turned my face up to the sky—well, to the ceiling—hoping some weather god was listening to my plea.

15

The Joy of a Little Scottie

The final group of the day, thirty-two people from south-ern Alabama, had chartered their own bus. They'd planned to see autumn leaves. They'd counted on seeing autumn color. With none of that available, they were royally ticked off. It was hardly my fault that we had empty branches and three feet of snow this time of year, but I was the one who had to put up with their bellyaching. The trees in Vermont are usually bare by Columbus Day, but you can't convince a South-erner that winter shows up so early this far north. At least they bought what seemed like a truckload of shortbread, and a heck of a lot of tartan ties and shawls. I'd have to put in another order soon.

By three o'clock I was about to give up on the day when the bell over the door jangled. I looked up as Sam walked in with a navy blue duffel bag slung over his shoulder. "You're not working today," I said. "Why the visit?" I didn't know why I even asked. He was probably here to see Gilda, but she was over by the side window waiting on the one and only customer we had at the moment.

He gave me a noncommittal wave and set the duffel down gently on one of the benches near the display of ghillie brogues. The blue and green tartan-patterned carpet in that part of the store muffled his footsteps, but I heard the distinct sound of the duffel bag's long zipper. Well, if he didn't want to answer me, I'd put him to work. "While you're here, you can go help your brother in the back. There are a couple of boxes too bulky for one person to lift." I knew they were too *heavy* to lift, as well, but I was smart enough not to mention the excess weight. Shoe, with his baseball-hardened muscles, would object to any implication that he wasn't strong enough. Sam was a little less sensitive, but I'd learned over the years to be respectful of the male ego. Testosterone poisoning was no fun to deal with.

Sam looked over at the customer and lowered his voice. "What's the hurry?"

"Those boxes are blocking the back exit, and I don't want to risk a fine if the fire marshal stops in." The ScotShop store-room, protected from public view by a sign that said *Staff Only*, was filled to the brim.

Sam nodded, but he didn't move. He just stood by the shoe display grinning like a demented monkey. Before I could ask if he was nuts, I heard an inquisitive *woof* behind me, in the general vicinity of my ankles. I spun to my left and promptly fell in love.

"Who is this?" I bent to touch a little nose and then scratch a pair of perky black ears raised like little flags above a set of chocolate brown eyes—dark chocolate, the best kind. His wiry eyebrows splayed out a good inch or two above his eyes. "Where did you come from?"

"That's Scamp." Sam moved toward me, but paused and

picked up yet another tartan skirt that had gone askew on its hanger. He lowered his voice even more. "Gilda took care of him while she was in rehab." He straightened the skirt and put it back where it belonged. "It was part of their program. Each resident got to care for a dog who wouldn't have a home otherwise."

"How could any dog as cute as this one not have a home?"

From his six-foot height, Sam peered down. "I guess nobody wanted him. He can't qualify as a show dog."

"Why not?"

"His bite is off."

"What does that mean?"

"It's something that disqualifies show dogs. Something about the way his jaw is formed."

I looked back down at the little fellow. I could see what Sam was talking about. His lower jaw did thrust forward. On a person it would have looked pugnacious, but on him, it just looked cute.

"The puppy mill where he was born was raided and shut down, and there weren't enough foster homes available. It's a miracle they hadn't already put him down."

I'd read about puppy mills and thought they *all* ought to be shut down. But shutting down this one was better than nothing. "Poor little guy."

"Somebody in the rescue organization that took the dogs thought he had the right temperament to help people. Somebody with big bucks paid to have him neutered, and subsidized all his food as long as he was in the rehab program." He smiled over at her. "Gilda gets to keep him as long as she goes to her AA meetings every day."

"Sounds like you're one lucky little dog." I knelt, and Scamp leaned his head against my skirted knee. I obliged him with a good scratch under his chin. "Where's Gilda been hiding him?"

"Shoe and I help. Whoever has the shift free, we take care of him."

"I'm happy to meet the little guy, but why did you bring him here?"

Sam looked toward Gilda again. I could see her between the racks of full-sleeved poet shirts. The customer was bent over a selection of tartan scarves; Gilda looked quickly over at Sam and smiled. Her blond curls shone in the afternoon sunlight slanting in through the tall windows.

I glanced at Sam. Still smitten. He obviously hadn't heard my question. He gulped. After a couple of seconds he returned to the land of the conscious. "Is it okay if I leave him here?"

Scamp let out a quiet but enthusiastic *woof*—in people talk it would have meant *yes*—but Sam gave a quick hand signal, and the dog subsided. Sam looked vaguely surprised, but I didn't have time to ask him why. At least the dog was quiet. That was good, but before I agreed, I had to be sure. I bent closer to Scamp's head, and he rewarded me with a brief lick on my chin. His long beard hair brushed my hand. He wasn't smelly. That was definitely a point in his favor. "Will he leave the merchandise alone?"

"I walked him right before we came here."

"What does that have to do with my merchandise?"

"Scotties have a lot of energy. They need long walks to settle them down. Especially a Scottie as young as he is."

"Then why were you carrying him when you came in here? I assume that's what the duffel bag was for."

"It's not a duffel bag; it's a Sherpa."

"A what?"

"That's what it's called. Owners use them to carry the dogs on airlines."

"That still doesn't answer my question."

"The snow sticks to his fur, so I brushed him and dried him before I brought him in here. No need to have any more melting snow than necessary, and I didn't want him to be wet all day, even though his outer coat is virtually waterproof."

"Thank you." I didn't mean to sound so dry, but what was I going to do with a dog shedding all over the kilts?

As if he'd read my mind, Sam said, "Scotties don't shed, and he's a good dog."

"I don't want him jumping on my customers." *Or on me*, I thought. "What if somebody's trying on shoes? Will he try to jump in their lap?"

"He won't. Scotties aren't lapdogs. If you had a couch in here, he'd be perched up on the back of it. They like to be up high."

My brother's companion dog, Tessa, never jumped, but I hadn't ever given any thought to the training that had gotten such a positive result. Maybe it was just her personality. "Okay. He can stay." I stood up. "Don't start grinning yet. It's going to be on a trial basis. Anything he messes up, you and Gilda pay for."

"That's fine with me. He'll be so good you'll hardly even know he's here."

As if to underscore Sam's comment, Scamp burrowed under a rack of low-hanging sweaters. They rustled from side to side as he settled down. Finally, all I could see of him was the tip of one front foot peeking delicately from under a luscious off-white fisherman's knit. Thank goodness he didn't shed that black hair of his.

Shoe walked out of the back room and sketched a wave at his brother.

Something still bothered me. "If Scamp is such a good dog, why do you want to foist him off on me?"

Sam glanced toward the cash register where Gilda was ringing up a purchase. He leaned a little closer to me. "Gilda said she was lonely at work, and I thought Scamp might be the answer."

Gilda? Lonely? That was ridiculous. I was here. How could she possibly be lonely? But, if she was, why hadn't she confided in me? I looked around at my three employees. We'd grown up together, shared adventures and scrapes, laughed a lot, had our tiffs and made up afterward.

I was the boss—that was why. I was removed from them now. I hadn't even recognized Gilda's drinking problem over the past few years. I'd believed her when she said it was migraines, when all along she'd been having the most horrific hangovers. Sam had known, and so had Shoe, but they hadn't clued me in. What else were they hiding from me?

Karaline came by an hour later. Her Logg Cabin Restaurant closed at three, but late lunchers frequently lingered over coffee and desserts, and then she had to get the place ready to open early the next morning. I could see the bulge her cash bag made under her parka. Luckily the bank was fairly close, and robbery wasn't a big problem in Hamelin. It wasn't a problem at all, in fact.

She surveyed the store. Gilda was straightening the merchandise on the big bookcase we used to display nonbreakable items, and Shoe was in the back room out of earshot. "Where's Dirk?"

"Hello to you, too, Ms. Logg," I said. "I'm doing just great. Thanks for asking."

She looked around. "So, where is he?"

I wasn't about to tell the only other person in town who could see my ghost that I'd rolled him up in the shawl again. "He, uh, he's taking a nap."

"Ghosts don't take naps."

"He left."

She leveled a long stare at me that might have gotten ugly, but Scamp, who was proving to be an absolutely perfect doggie, chose that moment to introduce himself. Karaline looked down at the nose snuffling her boot, and the stare turned into an openmouthed grin of delight. "You got a dog! He's so sweet!" She held her hand down for him to sniff. "He's so—" She broke off and twisted to try to look more closely at him. "He's a boy, right?"

"Don't bother trying to look. He's so furry underneath nobody can see anything. But yes, he's a boy."

"And such a sweet little—"

I interrupted. Not that I didn't agree with her, but the gushing did not become her. "He's Gilda's, but she said he could be the store dog."

"What about hair on the merchandise?"

"Scotties don't shed the way other dogs do." *Don't I sound like a Scottish terrier expert?*

Scamp swiveled his head to look toward the front of the store, and the bell over the door tinkled merrily. He tilted his head and moved back between two hanging sweaters, as if he were getting ready to pounce.

He proved to be very choosy about the people he greeted and those he didn't. Gilda said it was because Scotties were such good judges of character. All the rest of that day and the next, I learned to watch his reactions. If he turned away from someone, ignored them, I tended to wonder if they were potential shoplifters. Either that or dedicated dog-haters.

* * *

By the time I made it home that evening, I was in a great mood. Dirk was not. "For why did ye wrap me awa' from ye?"

"I didn't do it on purpose."

"Did ye no?"

"No, I didn't know."

He tilted his head to one side and raised one eyebrow.

"Why are you looking at me like that?"

"I canna ken what ye are talking about, foreby."

I tried to think of a way to smooth this over. "We have a new addition to our staff at the ScotShop."

"Och, aye?" But he didn't sound as interested as I'd hoped he might.

"His name is Scamp. I think you'll like him."

He crossed his arms. "Will ye gi' me the shawl? If ye dinna need it for the warmth."

I guess he wasn't in any mood to forgive me right at the moment. "I'm sorry, Dirk."

"My name," he said, "is Macbeath."

I handed over the shawl.

Wednesday morning, Emily didn't know what to do with herself. She looked around vaguely, hoping to see her knitting, but then she noticed an untidy stack of books. She moved the entire stack an inch to the left and straightened it so all the spines lined up perfectly.

Mark should have been home by now. Or at least he should have called her. Had she mistaken the timing? No, but maybe he'd gotten a ride back to Burlington? That didn't sound right but, just in case, she called his office. There was no answer, but that didn't prove anything, so she called another number she had. One of the graduate students answered.

"This is Mrs. Wantstring. Is my husband there?"

"I haven't seen him, but, uh, I think I saw his car outside."

Emily didn't even say thank you. She just hung up. He'd abandoned her. Something bothered her, but she couldn't place it.

Hot chocolate would help.

Then, a little later, she'd drive over to the ScotShop and talk to Peggy. That always made her feel better.

16

Dog on a Throne

Thursday morning, oblivious of even the sunshine on my face, I overslept. Shorty finally succeeded where the sun had failed by patting my cheek softly three times and meowing at me. I pulled myself out of bed, aware of every muscle. I shouldn't have been surprised. This happened every winter. I'd go skiing for the first time of the season, and pay for it with four or five days of aches and pains. It wasn't like that twenty years ago when I was ten years old. Nothing ever ached back then.

I took a long hot shower—best medicine ever for sore muscles—and pulled on my dark blue silk long john top and bottom, a floor-length heavy green and blue plaid wool skirt, and my old winter standby, a deep green fisherman's knit sweater. The cowl-like neck of my navy silk long john top draped becomingly—if I did say so myself—over the thick wool of the sweater. I ignored my face in the mirror. I'd taken one quick look and hadn't liked what I'd seen. My hair hadn't yet recovered from where part of it had been shaved where I had to have stitches last summer. I'd cut it fairly short, but it was still in that in-between stage that made me look like a stale, warmed-over pancake on one side and a dandelion head on the other. Thank goodness I was used to wearing a Scottish kerchief. It covered a multitude of hair disasters. I'd left mine downstairs. There was no way I'd forget it, though. I had my priorities straight.

The shop opened at nine. I'd planned to get some paperwork done, and now I wouldn't have time. I absolutely refused to miss breakfast. Gilda would have to open without me. I tromped downstairs. What was Dirk doing in my favorite chair? Before I could say anything, he scanned me up and down. "Will ye be working at the wee shop today?"

"Yeah, and I have to hurry. I'm running late." I slipped into my boots so I could get the newspaper without freezing my toes off.

"Ye need more clothing. Ye will freeze in this cold. Why can ye no wear breeches on a day such as this one?"

Dirk had quickly grown accustomed to short skirts on women in the summer and long, leggy jeans in the autumn. Despite his initial fourteenth-century shock at seeing women's legs, he'd gotten over it real fast.

I stuck one booted foot forward toward him and raised my skirt a few inches above the boot top. "I'm wearing long johns."

"Long jahns? Would *long jahns* be those blue stockings?"

"They're not socks. They go all the way up, and they provide insulation so I don't get cold."

"All the way up where?" He sounded scandalized. And interested.

"They're like jeans, only softer, and they . . ." I gestured up the length of my leg to my waist. Not that it was any business of his. I bypassed my kerchief and pulled on a knit cap to keep my ears from freezing. "Anyway, I like wearing long skirts to work. If customers see me wearing them, they're more likely to buy some for themselves."

"Ye have six of those skirts that I have seen so far."

He was counting?

"Why need ye so many skirts?"

I refused to be sidetracked by how cute all those *r*'s sounded when he said "skir-r-r-rts." "I happen to have ten of them. Not that it's any business of yours."

"Ye needna whinge so."

He sounded so . . . so superior . . . I wanted to deck him. But with shoulders as broad as his were and biceps as massive, I doubted I'd make much of a dent. I brushed past his chair—my chair—grabbing the shawl off the back as I went. He stood to follow me, but I closed the door in his face.

It was too cold to linger outside. I waved to my next-door neighbor, grabbed the newspaper, and scooted back into the warmth of my living room. Dirk had retreated to the woodstove, although I couldn't for the life of me figure out how he could possibly need the warmth of it. I ducked into the kitchen rather than argue over woodstove proximity. A hot cup of java would warm me just as well, and I could wrap my cold fingers around it.

Humming despite my irritation with Dirk, I started a big pot of oatmeal and, coffee in hand, I spread open the *Hamelin Piper*. The headline blared the news that our police chief had been "MISSING SINCE SUNDAY." Good grief. I set down my coffee mug and reached for the phone.

Dirk sidled into the kitchen and looked at the paper. "I told ye we should ha' looked in the wee cabin."

"Oh, hush up. You didn't think it was all that important or you would have insisted." The trouble was, I knew he was right and he *had* tried to insist that we check on Mac; but I wasn't going to admit that to him. "Anyway, everything was just fine when we were there."

"How can ye be sure of that?"

"He was cussing so loud."

Dirk obviously missed the reference, but he must have gathered the gist of what I said, because he quirked an eyebrow at me. "Are ye saying he swore?"

"Yes. So he couldn't have been hurt."

"Mayhap he swore *because* he was hurt, as I seem to recall I mentioned to ye at the time. Did ye not even consider that possibility?"

I slapped the phone back down on the counter. "Why are you grilling me like this?"

"What would be this *grillink*?"

"Grilling. Interrogating. Bothering."

"I am asking questions that need to be asked."

"You're bugging me. It's not my fault Mac hasn't come home for four days."

"Ye needna shout at me."

"I am not shouting," I shouted. "I'm being assertive."

"Ye are being stubborn because ye think ye were wrong to leave him."

I jammed both my fists onto my hips. "You . . . you . . . you can't say that to me."

"Aye. That I can." He crossed his arms, and I saw the muscles bunch under his billowy white sleeves.

I'd been with this man, this ghost, every day for the past five months and he'd been correcting me for three quarters of them. "Go away!" This time I really was shouting. "Leave me alone!"

He looked at me like I'd hit him. "I canna leave, as ye verra weel know." His brogue got thicker with each word.

"Oh, yes, you can!" I grabbed the shawl from around my shoulders and bundled it up as tight as a Tootsie Roll. He. Was. Gone. I strode into the living room and tossed him— tossed *it*—onto the couch. Good. Riddance.

I picked up the phone, got hold of Murphy, and explained what had happened up on the Perth.

"When you say, *We were skiing*, just who else are you referring to?" Police sergeant Murphy sounded quite reasonable when he asked this most unreasonable question. Unreasonable because I didn't want to answer it.

I was referring to my ghost—the one I'm not talking to. "Uh, it's the royal *we*. Like Queen Elizabeth?" A pregnant pause filled the phone line. "I, uh, like to imagine I'm with someone when I'm skiing," I said, scrambling to fill the silence without mentioning Dirk. I wasn't even going to think about him anyway. Damn Scot.

"Oh?" Murphy sounded skeptical. I couldn't blame him. "Like who?"

Harper. Cancel that thought. "I talk to the birds and squirrels while I'm skiing," I told Murphy. *And my resident ghost whom I just banished.* "It's sort of like having company."

"So you're telling me you didn't go into the cabin but you're sure Chief Campbell was there?" Murphy's Irish brogue got stronger with each syllable.

"That's right." I shoveled in another mouthful of oatmeal and chewed fast, hoping I was chewing quietly enough that he wouldn't hear me.

"And how would you—and your squirrel friends," he added in a tone I thought was unnecessarily mocking, "know it was the chief if you didn't see him?"

I swallowed. "Well, I already told you. His skis were parked beside the door."

"You recognized his skis?"

"Well, no, but we knew—I mean, I knew he was there."

"You and the squirrels knew he was there?"

"We . . . I heard him swearing at the firewood."

A few seconds of silence during which I heard muffled choking. Or maybe it was laughter. "I'll get right on it, Ms. Winn." He must have believed the swearing part. "We'll send somebody up there to look for him."

It's about time. "Thank you," I said. Maybe Mac had strapped on his skis and gone farther up the mountain after he got his fire started. Maybe they'd never find him.

I left for the ScotShop in a dire mood, but when I got there, my mood changed instantly. I found a crowd of people oohing in front of one of my display windows. Yesterday it had contained four kilted mannequins, several artful stacks of Fair Isle sweaters, and a selection of books, bookends, and other items. Now, nestled between two of the mannequins, was an ottoman covered in a tartan shawl that I recognized as one of Gilda's. Scamp sprawled in Scottie splendor on the ottoman, basking in the admiration, his head resting on a soft fat Loch Ness Monster pillow.

"Come on in," I told the crowd. "Feel free to browse."

"I want to buy the dog," one woman said. "Is he for sale?"

"No, but you can buy one of those sweaters next to the dog's throne."

I sold four sweaters, two Monster pillows, and five boxes of shortbread, thanks to Scamp. He was hired.

17

Blue Enameled Box

Sergeant Marti Fairing pulled the report from the printer and attached it to the file, although she hated to waste the paper. At least she had an answer, of sorts. The license plate was still fuzzy, and she couldn't tell for sure whether one of the characters was a 1 or a lowercase *L*; then there was a question whether another character was an *A* or an *R*. That left her with four possibilities. A1, AL, R1, or RL.

She ran the plate all four ways and ended up with three hits. Great. Now she had three suspects for a stupid report she shouldn't even be wasting time on. But there wasn't much else to do. She'd asked around. Nobody had seen a gray car with a crushed right rear taillight.

She looked back at the three possibilities. One from Bennington, one from Burlington, and one from Winooski. Pat Featherstone, Zebra Harvey, and Cessford Kerr. She was gonna put her money on the Featherstone guy. Sounded like the kind of a flake who'd back into somebody's car and leave the scene. Or Cessford. Who'd name a kid Cessford? Of course, when it came to that, who'd name a kid Zebra? Heck, it could be any one of them.

She almost wished she hadn't pulled the report. Maybe a nice robbery would show up before the end of the day. She took the entire fender-bender file, as she called it, and stuffed it under the items in Harper's in-box. Everyone had been threatening to put him on traffic. First he was gone for a week. Then he hared off to Poughkeepsie four different times on some sort of special assignment. Rumor mill had it that Archie—the town moderator—had requested it. No telling what sort of strings got pulled there. Still, Harper was okay. She could imagine his full-throated laugh when he found it. He always reminded her of her big brother.

She couldn't wait to tell him about how she'd picked the locks on Mac's house. When he hadn't shown up for work yesterday and everybody got worried, they thought maybe he'd had a heart attack—wouldn't that have been lovely?— and she'd volunteered to be the one to check out his house. But he hadn't been there.

Murphy had skied up the Perth about an hour ago to check out Ms. Winn's story—Fairing privately hoped Mac had fallen off a ledge. It was probably a good idea Murphy had gone. If he'd sent Fairing and she'd found Mac incapacitated, wouldn't she have just loved to turn around and leave him?

When the phone rang a moment later, Moira routed it to her. Well, of course she did. Fairing was the only one around. "Fairing here . . . He broke what? . . . Murder?"

She called for an ambulance and the mountain rescue crew.

And to think she'd wished for a simple robbery. Or a heart attack.

* * *

Karaline made her usual afternoon stop at the ScotShop when the Logg Cabin closed for the day. In between customers, I told her about Mac—how it turned out he'd been missing for four days. She was about to answer when Scamp scrambled to his feet and pointed his long-bearded snout toward the front door.

Karaline's face broke into a smile, and I turned to see what had caused such a look of joy.

Harper!

He shut the door behind him. He looked older, somehow. Worn. Gaunt. Tired.

Without quite knowing how it happened, I stood in front of him, the memory of that one time he kissed my cheek surrounding us both. Well, surrounding me anyway. He looked too exhausted to care. There were deep shadows around his gorgeous charcoal eyes, and I thought maybe he'd lost weight, but I couldn't tell for sure what with his heavy parka. "Hello," I said. How dull could I get? His eyes brightened for a second. Or maybe that was only my imagination. After all, he'd stood me up three times, but who was counting?

From behind me Shoe called out, "Yo, man."

Harper nodded in Shoe's general direction without making eye contact, and Shoe for once must have taken the hint. His footsteps ended at the bookcase. Harper dropped his gaze to the floor. "I came by to apologize."

I gestured to Gilda to take care of things and led Harper and Karaline into the back room. There was no way I was going to let him off the hook that easily. He'd have to come clean in front of a witness. We sat at the battered old table that had seen so many late-night conversations. I poured him the last bit of coffee, unplugged the pot, and tried not to glare at him. Tried not to be too hopeful, either, but he didn't have to know that.

"My dad was in jail," he said.

That was about the last thing I'd expected to hear him say.

"In the Amazon jungle."

No. *That* was the last thing I expected.

"He died the day after I got there."

Karaline and I reached out at the same time. She touched his left arm. I took his right hand. "I'm so sorry," I said.

"It's not your fault."

What a *man* thing to say. I knew it wasn't my fault. I was expressing empathy, not apology. Karaline and I both let go, but I doubt Harper noticed.

"I brought his ashes back in a blue enameled box. I wanted to explain, but then Poughkeepsie called Archie, and Archie called me, and I had to—" He stopped abruptly.

He was hiding something. Maybe not hiding, exactly, but not telling us everything. Poughkeepsie was the city where he used to work before he came here to Hamelin. Why would they call our town moderator?

He lifted his coffee cup and set it right back down. "That's why I kept having to—"

Shoe stuck his head through the doorway. "Unhappy customer needs to speak with you, Peggy."

"Can't Gilda take care of him?"

"It's a her, and no, she insists on talking to the owner."

Rotten timing. Karaline motioned me to go on. Harper didn't even look up.

Apparently I'd sold this unsatisfied customer a Graham of Monteith tie last summer, but her son-in-law was a Graham of Montrose. The fact that Dirk had upbraided me at the time for not selling her both of them—so she could be sure to have the right one—did not improve my mood. The only good point was that Dirk wasn't here to rub it in.

I exchanged one dark green tie for another that was so similar I had to look twice, but I handled the transaction with relatively good grace. Then she pulled out the matching scarf I'd sold her for her daughter, and I had to exchange that as well. I even did it without gritting my teeth. A happy customer was more important than a ten-day return policy. In fact, she was so happy, she proceeded to buy seven one-pound boxes of shortbread—"one for each grandchild"—and a scarf for herself, so there was quite a bit of positive cash flow, and she was smiling as she left. So was I.

Before I could get back to Harper—and Karaline, I added mentally—Sergeant Murphy, our only Irish cop in a town of Scots, closed the door behind him with a bang. I heard a muffled *woof* from Scamp that sounded distinctly like an objection to the loud noise, or maybe it was to the draft of frigid air that had blown in with Murphy. We'd have to get Scamp a little doggie coat to wear. Maybe in a nice tartan, although I wasn't sure which clan a Scottish terrier would belong to. Gilda would probably want him to wear her yellowish Buchanan plaid, but I was afraid it would clash with the blue and green carpet that covered half the floor. Scamp quieted immediately. That was good. I couldn't have him barking whenever he felt like it. Of course, he hadn't barked when Harper came in.

"Brrr! Too cold out there." Murphy threaded his way between the racks of kilts and long-sleeved white shirts, looking around as if checking to be sure nobody else was in the store. "I need to show you a picture. See if you recog—" He stopped in mid-sentence as Karaline and Harper came out of the back room. "You're back? It's about time. Fairing and I are threatening to put you on traffic detail."

I couldn't help it. I felt a rush of heat up my face as I realized what his words meant. Maybe Harper really had bounced from the rain forest to central New York. Truly. And he'd come here, to the ScotShop, before he'd gone to work.

"I'll be at the station in"—he looked at me—"in a while."

"Good thing you're back." Murphy's Irish lilt was prominent.

Harper gave an inquiring look and walked toward us. "You mean you missed me?" He was talking to Murphy, but I could swear he was looking at me.

Karaline stopped at the bookcase and readjusted a few items.

Murphy lowered his voice as Harper got closer. "We've got us a murder to solve. Guy up in that old cabin on the Perth."

For half a sec, I thought it might be Mac, but no; not even Danny Murphy would have been this casual if the dead person had been his police chief.

He handed an eight-by-ten photo to Harper. "No idea who this guy is. Do you recognize him?"

"No," Harper said and handed it to me.

There's something about death that sets a person apart. You can't be alive and look this dead, at least not as far as I knew. *Dirk could be dead and look alive*, I remembered, but that was different.

This guy in the photo, as dead as could be, looked vaguely familiar, but I couldn't place him. More than anything, he looked like the stone effigy of a dead king. Chiseled cheekbones ran parallel to his jawline. The only note of incongruity in the face was the delicacy of his soft feathery eyebrows. That and the obviously broken nose.

Karaline was finally satisfied with the way she'd arranged the shortbread display on the bookcase. It was amazing how quickly displays could deteriorate when customers rummaged their way through a store. I thought it was funny, too, how she could straighten things up in my store, but I never thought to straighten a thing in her restaurant. Maybe the next time I was over there I'd look around to see if I could find anything out of place.

She looked up at me, smiled, and headed across the store toward us. She obviously hadn't heard what Murphy was talking about.

I looked at the photo again. "He looks vaguely familiar, but I can't place him," I said as Karaline stepped up beside me.

"Oh my God." She reached for the photo. "It's Dr. W."

18

Mark My Words

"You know this man?"

I ignored Murphy and grabbed Karaline's arm. She looked ready to pass out.

"Who is Dr. Doubleyou?"

She hardly even glanced at Murphy. "He's . . . He was . . . a professor of microbiology at UVM."

Harper opened his mouth, but seemed to change his mind as Murphy challenged Karaline. "Was? What makes you think he's dead?"

"Don't be an idiot, Murphy," I snapped. "That morgue shot's pretty obvious, and you already said you had a murder on your hands."

Karaline kept talking as if she hadn't heard us. "He was my mentor. One of the finest men I ever knew."

Murphy cleared his throat. "When was that?"

"In college. I have a master's degree in microbiology," Karaline said. "I didn't pursue it. I had a chance to buy the

restaurant right after graduation and just went from there."
A wan smile played across her lips. "I have the cleanest restaurant imaginable, because Dr. W made sure I knew what
lurks in cracks and crevasses."

An unwanted picture of germs breeding in wild abandon
crossed my mind, but it vanished when I thought about that
man's dead face.

Murphy whipped out a notepad. "When was the last time
you saw him?"

"Is he really dead? Is that why you're asking all these
questions?"

I was right. She hadn't heard me snap at Murphy half a
minute ago.

"We found his body in the cabin up the Perth trail."

"The Perth," I said. "Did you ever find Mac?"

"What about Mac?" Harper's voice was sharp.

"The chief went out skiing on Perth," Murphy explained.
"Broke his leg and managed to get to the cabin, where he
found this dead guy." He motioned toward the photo.

"If his leg was broken," I said, "how did he get to the cabin?"

"Oh," Murphy said with the cheerfulness of someone
who's never fractured a bone, "he fell and broke it on the
way up the trail. Took him a while to crawl up to the cabin,
and then he had to get a fire started."

No wonder Mac had been swearing so much. How do
you crawl that far with a broken leg, much less build a fire
at the end of the trek?

"That must have been unbelievably painful. I can't imagine
breaking a leg." Karaline rubbed her left arm, and I remembered her telling me about falling out of a tree as a kid.

"Yeah," Murphy said. "It was pretty awful. Really bad
break to start with, and then he splinted it himself on one of
his skis." I saw Karaline make a face. "By the time we got

there," Murphy continued, "he'd run out of food and water, and he has two broken fingers from a log falling on him. If we'd gotten to him a few days earlier, he'd be in a lot better shape."

Thank goodness Dirk wasn't listening to this. The last thing I needed from him was, *I told ye we should hae gone to the wee cabin, never the mind ye didna care to see the constable.*

"Did Mac say when it happened?" I asked. I was hoping it might have been after I'd already left, but I'm afraid I suspected I'd made a really stupid mistake in turning around and leaving the cabin.

"Yeah. Sunday. That's the day this Dr. Double Something got smacked, too."

Harper gave Murphy one of those *time-out* signals, and Murphy shifted gears. "Can we get back to the topic now? I asked you when was the last time you saw the doctor—what was his name?"

"W, for Wantstring." She spelled it for him.

That was why his picture had looked vaguely familiar. I'd seen him walking with Emily that one time.

"I saw him about two months ago," Karaline continued. "He and his wife"—a faint shudder passed across her shoulders—"came into the Logg Cabin for a late lunch about half an hour before we closed. After they finished, Mrs. Wantstring left." She looked at me. "She said she wanted to talk with you, Peggy."

"That's not a surprise," I said. "Emily comes in here a lot. Usually to complain about Mark."

"Marcus," Karaline corrected me, tears in her voice. "He doesn't . . . He didn't like . . . He wouldn't let anyone call him Mark."

Harper cocked his head, but Murphy made a *let's get on*

with it rolling motion with his right hand. "What did you talk about when he stopped by your restaurant?"

"He told me he and a colleague had been working on a project of some sort for years. He said they'd entered a new phase. I think those were the words he used. He sounded excited, and"—she paused—"secretive."

"Secretive?" Harper's color had come back, but his voice was contained somehow, as if he were holding something back. What was going on?

"Yeah. You never know who might be listening. Most researchers are very careful about who they talk to."

"But he talked to you?" Murphy sounded skeptical.

"Of course he did. I knew him from my sophomore year all the way through my master's. I was one of his graduate assistants my last two years. We were very close."

Murphy raised an eyebrow.

Karaline humphed. "Not like that. I respected him more than any other professor I had." She paused for a moment. "Except maybe Dr. H. He was a new prof my last year in the advanced degree program, and I only had one class with him."

The bell clanged, and Emily Wantstring walked in. Beside me, I felt Karaline stiffen. I heard Scamp's claws scrabble a bit on the hardwood floor, and was afraid he might bolt out from under the sweaters, but a quick glance showed that both his feet had disappeared. Getting ready to pounce again? As Gilda tried to head Emily off, I quietly explained who she was to Harper and Murphy. It was Harper who walked forward. I didn't hear what he said to her, but her reply carried through the store.

"It's Mark, isn't it?" No tears. Not even much surprise. Shock, I thought. She pulled off her knitted purple scarf and tugged at the top of her turtleneck as if the room were suddenly too warm.

"We'd like you to look at a photograph." This time Harper's deep voice carried clearly across the intervening racks of kilts and sweaters. "We can do it at your house or at the station."

"What's wrong with here?"

I stepped to the door, turned the sign to *Closed*, and pulled the shade. It was almost five anyway. "Gilda, you and Shoe go ahead and leave. I'll do the closing once we're through here." She nodded and called to Scamp. Harper took a step backward when the little guy emerged from the back of the counter where we displayed tartan handbags. How had he gotten there? Last time I'd seen him, he was under the sweaters.

Scamp stood for a moment, sniffing Harper's boot. He looked up at Harper, studied my face and Karaline's, and sauntered back to Gilda, his little carrot-shaped tail wagging like crazy. He folded his ears, like fortune cookies. That meant he was happy.

I could tell Harper wanted to ask about the dog, but Emily stood beside him clutching her purple scarf in one hand and the zipper of her parka in the other, clearly not sure what to do with herself. Shoe and Gilda grabbed their coats from the back room and coaxed Scamp into the Sherpa. I locked the door behind them.

"But why?" The question burst from Emily like lava spewing from the mouth of a volcano. "Did they rob him? He never carried any money with him when he skied. He didn't have anything anybody would want."

"There weren't any identifying papers on him," Murphy said. "There wasn't anything like that anywhere in the cabin. We searched it thoroughly. Somebody cleaned him out."

Harper shot a stern look at the sergeant. I could understand why. I didn't think Murphy had meant to be unkind, but I could see that Emily was shaken. She reached out a hand and clutched Harper's arm. He pointed Murphy toward the back room and ushered Emily in after him. This wasn't the way they did it on TV, but Hamelin was a small town. Before he closed the door, Harper held up a hand, stopping Karaline and me from following. "We'll take it from here," he said.

Karaline studied the closed door for a moment, then turned to look at me. "Want a cup of coffee?"

"They won't let us back there," I said. "Anyway, I already emptied the coffeemaker."

"At the Logg Cabin," she said. "I'll brew a quick pot and we can sit by one of the front windows and keep an eye over here so we'll see when they leave."

Sounded good to me.

I debated whether or not to knock on the Staff Only door and ask for my coat, but it wasn't far from the ScotShop across the courtyard to the Logg Cabin, and my green sweater was thick and wooly.

Even if I were going to freeze, I didn't have much choice. Those few abrupt words from Harper—*we'll take it from here*—had shut me out. What I wondered was, *Is he shutting me out of my back room for now or is he shutting me out of the investigation—and out of his life—altogether?*

I had too many questions rolling around inside my brain, like what was a professor of microbiology doing camping out in that little cabin? *That's a ridiculous question*, I thought. All sorts of people like to go camping. But why now? PD, the grad student, had said Wantstring was on vacation, and I hadn't thought much about it at the time, but this wasn't any holiday season that I knew of. Surely classes would still be in session. And why the cabin? Emily had said he'd gone skiing. Why up the Perth trail? No feasible answer came to me.

My keys were in the back room in my coat pocket, so I

couldn't lock the ScotShop door. I just closed it behind me and went on with my internal list of questions as I walked around the courtyard. It didn't do to try to run on an accumulation of snow. There could always be a patch of ice underneath it.

One of the questions I asked myself as I walked was why he'd left his wife for the weekend. That one was easy to answer: Emily didn't like the outdoors. She didn't like being cold. She didn't like to ski. Three answers for one question. Still, if she'd had enough of a reason, she might have killed him. I narrowed my eyes against the cold air outside and tried to imagine Emily murdering her husband. I didn't even know how he died. Did she shoot him? Knife him? Poison him? Bludgeon him with a ski pole? I couldn't imagine any of those scenarios.

Before I could draft any more questions, Karaline unlocked the Logg Cabin door, and a rush of warm moist air billowed out, pulling us into its welcoming arms. I still had no answers, and the most important question of all—why would anyone want Marcus Wantstring dead?—followed us inside.

Emily sat on the chair the taller officer held for her at the little table in the middle of the crowded storage room. Murphy pushed the photo across the scarred surface. "Can you identify this man?"

She held her breath for a moment and hooked a finger in the top of her purple turtleneck, right where a cluster of white embroidered snowflakes spilled down over her collarbone. She tugged the fabric away from her neck. "That is Mark Wantstring. My husband."

Murphy pushed it a little closer to her. "Are you sure?"

"Of course I'm sure! You don't think I'd recognize a man I lived with for thirty-nine years?"

"Married that long, were you?"

Emily didn't want to answer that question. *I should have said thirty-seven*, she thought. Both police officers were looking at her. For once, she didn't keep talking.

19

Squirreling

Karaline didn't . . . couldn't seem to look at me, but I didn't feel like she was excluding me—just that her heart was close to breaking. She cradled her coffee mug against her peacock blue sweater. Warming her unhappy heart. The tears she'd held back while we were at the ScotShop spilled down her face and dripped from her chin, salting her coffee.

She murmured something so low I missed it.

I leaned forward. "Tell me about him, K."

"He had more of a sense of integrity than almost anybody I've ever known. He and Dr. H."

"You mentioned this Dr. H before, when you were talking with Murphy. What did the *H* stand for?"

"I don't . . . Oh, yeah. It was Harper."

"Like—" I almost said, *Like my Harper*, only he wasn't *my* Harper. He'd made that abundantly clear. "Did you call all your professors by their initials?"

She tapped the rim of her mug thoughtfully. "I guess I did.

It started my junior year. That was the year I decided I would definitely go on for my master's degree. I began to notice that all the grad assistants had nicknames. It was sort of a tradition in the department. You already met PD and Stripe. PD for Polka Dot. I wonder where Stripe came from?"

"She said it was a childhood nickname."

Karaline didn't seem to register my response. "The year I first was really aware of the nickname tradition, Dr. W's graduate assistants—there were usually two—were called S and O."

I opened my mouth, but she cut me off. "Don't ask me why. I never did find out. Maybe those were actually their own initials. But I just started referring to everybody like that. It was sort of a joke at first, and then"—she took a sip of her coffee—"then it became a habit. The next two assistants were Daffy and Duck. The year before I served as a grad assist—that was what we called ourselves—they went by Cleo and Ant. Then it was my turn." She stopped talking and was quiet for so long I thought she might have fallen asleep with her eyes open. "I was so excited when Dr. W told me he'd approved my application to be one of his assistants." Her voice was soft, wistful, sad.

"I'm sorry, K."

She nodded. "Anyway, the other student serving with me was . . . Mike, I think. He was R and I was K."

"How do you get an *R* out of Mike?"

Karaline chuckled, her sadness at bay for the moment. "Mike had this thing about scarfing down his breakfast just before he had to be at his first class, so he stored cereal in his locker and milk in the lab fridge, and I was always hungry, so I'd snitch some."

"I still don't get it."

"That's why we were *R* for Rice and *K* for Krispies."

"And here I thought the *K* stood for Karaline. So, other

than *R* for Mike, you just kept on calling everybody by their initials?"

"I'm not the only one. You do it, too. I call you P half the time, and you call me K."

"That's because you started it." I remembered how confused Dirk was at first. He thought her name was Caroline with a *C*, so he couldn't figure out why I called her K. I pulled my mind up short. I was not going to think about that . . . that . . . Scot. I didn't have to think about him and how right he'd been about Mac. He was gone. Maybe he wouldn't come back. Maybe, the next time I opened the shawl, it would just be . . . empty. Just a shawl. No ghost. No nothing.

I felt a sudden desolation, almost devastation. I shook myself. I was not going to think about him.

Karaline, who ordinarily would have asked me if I had ants in my pants when she saw me squirming around like that, was oblivious. She twirled her coffee mug counterclockwise, and a smile spread across her face. "We called him Squirrel behind his back."

"Squirrel?" I thought about the distinguished-looking face in the photo. There was nothing even faintly squirrel-like about it.

"Don't look so baffled. It wasn't what he *looked* like; it was what he *did*."

"Did?"

"He was always squirreling things away. Once, he slipped a CD in between two books on one of his bookcases, and he couldn't recall where it was, only that it was somewhere among the books, but he couldn't even remember which wall of his office he'd been standing by when he tucked it away. To top it all off, the CD wasn't in a case. So it didn't take up any room at all. It took us almost an hour to find it. Do you have any idea how many books a college professor has?" She laughed. "Luckily, his printed manuscripts were always in big three-ring binders, so he couldn't hide those away—unless he really worked at it. Another big problem was his thumb drives. He could never keep track of USBs. I found them everywhere. Just like his stashes of candy hidden around the lab and all over his office. His favorite was Tootsie Rolls."

I thought about the tight roll I'd made of my shawl when I banished Dirk.

"What's wrong, P? You look like you've seen a ghost." Then she obviously thought about what she'd just said and glanced around toward the door. "Did Dirk just show up?"

"He can't show up."

"I know that. He can't open doors."

"No. It's more than that." Why was I breathing so hard all of a sudden? "I sent him away."

"You what?"

"Don't look at me like that. He was being a royal pain in the tutu, so I folded him up."

"Again? He doesn't like that," she said in a low, steady tone.

"Well, I don't like being told what to do."

"So you consigned him to shawl purgatory?"

"Shawl purgatory? Where did that come from?"

"You're changing the subject," she said. "Deliberately."

I set down my mug and folded my arms. "Yes, I am. What goes on between me and my ghost is my business."

Karaline stood up so fast her chair fell over.

I hated being sulky. "I'm sorry, K. I don't know what's wrong with me lately."

She righted her chair and sat back down. "I know exactly what's wrong, and I'm going to tell you"—she held up her hand—"so you just sit there and take it."

"You sound like Dirk," I muttered.

"As far as Dirk is concerned, from what I can tell, he sees right through you."

He's *the ghost,* I thought. *I see through* him.

"And you don't like having him tell you what you *should* be doing instead of what you *are* doing, especially when he's right."

Sulk was out. Indignation was in. "*Nobody* likes being told they're wrong all the time."

She ignored that. "The other thing that's wrong with you is Harper."

I glared at her.

"One minute he was here—and I saw the way you two looked at each other—and then he was gone almost from one day to the next."

Almost from one heartbeat to the next, I thought. "He stood me up."

"Yeah? So? His dad died. And then work got in the way."

"He could have called."

She ignored that, maybe because she knew I was right. "Now he's back and you don't know what to do. He didn't even kiss you hello."

Not that he ever had, I thought. "What did he tell you after I left to take care of that customer?"

She stirred more cream into her half-empty cup. Stalling for time, I thought.

"He didn't say much. I think he'd rather tell *you* about it."

"Not a chance." I pushed my mug away from me. "He'll be all caught up in the murder investigation now." I readjusted my kerchief and tucked away a stray lock. Forget that—my hair wasn't long enough to be a *lock*, only long enough to tickle my ear. "He won't have time for me." I sounded like a frustrated adolescent. "Let's not talk about Harper. Or Dirk.

Tell me more about Dr. Wantstring. What was this project he was talking about?"

"I really don't know anything specific. What I told Harper and Murphy was all I know."

"That's all?"

"Yeah." I must have looked skeptical, because she added, "If I knew anything, don't you think I would have told Harper and Murphy—and you," she added almost as an afterthought.

"Wait. You said he was secretive? Maybe he's working on some hush-hush government project?"

Karaline looked at me as if I'd gone out of my mind. "At UVM? In the microbiology department?"

I looked into my half-empty coffee mug. "Yeah. I guess you're right. But still, he's dead." I took a sip of the rapidly cooling coffee. "Are you sure he didn't mention any more details?"

She gazed out onto the snow-filled courtyard. A man enveloped in a bright blue parka had brushed the snow off one of the courtyard benches, and sat there using his cell. A tourist, by the look of him. Awful cold phone booth, I thought.

"He wouldn't say anything more. He was such a private person." The pain in her voice was almost palpable. "He never talked much about himself or his wife. I never understood their relationship. They seemed like such . . . opposites."

I decided to take the high road. Dirk would have been proud of me—but I wasn't thinking about him. "Maybe she made him laugh," I said, wondering even as I said it whether that would be enough to sustain a marriage. I looked beyond the cell phone guy. The front door of the ScotShop was still firmly closed. "I wonder what's keeping them so long?"

"They're trying to decide how she killed him. Don't you know the spouse is always the prime suspect?"

"Emily wouldn't have the gumption to kill anybody." Then

again, I remembered her constant bickering. She'd been so upset the day he'd left her to go up to that cabin. Hmm . . . maybe . . . No . . . impossible. Emily couldn't be a murderer.

"Even if she's innocent," Karaline said, "they'll have their sights on her until they find who really did it."

"Could he have been killed because of whatever he was working on? PD said the same thing—that he'd gotten secretive, remember?"

Karaline's eyes widened. "Oh my God." She was getting into a habit with that phrase.

20

Better Than a Bear

I looked out the Logg Cabin's big front window again, just as the door to the ScotShop opened. Murphy and Emily turned to their left, toward the police station. Maybe she had to sign a formal statement. At least she wasn't in handcuffs, but Karaline was probably right—Emily was a suspect for sure.

Harper stepped out, looked around for a couple of seconds, and headed toward the Logg Cabin. He must have seen us in the window.

"Looks like his radar is turned on," Karaline said.

"What?"

"Nothing." She walked over to let him in and locked the door behind him.

"I need to talk with both of you." He stamped the snow from his boots and took off his parka. "Eventually you'll need to sign statements at the station, but I'd like to have an informal discussion, if you don't mind."

"Fine with me," I said.

"Sit," said Karaline.

"Can we go back there?" He tipped his head toward the alcove near the kitchen. "Away from this window."

Karaline led the way and sat us at the same table where Harper and I had sat once before. I wondered if she did it on purpose. Once again, Harper took the seat that would put his back against the wall. K took a moment to disappear into the kitchen, where I assumed she was refilling the carafe. She came back and poured Harper a mugful without asking. When we settled in, he turned to me. "Tell me what you know about Emily Wantstring."

What did I really know about her, other than that she seemed to be lonely? "She talks so much about herself, but I don't really feel I know her." I rubbed my hand across my forehead. "I'm not proud of this, but I usually tune her out. The only concrete thing I remember is that they had their thirty-seventh anniversary last month. Other than that, all she did was complain about how lonely she was."

"The thirty-seventh? Not the thirty-ninth? Are you sure about that?"

"Yes. She talked about it quite a bit."

"Have you talked to her since Sunday?"

I thought back. "Let's see. Sunday. I remember looking out at the two-foot snowfall when I woke up. Then . . ." Then I'd had breakfast with Dirk, but I couldn't very well say that. Anyway, I was not going to think about Dirk. He'd been fascinated by the waffle iron. In fact, I'd made five waffles instead of my usual two just so he could watch the butter melting in the little square holes. When I poured on the maple syrup . . .

"Then . . ." Harper prompted.

I put Dirk firmly out of my mind, although it *was* a shame he'd never heard of maple syrup, that northern ambrosia. I took a breath. "Then Emily called me after breakfast. She was angry because Mark . . ." Karaline shifted in her seat. "Marcus," I corrected, "had gone off into the woods. She doesn't like skiing."

"He loved it." Karaline's voice was so sad, I lost my train of thought and Harper had to prompt me again.

"She was angry?"

"No, I didn't mean that. She was upset at being left alone. She complained about being cold."

A line formed between his eyebrows. "She told me they'd bought a house in that new development. They're supposed to be well insulated."

"Snore," I drawled, and we all three laughed. The ads for Eco Estates showed a fat mama bear with two roly-poly cubs curled up asleep and snoring in a roomy den. A people den; not a bear den. I did wonder how they'd gotten the bears to cooperate. Probably photoshopped, I thought. The tagline read: *Better insulated than a bear.*

"Maybe she forgot her fur," Karaline said. That brought us back to the topic.

I ran my phone conversation with Emily through my memory bank. "She really did sound cold. At one point, her teeth chattered."

"Maybe she was calling you from outside," Karaline suggested, "like the guy out there in the courtyard."

"That sort of defeats the purpose of a bear-insulated house, doesn't it?"

Harper pushed his coffee cup aside. "Could you hear any background noise?"

"No. I just told her to make herself some hot chocolate, but I can't help wondering if Emily really was outside while we were talking."

"Why would you think that?"

"I'm not accusing her of anything, Harper. I just can't get over how cold she sounded."

He drew his brows together. It was obvious that he would already have considered Emily a suspect, just as Karaline had said, but I sure hoped I hadn't added fuel to that fire.

After Harper left a few minutes later, I turned to Karaline, who'd pushed her chair back from the table. "Do you think Emily could have been calling me from that cabin? Maybe she did kill him."

She bent forward, elbows on her thighs, and hid her face in her hands. "God, I hope not." A minute or two later, she said, "We goofed. We should have told Harper about the break-in."

"Emily probably told him when he questioned her."

We talked for almost an hour, accomplishing absolutely nothing. It was all conjecture at that point. Over three or four more cups of coffee, Karaline mourned her beloved mentor and shared stories from her days at UVM. Outsiders thought *UVM* meant University of Vermont, but it really stands for "Universitas Viridis Montis." That's Latin for "University of the Green Mountains."

I idly wondered what Dirk would have thought of all this—he'd learned a little Latin, and a fair amount of Greek no less, from Brother Somebody or Other when he was a boy. I pulled myself up short. Why was I thinking about that ghost again when I was so mad at him? And why was I mad at *him*, when I was the one who'd been too stubborn? He was right. I was wrong. It wasn't a pretty picture. Maybe I should apologize?

As if she knew my mind, Karaline asked me about what happened when Dirk and I had gone up the Perth trail. "You really heard Mac? You could tell it was him?"

"Oh, yeah. He was swearing worse than I've ever heard. I know I should have checked on him right then," I admitted, "but it never occurred to me he was hurt or that he had a body in there." I resolutely put Dirk's voice out of my mind. His voice when he'd said, *Mayhap he is injured.* I was not going to dwell on that. I couldn't keep myself from wondering, though, what might have happened if we'd gone to help Mac.

She thought for a moment. "You don't suppose . . ."

"What?"

"What's the possibility that Mac killed him?"

I thought about it, but only for a few seconds. "Maybe. All we have is Mac's word that Dr. W was already dead when he got there."

"And neither one of us trusts him as far as we could spit."

"I can't spit very far, K."

"That's what I mean," she said. "Still, if his leg was broken that badly, I doubt he could have killed anybody."

"Maybe . . ." I tried to picture the scene. "Maybe Mac broke his leg *after* he killed Dr. Wantstring. Would that have been possible?"

She screwed her mouth up so much I thought it would wind itself off her face. "You know darn well I'd love nothing so much as to pin this on Mac, but what could he possibly have had against Dr. W? Motive, you know? Motive is essential if what you read in books is to be believed."

"Maybe Mac has been secretly in love with Emily and saw this as a way of eliminating the competition?"

Karaline groaned as hard as my stupid suggestion deserved. "You're right, K. No motive."

"No motive that we know of," she said. "I still want Mac to be the perp."

"Perp?"

"It's the sort of word Mac would love, don't you think?"

"Yeah. He would."

"What did Dirk have to say about Mac?"

"I'm not talking about him."

"Cut the fake indignation, Peggy Winn. It does you no credit."

"It's not fake. I'm saddled with a ghost I don't want, one who gets all bossy and self-righteous. Just because he's from the fourteenth century doesn't mean he's better than any of us."

"Are you in love with him? I thought you were in love with Harper."

For want of a better response, I stuck out my tongue. "I'm not in love with anybody. I'm just fed up with having him on my heels telling me what to do every minute of the day."

She gave me a knowing look, and I wilted. "Okay. I give up." I uncrossed my legs and recrossed them the other way. "If you must know . . ."

"I must."

"Dirk said we should go to the cabin and be sure Mac was okay."

"And what did you do?"

"I, uh, I turned around and left."

"Great decision, P."

As much as I hated to admit it, I couldn't shake the feeling that if I'd gone to the cabin, Dr. Wantstring might still be alive.

She stood and picked up our three coffee cups in one hand and the carafe in the other. If I tried that, there'd be at least two items on the floor. Turning toward the kitchen, she said, "At least there was nothing you could have done about Dr. W."

"Oh, yeah." I felt better, but not by much.

I went next door, retrieved my parka, and locked the ScotShop. I drove Karaline to the bank so she could make her deposit. I hadn't taken the time to close down the cash register, and I sincerely hoped nobody was going to choose tonight to break in. I dropped Karaline off at her place and drove home slowly in the early-winter dark, weighted down by Karaline's sorrow, by Harper's inexplicable actions, by a nagging fear that I was somehow responsible—not for the death, but for having made the situation worse. There were also my suspicions about Emily and Mac.

From all Karaline had said, Dr. Wantstring was something of a paragon. Why would such a good man have been murdered?

Unless it was by his wife. Was he a closet abuser and she'd finally had enough? I couldn't believe that. Karaline respected him too much. Or had Mac done the dirty deed; was he a closet maniac? I disliked the arrogant son of a gun so much I wanted to believe it. But couldn't.

A block from home I made a U-turn and headed out of town, despite the heavy snow. The Hamelin Clinic was too small, so Mac had to be in the Arkane hospital. I owed him an apology for not checking on him when I heard him swearing, and the sooner I got it out of the way, the better. I seriously considered not saying anything, but I knew he'd be able to read my statement in the official files, and I thought it would be better if he heard from me that I'd been there and left, rather than from reading it in some dry police report.

I'd even seen where he'd fallen, and the flattened swath where he dragged himself to the cabin. Why hadn't I listened to Dirk?

21

There's No Place Like Home

At the hospital, I asked for Mac's room number and peeked in at his door. He had more plaster and wire on him than a modern art exhibit. I put on a cheery voice. "You up for a visitor?"

Mac had one continuous eyebrow, as springy as a Brillo pad. It stretched over both eyes. Right now it was drawn down in a disgusted-looking *V*, like an arrow pointing at the bridge of his wide nose. "A visitor? Do I have any choice?"

Oh boy, is this going to be fun or what?

With surprisingly little encouragement, he regaled me with a step-by-step account of his entire saga. When he told about burying his other ski, I remembered stopping there and stepping on something. He should have had bright blue skis. Then I would have known something was wrong. Nobody leaves a ski buried for no reason. As it was, I'd thought it was a smooth brown snow-covered branch. Not that I'd paid much attention to it. I'd been thinking about Robert Frost the whole time Mac was getting two fingers broken and struggling to get a fire started.

I'd also argued with Dirk about . . . what? About something I couldn't even remember now.

"So I want you to go get it for me. Leave it at my house."

"Get what? Leave what?"

"My ski, dammit. Haven't you been listening to me?"

I was about to retort in kind, but I remembered that I'd come here to apologize—and he was right: I had *not* been listening to him—so I swallowed my irritation. "I'll get it." Naturally, he never said, *Thank you.*

He rattled on for quite a while. When he got to the part about the ax that caved in the back of Dr. Wantstring's head, I interrupted him. I didn't want gory details. "I have to apologize to you," I said.

"It's about time."

"About time for what?" I was truly mystified. How could he know already? Had someone from the police department called him about it already? I decided to play innocent. "What do you mean?"

"That time you laughed at me when I was in second grade and you were in kindygarden."

He said it wrong, but I was too astonished to correct him. "In second grade? Kindergarten?" *Okay, so I did feel a need to correct him.* "What are you talking about?"

"Danny pushed me on the playground during recess, and you laughed at me. You've owed me an apology for years."

"Why should I apologize for that?" I had to think for a second, but then I remembered. "Danny didn't push you. You fell." The picture of Mac flailing as he tripped over his own two feet and toppled to the soft grass was still funny, even though I hadn't thought about it in almost two dozen years.

"He pushed me. And you laughed, and that made everybody else laugh, too."

"I didn't laugh long. If I remember right, I ran over and helped you stand up, even though you weren't really hurt."

"Yeah." He held up his left hand, the one with the cast on the fingers, and I wondered if he was trying to make a rude gesture. No. That wasn't Mac's style. "First you laugh at me, and then"—he held up the index finger of his right hand—"you humiliate me."

"Humiliate you? You're nuts."

"So, apologize."

"In your dreams." I turned and stalked out. Let him read about what I'd done in a police report. I didn't care. And if he thought I was going back up the Perth trail to pick up his lousy ski, he had another think coming. Let it sit in a snowbank for the rest of the winter. He'd find it come spring.

Not that I felt vindictive or anything.

Home felt empty. Even Shorty had disappeared. My fuzzy gray cat liked to nap on my bed, or a chair somewhere, or behind the woodstove, but he always bestirred himself to acknowledge me when I came home. I headed toward the warmth and opened the damper a little more to let the fire blaze up a bit. Damn Mac Campbell. But my heart wasn't really into resenting him. He wasn't worth the effort.

I rubbed my hands together to increase circulation and scooted upstairs to change into heavy sweatpants, thick socks, and my favorite fisherman's knit sweater. I may have grumped at Emily about complaining when the weather turned cold, but . . . well, it *was* cold. Remembering my advice to her, I clomped down the stairs in my felted indoor slippers and headed for the kitchen. Hot chocolate would do the trick.

Humming to myself, I gathered all the ingredients. Soon, my hands wrapped around the steaming mug, I went back and sank into the overstuffed chair closest to the woodstove. I deliberately avoided looking at . . . at the shawl. *I told ye we should ha' looked in the wee cabin. Ye need a husband to protect ye.* How dared he preach at me like that? I didn't need him. I didn't need anybody. I had a perfectly good life. I had enough food and a warm house. I didn't need a bunch of fourteenth-century bother. I didn't need anybody telling me what to do whether I wanted advice or not. Not that I ever wanted advice. My life was very well-ordered. I knew what I wanted. I knew what I needed. I didn't need a bossy ghost and a million spiderwebs. I didn't.

Shorty materialized and jumped onto the couch, where he bumped his head against the shawl. From there he vaulted into my lap. I set the mug down and stroked him absentmindedly. See? I had a cat who loved me. I had my twin brother and my dad who loved me. And I loved them, too, although I noted with a teeny part of my mind that I hadn't included my overbearing mother in that list. Not to worry about that now. I went back to the important matters. I had Karaline, who was the best friend a woman could wish for. I had the ScotShop. What more could I ask?

The rolled-up shawl sat there accusingly. Shorty kneaded my tummy. He raised his deep green eyes and peered into mine. He meowed loud enough that I flinched. Oh, all right. I leaned far to my left and touched the end of the roll. It seemed to emanate warmth. No. That was just my imagination. With Shorty weighing down my lap, I could just barely get a grip on the edge of the shawl. I pulled. How could something with a two-hundred-pound Scotsman in it weigh so little? I held it in my lap for a long time before I unrolled it.

When Emily left the police station, she'd felt somewhat drained, but by the time she pulled into her garage, she harbored an exhaustion that threatened to overwhelm her. Maybe she could knit for a while. That calmed her down sometimes when she began to feel frantic. Only, she didn't feel frantic now. She just felt empty.

She ran her hands up and down along her upper arms, trying to bring some feeling back. What was it Peggy Winn had told her about how to get warm? Hot chocolate. She headed for the kitchen, wondering where Mark might have wanted to be buried. They'd never talked about it.

She had to call her sons. But how could she tell them their adored father was dead? She knew they'd loved him the best. And why not? Mark was the one who had showered them with attention, first while Emily was on the road so much for twelve seasons, and later when she was simply trying to survive. They both worked in microbiology now, just like their father. Oklahoma and Iowa. One was at a prestigious university; the other one worked at a research firm. She couldn't imagine they'd want to disrupt their lives, their own families, to come home. Now, if *she'd* been the one to die, they would have been at their father's side in a heartbeat to support him through his grief. She knew this without even thinking about it.

She'd call them a few days before the funeral, and she'd send them a copy of the obituary. That would be enough. If they chose to come home for the funeral, though, whatever would she talk to them about? She didn't even know when the funeral could be scheduled. They'd told her the . . . the body . . . Mark's body . . . was at the medical examiner's office. She supposed they meant . . . Emily's throat tightened, and she tugged at her turtleneck. They meant the morgue, but they'd been too polite, too kind, to use that word.

Since she had to wait for . . . for the body to be released, she had a good excuse—a good reason; that was what she'd meant to say—a good reason to wait about calling the boys. And what about calling her sister? Why hadn't she done that?

Emily crossed her arms. Josie was way too busy to be bothered with this. She wouldn't be able to take any time away from her important work. Time enough to call her when the funeral was scheduled.

22

Birthday Party #1

Sergeant Marti Fairing looked around the cramped space of Hamelin's police headquarters. Balloons dangled from Murphy's chair and floated over his desk. Moira, the dispatcher, pushed the microphone on her headset back out of the way and called out something to Joe, one of the other junior officers. Harper sat hunched over at his desk, like a broody hen on an egg-filled nest, moving bright yellow sticky notes from one position to another. From where Fairing stood, it looked like there was a word or two on each note.

She began a circuitous stroll around the room, dodging desks and out-of-position chairs, as the hilarity quotient of the spontaneous birthday party built. She managed to peer over his shoulder for about three seconds before he jerked his head around.

"You spying on me?"

"Just wondering what's going on. You're not exactly joining in the fun."

Harper went still. Fairing had seen him do that before a couple of times. *Maybe he's laying another egg*, she thought. But then he shrugged and began stripping the sticky notes off, one at a time, and sticking them onto a leather notebook, kind of like one of those blank books people used for diaries. Fairing saw enough words to pique her curiosity even more. *Wantstring*, one of them said. *Financing?* Fairing wondered about that question mark. *Dad. Poughkeepsie.*

Poughkeepsie? What did the dead guy have to do with where Harper used to work?

"Harper!" Moira's voice boomed from across the room. "You gonna join us anytime soon or do we have to put you on traffic duty?" Moira, the transplanted Southerner whose accent hadn't faded a bit in the three decades she'd served as Hamelin's police dispatcher, beckoned, and Fairing poked Harper's shoulder. "Better do what she says."

"Murph already threatened me with traffic," he muttered.

Fairing made an elaborate fake curtsy—hard to do with a duty belt on her hips. "You can have it anytime you want. We've got us a doozy. Woman calling two or three times every day."

Harper twirled a pencil around on his desk, as if he weren't up to repartee. "Why's she calling so much?"

"Wants us to find out who backed into her car last Sunday."

"Any leads?"

Fairing snorted. "If you can call them that. The woman whipped out her iPhone and caught a picture of the car leaving the lot—gray Ford. I ran the potential combinations from what I could see of the license plate. I've got three possibles, but nobody around here."

"So?"

"Silly to pursue it when we have a murder on our hands. There was hardly any damage to her car other than some scraped paint. Other car broke its taillight."

Moira held up a candle-bedecked birthday cake, and her long fingernails glittered in the light of her desk lamp. "All right, you two; hush up so we can get this party started. You get over here, too, Murphy. Did you think we were going to let you turn two dozen years old without us singing to you?"

Usually by this time of the evening, the place would be almost deserted, but with a murder on deck—and a birthday cake—everybody seemed to have congregated. Fairing waved a hand in acknowledgment and stepped away from Harper's desk. Something was going on to make him so pensive, and Fairing thought maybe she ought to find out what it was. One of those sticky notes had the murdered guy's name on it.

She heard Harper's footsteps pause behind her, and she turned in time to see him step back and slide the leather notebook into his top desk drawer.

"Harper!" Moira sounded like she was getting irritated. "We're havin' cake and ice cream over here, and you're the party pooper."

"You're the boss," Fairing called. "Hurry up, Harper, before the ice cream melts."

Mac took a peek and then slammed the metal lid back down on whatever this was—a poor excuse for food, especially for a man who needed all his strength just to heal. He looked around the hospital room that was, for the moment, the closest thing he had to a home. Not that he was planning on staying long. Nope. He'd be out of here in no time, once he was out of traction. Once he'd gained back a little weight. He was healthy as a horse. And he sure didn't want anybody like that Peggy Winn coming in again and seeing him in this hospital johnny.

He'd handled himself pretty well on that mountain, all

things considered. Getting his leg splinted like that—he deserved a medal or something. Crawling up that slope and down into the clearing, up those steps and . . . His thoughts veered away. Mac wasn't squeamish—he didn't know the meaning of the word—but the way the back of that skull was caved in wasn't something he wanted to think about before he had to eat a lousy hospital meal.

He'd told Murphy to get the investigation started. Somebody killed that guy, and by golly Mac wanted whoever it was under lock and key before he got out of the hospital. No reason they couldn't catch the perp sooner rather than later. Mac tried to shift his weight, but his hip hurt like the dickens. His leg felt like a red-hot poker was rammed up from his toes to his knee. He needed out of here. Soon. Anyway, tomorrow was his birthday. Maybe somebody would bring him a cake.

A nurse opened the door. "Feeling any better?"

Mac saw her name tag. Amy something-or-other. He told her exactly what he felt like, but she pretty much ignored him. She just looked him over and walked away, toward the computer on a little cart beside his bed. She didn't even wish him an early happy birthday, and it must have said it right there in the computer.

The whole time I sat there holding the rolled-up shawl, I kept wondering how my life would be different if I hadn't found this shawl in that mysterious store. Dirk and I had had a lot of fun together. On the other hand, he put a crimp in my love life. No. That wasn't fair. I didn't have a love life, but I knew darn well he'd be jealous as all get-out if I did. Not jealous. Just . . . protective.

Shorty meowed at me again.

"Oh, all right."

I unrolled the shawl and slowly lifted it to my shoulders.

Shorty jumped down and meowed at the figure that appeared in front of us. Dirk said, "This isna the same day, for ye are wearing different . . ." He waved his hand, apparently not knowing the word for "sweatpants."

He'd missed 653 years; he had no way of telling what day this was. Even though I'd dismissed him only this morning, I didn't have to say so. "It's Thursday," was all I said and went back to my hot chocolate, knowing he might think he'd been in there a whole week.

I patted my lap, but Shorty ignored me and wandered over to the couch to lick up a spiderweb, his new favorite snack.

23

Wooden Box

Emily had to go out and get the mail even though it was already dark. She couldn't just sit and rot, although that was precisely what she felt like doing. Sit and rot. Or sit and cry. She wound a heavy scarf around her neck twice and shrugged into her heaviest parka. Her good boots had slouched onto their sides, and she didn't feel like bending down to work them over her heavy socks. So she eased her left foot into a pair she almost never wore. She should have dropped them off at the Goodwill store years ago. Why had she even brought them here, to Hamelin? They'd been sitting in the mudroom for such a long time, they shimmered with a faint coating of gray dust.

The first boot went on just fine. When she tried to put on the second boot, though, her right big toe jammed into something hard. The mail could wait. Emily pulled out a small square wooden box. She recognized it as one her husband had brought back home from one of his visits to the Amazon.

It had a lid with a tricky way of opening it. She'd seen Mark open it with a simple push, pull, twist, but she'd never bothered to ask him how it worked. Was there anything in it? She thought maybe he'd put a paper or something in it, but she hadn't been curious enough to pay attention. It always used to sit on the coffee table, but she couldn't recall when it had gone missing. And now here it was in an old boot. She shook it gently. Nothing rattled inside, but then, it wouldn't, would it, if it were just a piece of paper he'd put in there? She took it into the kitchen where the light was better.

Mark always liked to hide little things in odd crannies. He stuffed treasures—some not so valuable, like ballpoint pens—wherever he happened to be standing, the way a squirrel puts nuts into any available hole. But this particular acorn didn't make sense.

He'd never hidden anything in shoes before. Not that she knew of. The mail forgotten, Emily took off her coat and played with the box, twisting it this way and that. She always complained about the way he scattered things everywhere, all around the house, not that the complaining did any good. He probably did it at his office, too, although she'd been there only two or three times, and it had looked tidy enough. Why had she ever complained about such a stupid thing? She should have found his habit of squirreling things away endearing, rather than irritating.

All her married life with him—and the two years before the wedding—she'd found keys and coins and pens stowed here and there around the house. He even hid Tootsie Rolls, tucking them under couch cushions, between books, in the medicine cabinet. More frequently than she wanted to admit, she'd eat them as soon as she came across them. She liked Tootsie Rolls just as much as he did, but where he wanted to save them, she felt she'd better take her pleasure where she could find it, because you never knew when life was going to . . .

She leaned against the bright orange chair. Life had taken Mark just the same way it had taken her voice. Here she was worrying about finding all her husband's little doodads, when what she really wanted to collect was Mark himself. She wanted her arms around him. She wanted his arms around her.

She unwound her purple scarf. No wonder she'd been so warm. She used the end of it to wipe her eyes and then draped it over the back of Mark's blue chair. His favorite scarf had been cashmere in a soft brown, the color of beach sand. He always left it hanging over his kitchen chair whether they were in Burlington or here, so he never had to go looking for it. She'd given him that scarf when she got her first paycheck from the Met. She couldn't remember having seen it lately. He wouldn't have taken it skiing.

It had to be around somewhere. Just like the mail, she forgot about the box and was now intent on finding the scarf. She went into the bedroom, but before she could begin the search, she had to sit for a minute on the edge of their bed. She reached out to the pillow, his pillow, and pulled it up to her face. She missed his smell when he was gone. Was this faint scent all she'd ever have left of him? That was nonsense. Standing, she placed the pillow back, straightened the bedspread, and began a methodical search of every drawer. She opened each jacket hanging in the closet, thinking he might have tucked the scarf around the hanger, but the light brown scarf might never have existed. She looked in the car. She went out to the living room and picked up the silver-framed photo of the two of them that cold day years ago when they'd driven down into the Berkshires, proof that she wasn't losing her mind. But where had the scarf gone?

She set down the photograph and her hands stilled.

Should she mention to the police that it appeared to be missing?

Mark had taken it with him, after all, even though he never wore it when he was skiing. That was the answer. She'd call Sergeant Murphy tomorrow and ask him to return it.

Fairing studied Harper over her plastic bowl of ice cream. He'd been gone a lot lately, and she wondered what all that was about. He'd been pensive. Not the Harper she was used to. She tossed her empty bowl into the trash and looked at him until he glanced up at her. "Have you been to see the chief yet?"

"No. Why?"

Moira, who never missed a thing in the station, spoke up. "You've been gone long enough to forget what he looks like." She glanced at the oversized clock on the wall. "Still a couple of hours left for visiting time." She winked at Fairing. "Serves him right for leaving us for so long."

Harper heaved an exaggerated sigh, but Fairing thought he'd gotten to his feet a little too quickly. Was he looking for an excuse to leave? "All right, you convinced me."

As he left, he didn't look back, didn't thank Moira for the cake, didn't make eye contact with anyone. What was going on? Fairing wondered if it had anything to do with that leather-covered journal and the sticky notes.

Mac heard three sharp taps on his door, but he ignored them. There was a pause, and then he heard a woman's voice. It sounded like that nurse, and the other voice was Harper. About time he came back from his vacation. *Undercover work*. Ha! Not a chance. He ought to fire the guy, but Archie

was on Harper's side. And Archie was the town moderator—
the Vermont version of a mayor. Technically, he was Mac's
boss, although Mac didn't like to think about it that way.

"If I had to guess," he heard Harper say, "he's either on
death's door or—more likely—just too grumpy to respond.
But you're hospital personnel so you can't say that. Am I right
on the second one?"

"Those are your words," the stuck-up nurse said. "You
didn't hear a thing from me."

"I'll take my chances, then. Okay if I go on in?"

"If you're up to it, be my guest." Mac could hear a grin
in the nurse's voice. What the heck was so funny?

"I'll be on my guard."

Mac closed his eyes and pretended to be asleep. But he
didn't want Harper sneaking up on him, so he snapped his eyes
open and glared. "What're you doing here? When did you get
back from that *emergency* of yours?" Mac sneered. "I should
have fired you for taking off like that and not reporting in. Have
you been to the station yet? What have you found out so far?"

"Just thought I'd check in with you, let you know what's
happening."

"So, how's the case going? What have you got to report?"

"Nothing much. We're still interviewing people. Nobody
has anything against Wantstring."

"Against who?"

"The victim. He's a microbiologist at UVM."

"Micro-what? Who identified him?"

Harper explained, and Mac's mood went even further
downhill from there. "You mean you've known who this guy
was for the past four hours and nobody thought to tell me?"

"The whole department's been called in," Harper said.
"Everybody's been out interviewing. Murphy's leading the
team, and doing a damn fine job of it."

"But he hasn't caught the perp yet."

Harper checked his watch. "It's been only a little more than ten and a half hours since we found out anybody was even dead. How many murders have you solved in that time?"

Mac's explosion brought Amy, three other nurses, and two interns on the run. By the time everything was sorted out, Mac—far from being embarrassed that he'd disrupted hospital routine so severely—felt pretty good about his own importance. He grinned at the nurse, but she just shooed everyone out and then left Mac alone.

It wasn't fair. It was all Harper's fault. And that Peggy person.

24

Puzzles

Sometimes I simply don't understand myself. I'd been so grumpy with Dirk Thursday night, when all he'd been trying to do, for the most part, was to protect me. Once I unwrapped the shawl, I'd tried to apologize, but it hadn't come out well, and he'd been—not exactly affronted, but, well, a bit defensive. Or so it seemed to me. So I'd flounced off to bed in a huff. It was no wonder sleep eluded me until well after midnight. I woke about five hours later to find spiderwebs practically encasing my bed. "Dirk!"

"Aye?"

"Why are there spiderwebs all over the place? What are you doing in my room? I don't want you coming in here. Well? What have you got to say for yourself?"

He looked affronted. "Since ye request an answer, I have several comments to make in response . . ."

All those *r*'s of his practically had me laughing. But not quite.

". . . to your questions and comments. Are ye willing to hear me out, or will you be r-r-r-r-rolling me up again in yon wee shawl?"

"Quit the sarcasm. Why were you in here?" I brushed away one web. There didn't seem to be a spider in it.

"I came when ye began wailing."

"I did not wail."

"Yes, ye did. 'Twas a nighthorse. . . ."

"Nightmare."

"Aye, and ye were caterwauling like a stuck pig."

"I was not, and I didn't have a nightmare."

"'Tis good ye canna remember it."

Since I couldn't convince him—stubborn ghost that he was—I went on to my next complaint. "I don't want you coming in my room."

"I wouldna if ye hadna poterunged so, and"—he held up his hand to stifle my comment—"if ye dinna want me here, ye maun close the wee door."

"I forgot." I sincerely hoped "thotairoongeying" wasn't something totally undignified.

"And a good thing it was that ye did. I have sat wi' ye for hours to be sure the mare would not return."

Apparently it hadn't. With as much grace as I could contrive, I said, "Thank you. Now go away so I can get dressed."

Well before dawn on Friday morning, Emily gave up on sleep and hauled herself out of bed. She pulled her bathrobe closer around her and brewed a pot of coffee. While it perked, she studied the wooden puzzle box. It was all a puzzle. How to open the box. Why Mark was gone. Nothing made sense. Without Mark, nothing would ever make sense again.

Dreading what she might find, she sidled into his home

office, wishing her friend Sandra, her neighbor from Burlington, could be here to help. Maybe she should call? Sandra didn't even know Mark was dead yet.

She rummaged around in the wide top drawer of his desk, studied the contents of the drawer next to it, ate one of the Tootsie Rolls she found there, and opened the bottom drawer. Files, more files than she'd expected to see. Why wasn't all this in his desk in Burlington?

She flipped through the tidy labels. There was a time early on in their marriage when she would have helped him set these up, typing the labels on their old secondhand Remington typewriter, the one that had served him so well all through grad school. The Remington had been gone for a long time. These labels were handwritten in Mark's careful script.

About a third of the way into the drawer, she saw a folder labeled *E.F.W.* Her initials. Each dot looked more like a comma than a period. That was Mark, all right. She pulled the file folder out and opened it across her lap.

The first page was a folded piece of blue stationery, with handwriting in green ink.

If you've found this folder, heart of my heart, then I'm most likely on the other side of whatever bridge forces people apart. They would have had to take me kicking and screaming, though, because my joy in life was being with you.

I know—I can almost hear you saying it—if that was your joy, why did you take off to the Amazon every year for weeks at a time?

If the very first sentence of this note is correct, then I probably feel now that those were wasted weeks (although I hope my students wouldn't think that!).

Keep looking through this folder. You'll find a life insurance policy, my final gift to you.

If you need anything—

The next few words were crossed out heavily, but she could see it was something about his friend Denby. Above it, he'd written,

Sandra and Ron will be able to help you.

All my love,
Your Mark

Emily held the letter to her heart for a long time. She didn't care about the insurance. She wanted her husband back. He'd even signed it *Mark*, the way she addressed him, when she knew he preferred Marcus. Maybe he was trying to make her feel more at ease.

Eventually, she wandered back into the kitchen, wondering whether she should notify the police about the insurance policy. No. That was her business, not theirs. Emily wandered into the den, flipped on the TV, and tried to forget about all this; but she couldn't forget that the seat beside her was empty.

She couldn't forget about the note she held clutched to her heart.

Fairing made it to work extra early on Friday morning, followed moments later by Harper. Murphy was already there, hard at work at 0600.

Fairing threw her parka across the back of her chair. "What did you do, Murph? Sleep at your desk?"

"Glad I didn't. Amazing what you can find on a computer when there aren't any jokers around to distract you."

"I take that personally," Fairing said. "What did you find?"

"Only a little bitty five-million-dollar insurance policy on Marcus Wantstring."

Fairing stiffened. "Five? Talk about a motive."

Harper shrugged out of his parka. "For anybody else it might be a motive, but I'm betting Mrs. Wantstring is innocent."

Fairing pointed a finger. "Didn't you always warn us not to make assumptions?"

"This is not an assumption," Harper said. "It's a fact."

It wasn't two minutes past seven when the phone rang. Murphy answered it, listened, made one or two comments, and then tried not to slam the phone down. In fact, he didn't slam it. He just set it down with definite intent.

Fairing looked up from her computer. "You want to explain that," she said, "or are you going to leave us guessing?"

"Mac wants me to bring the reports—everything we have so far—so he can read them. Now."

Fairing tapped her fingers lightly on the keyboard. Not enough to type anything, just enough to show her irritation. "Mac never reads anything."

She hadn't called him "the chief." She never did. She didn't like the man, but she tried not to be too obvious about it. After all, she hadn't been here long enough to accrue much seniority.

"Maybe he's running out of things to do in the hospital," Harper said. "He's strung up like a rabbit in a snare."

Fairing muttered something, just loud enough so they'd almost hear it. "Serves him right."

Murphy cleared his throat. "I'm printing this report I just finished to take to Mac."

"What is it?"

"All the highlights," Murphy said. "Everything we've learned so far."

"Yeah," Fairing said. "Precious little."

Harper pointed a finger at her. "You ought to go visit him."

"Who, me?" Fairing let out a snort. "Visit Mac? You have to be kidding."

"No, I'm not." He stood and headed toward the printer. "It might do you good to see him helpless like that."

She mulled it over, and a slow grin spread across her face. "If I deliver the report, you can handle the fender-bender lady when she calls."

I decided on a short tub bath. I woke up when the water began to turn the temperature of a leftover cup of coffee. Good thing I hadn't slipped under and drowned.

By the time I decided on what to wear—my green silk long johns, tartan skirt, and navy sweater, with a kerchief, of course—I had to hurry if I wanted breakfast at the Logg Cabin before I had to open the store.

"You stay here, Dirk. I'm not going to roll you up, but it would be better if you stay here today. I'll run by the Logg Cabin for breakfast, do the store, and I'll be back by six at the latest."

"I would like to see Mistress Karaline."

Hadn't we had another conversation just like this a few days ago? "No. I need to talk with Karaline about the murder, and I can't have you distracting us by asking questions."

He spun around. "Murder? What murder?" His *r*'s rolled around like balls in a bowling alley.

"The . . . Oh, you weren't around yesterday, and I forgot to mention it last night."

I gave him a quick summary, but I kept getting side-tracked answering questions about microbiology and why Mistress Karaline needed to study wee bugs in order to cook wee meals for wee people and how wee Mistress Emily was faring.

Well, maybe I exaggerate, but I didn't like all those questions. I felt like I was drowning in a sea of "wee"s. I made a dismissive gesture. "I don't know how she's doing. I guess she's okay."

"Ye mean to tell me ye didna sit wi' her last night?"

"You know darn well I didna—didn't—sit with her. I was here at home all night long. Anyway, I don't know her that well."

"All the more reason to help her. I misdoubt she has many friends in this wee town."

"With the way she talks nonstop, she probably doesn't have *any*." He skewered me with one of those looks I was beginning to dread. "Quit looking so superior," I said. "I wouldn't know what to say to her."

"Ye needna say anything. Ye need only to sit wi' her."

"And who made you the expert?"

He lowered his voice and his eyebrows at the same time. "My dear mother. She sat night after night with anyone who needed her, any time there was a death."

Insufferable. How dare he throw his mother in my face? I couldn't possibly compete with a dead—probably in his mind a sainted—woman. "I'm going to breakfast."

"This time I intend to go wi' ye, and ye canna stop me."

"You insufferable, arrogant . . ." This time I rolled the shawl deliberately, while he was watching me, and he gradually disappeared from his feet up to his head.

I didn't have the slightest pang of guilt.

Well, maybe *one*. And that *one* was a big one. Shorty

meowed at me as if to reinforce the thought that I was being hopelessly immature. It was like I was five years old or something.

But did I unroll the shawl?

No. No, I didn't.

Sometimes I don't like myself.

25

Catch a Thief

Mac looked at the meager printout Fairing had just delivered. They hadn't done much if this was all they had to show for it. The first page was headed, *Day 1, Thursday*, and the date. Like he didn't remember that day. Yesterday. The day they'd finally found him. Why'd it taken them so long to come looking for him? How had they known he was there? He'd been too far gone to ask about it at the time.

He read the first sentence about a phone call from Peggy Winn.

Then he read the rest of that paragraph. She'd turned around and left him! Damn that woman. Knew he was there and didn't ski across the clearing to help him! Mac ratcheted his anger up five notches. Six. He took it out on Fairing.

Fairing walked in, made sure nobody was on the phone, raised her voice, and said, "I'm going to string you up as high as Mac's leg."

Harper grinned. "Can I deduce that you thoroughly enjoyed delivering that report?"

"Quit Sherlocking it. You just deduced yourself out of any more favors. Next time Mac Campbell wants a report, you can take it yourself."

She shed her heavy parka, draped it over her chair, and started typing. Her fingers stilled for a moment. "He *did* look like a snared rabbit." Smiling, she went back to her work.

A few minutes later she heard Harper expel a volley of pent-up breath. She looked up, cocked her head inquiringly, and, when he shook his head, went back to what she was working on. *An entire conversation without any words*, she thought. *Wish I knew what the heck we just said.*

When I reached the Logg Cabin, Karaline crossed the room to greet me, but I could tell her mind was on the comfort of her customers.

"Can you take a minute to talk, maybe have a cup of coffee with me?"

Karaline looked around her well-run establishment one more time. "Uh . . . sure. We had a rush from seven to eight, but it's slowed down a little. Have a seat back there in the corner at the two-topper."

I knew that was restaurant-speak for a little table just big enough for two people.

"You want breakfast, too?"

"Yep. Short stack of pancakes, bacon ex—"

"I know, extra crispy. Let me put in the order and I'll join you in a minute."

It took a little more than the promised minute, but she had two full coffee mugs in one hand and a coffee carafe and cream pitcher in the other when she sat across from me. How did she do that without spilling everything?

"Where's Dirk?"

"He stayed home today." That was technically true. I just didn't mention that he hadn't intended to stay there. On a normal day, she probably would have taken me to task over my comment. She knew, after all, that Dirk liked to be in the thick of whatever was happening, but today she just sipped her coffee. I studied her. Her normally aquiline, model-sharp features looked gaunt. "Did you sleep at all last night?"

"Not hardly." She slapped her hand over her mouth and let out a jaw-cracking yawn. "It seemed like all night long I'd doze for a while and then wake up remembering something funny Dr. W had done or said." She folded her arms across the white bib apron that covered her fire engine–red sweater. The Logg Cabin logo, stitched in black, peeked above one of her wrists. I thought for a moment that she might be shutting me out—body language, you know, says that crossed arms mean a closed attitude—but then she raised her shoulders almost to her ears and tilted her head back in a noisy stretch. I could hear her joints creaking from across the table.

Uncrossing her arms, she said, "He never acted like he had to entertain us to get us to learn, but he was just so . . . so funny and open with us. His humor was . . ." She seemed to grope for the right word. "It was organic, so much a part of him that we laughed and learned all at the same time."

She paused for a moment while Dolly placed my pancakes and bacon in front of me. "Thanks, Dolly," I said. "This looks great."

Karaline ran a quick eye over my food, nodded to herself, and took up the story. "Dr. W firmly believed that too many college educations result in ivory-tower people who aren't prepared for the real world when they get out into it. Microbiology is all about microbes." She looked at me, probably expecting me to say something like, *Yeah. So?* But I held my peace. "You can study all the books in the world, but coming up against the real thing can be a definite eye-opener. Do you ever wonder why the restrooms in the Logg Cabin absolutely sparkle?"

"Can't say I've ever thought about it. I've seen some pretty awful public bathrooms—enough to make me appreciate yours."

"Yeah. Well, there's a reason for that. The first class I ever took from Dr. W, he assigned us homework."

"Yeah?"

"We had to collect water samples from drinking fountains, sinks, and toilets. Not just the supposedly clean water coming out of the faucet or fountain, but the droplets that were splattered on the sides, counters, and nearby walls."

"Yuck!"

"Right. Then we prepared slides and looked at what swarmed inside each drop. In fact, one guy threw up when he found out what had taken up residence near the toilets at his dorm. I never let him live it down."

She gazed across her restaurant, and I could almost hear her calculating how many people were there, how many needed attention—not many from the look of it—and whether her staff was functioning at a high level of professionalism.

"Dr. W wouldn't tolerate dishonesty in any form. One year, some of the undergrads complained that somebody was taking quarters out of the washing machine in their dorm—for some reason, they were mostly biology students on that one floor. They pooled the money from the machines and used it to buy laundry soap and stuff like that. This went on for weeks, until Dr. W snuck into the dorm about four o'clock one morning. Wearing gloves, he spread silver nitrate on seven or eight quarters, put them in the machine, and went home."

"Silver what? What did that do?"

"Silver nitrate. A few days later, they were complaining again. Dr. W made everyone stand up and hold out their hands. There was one student whose fingers had turned black. He was expelled from the biology program. Dr. Wantstring wouldn't let him sign up for any more bio classes."

"Silver nitrate does that?"

"Yep. Even the slightest exposure will stain the skin black, no matter how little of it gets on you."

Dolly interrupted. "Can you come back to the kitchen?"

Karaline frowned.

"Nothing bad, I hope."

Karaline rolled her eyes at me. "One never knows."

26

Birthday Party #2

Mac Campbell struggled to hang up the phone. This would have been a lot easier if he'd had his cell phone. Everything would have been easier if he'd had his cell phone. He would have gotten off the damn mountain a long time ago if he'd had his cell phone with him that day so he could have called for help.

That damn Peggy Winn wouldn't have abandoned him, wouldn't have turned around and left. He already would have been out of there before she even showed up. He wouldn't have had to drag himself to the cabin. Wouldn't have had to search a dead man's pockets. Wouldn't have had to starve for four days. Wouldn't have gotten so dehydrated. Wouldn't have had to wallow in his own poo.

Mac had never been inclined toward introspection, but even he got tired of TV news shows and talk shows after a while, and there wasn't anything to do, strapped up like this.

Strung up like a fish dangling from a fishing line, like a deer strapped across the hood of a car. Nothing to do except think. Think about how unlucky he'd been.

He wondered if that Peggy Winn woman had retrieved his ski and ski pole yet. Well, of course she had. She owed him big-time after abandoning him like that, and he'd given her orders, hadn't he? She'd probably been so scared, she must have left the hospital and gone directly to the Perth.

He hadn't told her where to put them, though. She couldn't get into his house. He had enough locks on the doors and windows that nobody—nobody—could ever get in without keys. He didn't think even Peggy Winn would be stupid enough to leave a ski unattended on his porch.

Or maybe she would. There were plenty of people in the town—most of them, in fact—who put their skis out on their front porches and just trusted that nothing would happen to them. If Mac had been fair, he would have admitted—only to himself, of course—that nothing usually did happen. People around here didn't steal skis. Everybody had them. Nobody needed to take any.

He heard a knock. Or he thought he did. If it was a knock, it was so timid there was hardly any sound to it. There weren't any visiting hours this early in the morning, even though Fairing had come in like she owned the place.

Maybe it was that doctor who hadn't done Mac much good as far as Mac could tell. All he'd done was wrap Mac's leg in the heaviest cast he could concoct. And strap his fingers up like a Thanksgiving turkey leg.

Mac was sure now that somebody was knocking, but that stupid doctor wouldn't wait that long for an answer; he'd just barge in. Neither would the snooty nurse. She walked in all the time with hardly a second's notice. Did Mac even want anybody

seeing him like this? Yeah. Why not? He could tell them his
story. It was getting better with each repetition. "Come on in
if you have to." He craned his neck to the right to see who it
was. They could have put the bed in a better position so he
could see without getting a crick in his neck. "Oh. Ma. Why
haven't you come before this?"

She sidled up to the bed and laid a tentative peck on his
cheek. "You didn't call me until five o'clock this morning.
I didn't know anything had happened to you until you called.
I got here as soon as I could."

Mac crossed his arms over his chest, his broken fingers on
his right bicep. Might as well let her see what he'd been through.
How badly he was injured. She hadn't brought a birthday cake,
but he'd be willing to bet she'd scurry home as soon as he was
through talking to her and bake him something. She always
did. He could count on that. Even if she hadn't come to visit
him right after it all happened. "Sit down over there where I
can see you without hurting my neck. I'll tell you what happened." He'd told her already, on the phone this morning, but
maybe he'd left out something. Wouldn't hurt to go over it one
more time.

As Mac's mother got ready to leave two hours later, she pulled
a package of homemade cookies and a soft stuffed turtle out
of her handbag and placed them on her son's chest. "Happy
Birthday, dear."

Mac waited until she'd shut the door before he began to cry.

I finished my pancakes alone, while Karaline intervened in
whatever flap was going on in the kitchen. Any business

owner was used to problems. I hoped hers wasn't anything serious. I polished off my coffee, paid the bill, and made it to the ScotShop a minute or two after eight thirty. Gilda trailed in almost on my heels, followed by Sam, with Scamp peeking his little head out of the end of the navy blue carrier. The dog looked kind of like Groucho Marx. His spiky eyebrows made me want to laugh. "Aren't you worried he'll fall out of that thing?" I pointed.

They shook their heads in unison, left-right-left-right, looking like they'd been choreographed. "He can't get out," Gilda said. "There's a zipper."

"Yes, I can see the zipper." I couldn't help the look of skepticism.

She stepped back a pace to where she could see the carrier and squeaked in alarm. Scamp was already halfway out of it. "Scamp! What are you doing?"

"Looks like he wants out," I said. "And he's obviously got your zipper figured out."

"But he's not supposed to be able to do that."

"Maybe you'd like to tell Scamp that rule." I headed for the safe in the back room to pull out the day's beginning cash. I could hear Gilda's diatribe even through the intervening door. *I must not have closed the zipper all the way. I can't believe I did that. . . .*

I'd already opened the safe before I remembered that I'd never closed out the cash register last night. It felt like a week had passed since then.

Of course, a lot had happened yesterday. I'd seen Harper. We'd found out about Dr. Wantstring being dead. I'd tried to help Karaline through her grief. It was mostly just listening to her, but at least I was there. I'd talked with Harper at the Logg Cabin. I'd visited Mac at the hospital, and he hadn't even appreciated it, damn his hide. And I'd unwrapped Dirk. And then rolled him up again this morning, but I wasn't going to think about that.

Long day Thursday. Check.

Accomplishments Thursday. None.

I left the safe open—there wasn't anything in there anyway—just until I took the extra cash out of the register and locked it away.

For the next hour or so Scamp investigated every corner of the shop. If I had a nose like that, I wondered what I'd be able to smell. He turned up a couple of dust bunnies we'd missed in our vacuuming, and I had to admit he was a natural at charming the customers.

What Dirk had said, though, about Emily, kept haunting me. *All ye need do is to sit wi' her.*

Around eleven o'clock, Scamp pattered over and sat down in front of me. I bent to scratch his little head, but he scooted away, returned, and sat himself back down, his wide front feet perched on my toes. He was kind of hard to ignore. I looked into his twinkly dark chocolate eyes. They seemed accusatory, somehow.

All right, already. I'd check on Emily but I absolutely refused to leave before the end of the day.

And it was a good thing I ignored both the dog and the memory of Dirk's instructions and stayed at the ScotShop Friday until closing time. An unscheduled tour bus stopped, and we were inundated for almost an hour. Sales were healthy. Nobody complained. And I had enough stock on hand to replenish the shelves as they were depleted.

At five, I turned the sign on the front door to *Closed.* It didn't take long to close out the register, even with all the sales. For once everything tallied perfectly the first time around.

I dropped off the deposit and pointed my brown Volvo toward Eco Estates. I'd *sit wi' the grieving widow* for a little while this evening. Then maybe Dirk—and even the dog, for criminey sakes—would leave me alone. Dirk wouldn't know I'd been there, though, unless I told him.

Doggone him. He wouldn't leave my mind. I could fold him up and get rid of him, but I couldn't *get rid of him*, if you know what I mean. Even though he wasn't close by my side, he was in my head, and I had a harder time trying to get him out of there than I'd had shooing him from my personal space. I should have listened to Emily without judging her. I had no idea what she was going through, to lose a husband like that, somebody on whom she must have depended for the thirty-seven years they'd been married. Well, I had a little bit of an idea from all she'd told me about him, but I still didn't feel like I'd connected with her.

I swung by my house on the way to Eco Estates, changed my clothes to something a little less Scottish, and picked up the shawl. I waited to unfold it until just before I got out of the car in front of her house.

Dirk looked around in some surprise. The last time he'd seen me I'd been in my living room putting on my coat to go to breakfast at the Logg Cabin. Now the light was totally different. Early evening. I was wearing different clothes. And we were in my car.

"Sorry," I said. "I was angry."

"Why did ye no open the shawl before this? Am I right? Has it not been at least from morn till gloaming that I havena been here?"

Gloaming. The darkening shades of evening. "Right. I didn't want to startle you by opening it too soon." I opened my door and he slipped out beside me. "I decided to visit Emily and thought you might like to join me."

As we walked toward her front door, I heard him mutter, "Ye didna wish to face her alone."

Once again, he was right, doggone him.

27

The Joy of a Simple Song

Walking into Emily's house was like stepping into a blast furnace. She wore her usual turtleneck with a heavy hand-knit cardigan. I'd always thought of her as being pudgy, but now I wondered if it was just that she always had so many layers of fabric on her.

You know how you read about people being at a loss for words? That sort of thing usually didn't happen to me, but as Emily closed the door behind me I realized I had no clue what to say to her. *So how are you doing now that your husband's been murdered* did not seem like a viable conversational gambit. Neither did *I rolled my ghost up in a shawl this morning, but he's standing beside you right now.*

I kept my mouth shut.

"I'll make us some hot chocolate, Peggy. Hang up your coat and come on back." Emily headed toward the kitchen. "You were right, you know," she said over her shoulder.

"Right? About what?" I stuffed my gloves in my pockets

and snugged the shawl under the collar of my parka before I slipped out of it, wishing I had on a sundress instead of my usual heavy winter clothes. I started to head the way she'd gone, but at the last moment I remembered that Dirk would be stuck next to the coatrack if I didn't take the shawl with me.

"I thank ye," he said as I slipped it over one shoulder. There was no way I was going to wrap the thing around me in this heat.

"You told me hot chocolate would warm me up," she said as Dirk and I stepped into the kitchen, "and it does in so many ways. I must have drunk a gallon of that stuff since Mark . . . Marcus . . . since I found out he was . . ." The sentence trailed away into a vacuum. "It's not like being alone is a new experience. I've spent a lot of time by myself while Mark . . . Marcus is . . . *was* . . . off collecting all sorts of exotic bacteria."

All her self-correcting was beginning to wear on my nerves. Couldn't she just pick one name and stick to it?

"Even when he was teaching, he'd leave early so he could walk to work, no matter how rainy or cold the weather was. When we were first . . . together, I used to walk part of the way with him, but I haven't done that in years." She rotated the wooden spoon back and forth. "Yes. I'm used to being alone. He's been going to South America for three or four weeks every summer for . . ." She reached for a pot on the back burner, then stopped and rested her hand against her chest. Her heart.

Oh, dear. She wasn't having a heart attack, was she?

Apparently not. After a moment she resumed her broken sentence. ". . . for years. Those times, though, when he was gone, I always knew he'd be back eventually. I never doubted it for even a moment."

"I'm so sorry for your loss." It was trite; it was one of those standard comments, but it was the only thing I could think of to say.

She pulled the pot to the front of the stove. "Sit while I get this put together."

"Can I help with anything?"

"Of course not. You just park yourself on that chair."

Her eyes filled with tears. "Are you okay, Emily?"

She nodded, but it didn't look very convincing. "Mark used to say that very same thing when I'd come home and he'd be making dinner. If I offered to help, he'd say, *Of course not. You just park yourself on that chair.* Always those same words. It wasn't that he didn't want me working with him in the kitchen. It's just that he loved to cook." She drew herself up a little straighter. "So, now all I have left is the memory. Now, you go ahead and sit."

Her kitchen table was painted a stunning lemony yellow. The four wooden chairs ringing it were equally bright. One was Wizard of Oz green. One was an intense blue, the kind that, when I saw it in a picture of the Mediterranean, I always thought the color had been photoshopped. The other two were a deep neon red and jack-o'-lantern orange. It looked like a congregation of M&M's. All she was missing was the brown.

I chose the green chair and waited, since I didn't know what to say. Emily's kitchen was disturbingly silent. I usually hummed to myself—or talked to my ghost—when I was cooking, especially when I made hot chocolate, but Emily was silent. I wondered if it was always like this or if she was still stunned by her husband's death.

Eventually she set two delicate china cups on the table. Their muted vine-and-leaf pattern looked rather blah compared with the brilliance of the table and chairs. She sat in the orange chair across from me and poured frothy chocolate from a teapot that matched the cups.

All her actions were deliberate, almost choreographed, as if she were restraining herself out of fear that she might explode.

These cups didn't hold enough for more than a couple of good slugs. We sipped in silence. Dirk must have known what to say, doggone it. Why wasn't he helping me out here? Eventually I gestured to the chairs. "You must like bright colors." Dirk ran a finger along the back of the Mediterranean blue one. I wondered if blue was his favorite color. I'd have to ask him sometime.

"Bright colors." She raised a hand to her throat, tugged at her turtleneck, and trailed a finger along the front of her neck. I saw a faint scar I'd never noticed before. At least, I thought it might be a scar. I wondered if that was why she always seemed to wear turtlenecks. Well, not always. Not in the summer. But, thinking back, I realized that each time I'd seen her in warm weather, she'd had a pretty scarf wound around her neck.

She was silent for so long I thought she might not have heard me ask about the colors. I was just about to make another inane comment when she spoke. "I've often wished I'd given Marcus a bright blue scarf instead of that light brown cashmere one. His favorite color was blue. He always sat in that blue chair. He used to hang his scarf over the back of it." Her eyes became unfocused, like she was seeing something nobody else could. I wondered if I looked like that every time I glanced at Dirk. "I spilled some coffee on it once."

"Coffee? On what?"

"On his scarf. It left a brown stain that even the cleaners couldn't remove. But he refused to get rid of the scarf. I wish they could have found it. It wasn't with his things." She studied her cup. "All the color in my life used to come from music."

I waited for her to continue, but she didn't say anything else. Did she not want to talk about it? Only one way to find out. "Music? What do you mean?"

Instead of answering, she pushed her cup away, stood, and motioned me to follow her down a narrow hallway. We entered a room that must have been Dr. W's private study. An old-fashioned record player stood on the far side of the room behind a tidy desk. Emily looked at the vinyl record already in place. It was one of those little ones, what my dad called a forty-five, but I wasn't sure where the name came from. She turned a switch, setting the turntable spinning, and lifted the arm. She held it for several seconds. I could see that her hand shook.

Violins, cellos. I could identify some of the instruments, but quickly stopped trying and just listened to the glorious sounds, utterly transfixed by the voices. "The Flower Duet" from *Lakmé* had to be one of the loveliest, most haunting songs ever written for female voices.

After the song faded into that final ethereal chord, Emily lifted the record, tucked it into a paper record jacket lying nearby, and returned it to a shelf that held what looked like hundreds of other records. She leafed through them, chose another one, and placed it on the turntable.

Again, we listened in rapt silence. This time it was a solo voice and its power was almost palpable as the singer's notes soared. "My *Turandot*," she said when it ended.

"I know," I said. "When I was growing up, our neighbor, before she died, used to play opera records all the time. In the summer, when her windows were open, I'd sit in my backyard and listen to them." I leaned against Dr. Wantstring's desk. "Eventually she noticed me listening and invited me inside.

She taught me a lot, although I'm no expert by any means. *Turandot* was one of her favorites."

She nodded, but it looked to me like her thoughts were elsewhere. I couldn't think of a way to bring her back, so I just waited, wondering who'd recorded those two arias. I was fairly sure it was the same voice on each record. The quality of the records was too good to be Callas—all her recordings were fairly scratchy, even the remastered ones—so maybe it was Sutherland? Fontini? Nilsson? Someone pretty remarkable, that was for sure.

Tears glistened on Emily's cheeks. Dirk stood beside her in spellbound silence. I had no idea he was an opera fanatic. Well, of course he wasn't. Opera hadn't been around in the fourteenth century. Had I really not listened to any opera in the five months I'd had Dirk hanging around? I looked again at his face. Transfixed. Okay. Maybe he'd forgive me for wrapping him up if I pulled out a bunch of my opera CDs when I got home.

He leaned a bit closer to Emily, as if to comfort her.

I'd certainly been moved by the music—it was absolutely glorious—but I was nowhere near crying. I must have missed something. Maybe these songs were ones she'd enjoyed listening to with her husband? But her reaction seemed overly dramatic, even for a new widow.

"Mistress Emily is sad."

Of course she was sad. What did he expect me to do—answer him? I nodded. "What did you do before you and Dr. Wantstring married?" Why wasn't she chattering the way she usually did? And why wasn't Dirk helping me out here?

Her quick intake of breath was audible. She wiped a hand across her eyes and gestured to the record player.

I waited for her to answer me. Maybe she'd been one of

those women, so common in her generation, who never worked for a living and didn't want to admit it.

She must have seen the question still in my face. "The recordings," she said.

"What would be *reecordinks*?"

I ignored Dirk. "Recordings?"

She led the way into her living room and motioned for me to sit on the blue couch. She waited for me to settle in before she said, "That was my voice."

"That was you?"

"What was? Who was who?" Dirk couldn't keep quiet.

"Don't sound so surprised. I sang with the Met."

"The Metropolitan Opera?"

"What would be—"

"You needn't keep parroting me like that. I was singing with a smaller opera company when I met Marcus, but then a couple of years later, shortly after we married, I had a chance to audition at the Met and . . . and I was accepted." She leaned forward over her coffee table. The surface was so highly polished I could see her reflection upside down. She moved a magazine about a quarter of an inch to the left. I couldn't see that the repositioning made any appreciable improvement. It had looked tidy enough to start with. "Now," she said, "the only music I have is on those recordings of my voice." She gazed back down the hallway in the direction of Dr. Wantstring's study. "The ones I just played for you were only two of the hundreds we have."

All of a sudden all the pieces clicked into place. "The recordings. You? You were Emily Fontini, weren't you? I mean, aren't you? The Great Fontini?"

"What"—Dirk cleared his throat—"or *who* would be a *fonteenee*?"

"I don't know about the *great* part, but yes, I was Fontini. The verb is past tense." She grimaced. "That's right. Past tense. I was Emily Fontini. I certainly did have my name up in lights for quite a while." She tugged aside her turtleneck and fingered the scar on her throat.

I looked away from the pain in her face. She sounded exceptionally bitter, but I could see why, if she'd had a voice like that—and then had given it all up. But why? Why would she stop when she was so famous? "My neighbor," I said, "the one who introduced me to opera, thought Fontini was even greater than Sutherland."

Emily raised an eyebrow in a denial that I happened to see because I'd glanced quickly toward her. "No. Not at all. Joan was one of my idols. I was blessed to have been able to sing with her in three different productions, but I could never have surpassed her sublime quality."

Good grief. This woman I'd been berating for so many months had been on a first-name basis with one of the greatest operatic sopranos of all time, and—no matter what she said—had had a voice as wonderful as Sutherland's. Why hadn't I been kinder? Grasping for something to say, I asked, "Were your children born after you, uh, retired from the Met?"

"What a delicate way of phrasing your question. The answer is no. I sang twelve seasons and Mark . . . took care of the boys." She crossed her legs and leaned back against one of the many fat pillows scattered over the back of the couch. "He was so good with them."

I wondered why they weren't here with their mother.

"But then the cancer attacked my throat. With surgery and radiation, my larynx was so badly compromised I was never able to sing again."

I glanced up at Dirk, who stood poised, towering over her from behind the yellow couch. His face held a quizzical expression, and I could almost hear the queries ringing inside his head. *What would be a* lairynks? *What would be* raydeeasion? He still had a very fourteenth-century way of thinking about spelling, as I'd found out when I'd had to spell various words for him. Why wasn't he asking his usual questions? Not that I wanted him to, because there wasn't a way in the world I could have answered him. But it wasn't like him not to question something like this.

I needed to say something. *I'm so sorry* didn't seem adequate, but I said it anyway.

She didn't even acknowledge my words. Not that I blamed her. She hugged her sweater tighter around her, even though her house seemed to have gotten ten degrees warmer in the last few minutes.

"I'm so very sorry," I said again. This time I truly meant it. "I've listened to your recordings for years and never realized . . ."

"We didn't let many people know why I had to quit." She crossed her legs the other way, braced an elbow on her knee, and propped her chin on a fist that was closed so tightly her knuckles turned white. "Throat cancer. I didn't want pity. Especially not from anyone in my old life . . . my life at the opera."

I didn't know what to say. "I love your voice."

She turned her face toward the window, away from me. "Not anymore, you don't."

Dirk had spent so much time telling me what to say and when to say it, and now when I needed his advice—all right, his bossy directions—he abandoned me.

I finally made my excuses, draped the shawl around the neck of my parka, and left.

Opening the car door and pausing long enough for Dirk to get inside had become almost second nature to me. I waited until I was at least a block away from Emily's house so she wouldn't see me apparently talking out loud to myself.

"You could have said something in there. You left me floundering."

"*Flowndring*? What would be—"

"A flounder is a kind of fish," I explained. "When it's out of water, it can't breathe, so it flops around, and I think that's where the word came from." Or maybe not. I was making this up as I went along.

From the corner of my eye I could see him shake his head, sadly, slowly, as if mourning the passing of a minor intellect. Mine. "I didna say anything when we were with Mistress Emily because I didna know what type o' rare beastie that *canser* must ha' been to attack her and tear at her throat in that way."

"Huh? What do you . . . Oh, cancer. It's not an animal. It's a disease. Emily got very ill, very sick, and her throat was damaged by the illness. 'Cancer' is what the illness is called. It hits a lot of people nowadays. I imagine it does feel something like an attack." Obviously it did, if she'd used that word to describe what it had done to her. Poor Emily.

He cleared his throat—unnecessarily, I thought—and proclaimed, "And ye say that my time was bad. We didna have such . . ."

For once he seemed to be at a loss for words.

28

Another Wee Tiff

Saturday morning, Mac hid his turtle in the drawer of the little table beside the bed. He'd already eaten all the cookies. Then he called the station at seven.

"Hamelin Po-lice," Moira drawled.

"You've lived in this state for thirty years," he growled. "Why don't you learn to talk right?"

"And just what would I be saying wrong?"

Her words sounded syrupy to Mac. Why couldn't she talk faster? "What's been going on around there? Anybody arrested yet?"

"I am not a dee-tective," she said. "All I do is answer this little bitty phone. I don't know a thing about what's going on."

"Well, don't waste my time. Who's there?"

"I am," she said.

Mac missed the sarcasm. "Who else?"

"Fairing," she said. "I'll switch you over to her."

"No!" Mac didn't want to talk to any woman. Moira

didn't count. She was a dispatcher. Dispatchers could be women. Officers ought to be men. He'd had to hire Fairing, though. Not because he wanted to, but because she was the town moderator's niece.

He'd hired her after a blistering discussion in Archie's office. So what if she had commendations from the NYPD? So what if she'd performed heroic acts on 9/11? So what if she'd saved a bunch of lives? Mac didn't believe it. Some man had probably done those things, given up his life in the performance of his duties, and Fairing had taken the credit. Yeah, that was probably it. He'd hired her, but he didn't have to like it.

He called back twenty minutes later and asked to speak to Murphy. And again an hour later. Didn't the man ever do any work at his desk? Without his own cell phone and contact list, Mac didn't know any of his officers' cell numbers. He would have called them at home if he'd been able to, but if there was a phone book anywhere in the damn hospital room, he sure couldn't see it. He'd wait until they changed shifts. Three o'clock. He could get the new nurse to give him a phone book. That Amy person wouldn't give him the time of day.

I walked out to get the paper Saturday—I usually looked through it over breakfast—and the headline screamed:

SENATOR CALAIS KNIFED

I glanced quickly over the first few paragraphs, enough to know she'd been attacked outside the Capitol Building. But she'd survived. Good. I always voted for her.

I walked inside and spread the paper out on my kitchen table while I pulled bacon and eggs out of the fridge. Dirk wandered in from the front room, the shawl thrown negligently over his shoulder. "Will ye be eating wee eggs and fatted pig?" I'd tried to introduce him to the term "bacon," but he preferred his little bit of whimsy.

He bent over the paper. "Ahh," he said. "Oh?" A little later, as I lifted four strips of crisp bacon out of the fry pan, he asked, "Did ye read this stor-r-r-r-y?" His *r*'s rolled together like little lemmings char-r-r-r-ging toward the sea.

I turned the bacon over to drain off the fat from the other side. "What story?"

He cleared his throat. Oh, dear. I should have known what was coming. He started at the beginning and read the story word for word. Senator Josie Calais, it seemed, was just leaving the Capitol Building, walking down the steps to meet her husband. They had plans to go out to dinner. Dirk looked up at me and wiggled his eyebrows. "Did I no tell ye?"

"Tell me what?"

He kept reading. The gist of the story was that as the senator's husband climbed the steps to meet her—the reporter made a big deal about that for some reason—he saw a man lurch toward her, the blade of a knife glinting in the early-evening sunlight. He tackled the guy from behind. As the man fell, he managed to slash open the senator's leg from her knee almost to her ankle, without severing an artery. At press time her attacker had been arrested and the senator was, according to her husband, recovering and in fine spirits.

"That's ridiculous," I said. "Who in real life would say, *My wife is recovering and is in fine spirits*? Somebody made up that part of it for sure. I wonder how many stitches she needed."

"Ye werena listening as I read, were ye?"

"I heard it." I scooped scrambled eggs out of the skillet onto my plate. I sat and lifted my fork.

"She needed a man to protect her."

I stopped the fork halfway to my mouth. I'm afraid my mouth was open rather unattractively but I couldn't believe what I was hearing. "You . . . She . . . That's the most . . ."

Dirk just folded his arms over his chest as I spluttered. "Ye need a man," he said finally, in tones that brooked no dissent.

I dissented anyway, and we argued back and forth about freedom and individual choice, and a dozen other things that he approached from one point of view—a Middle Ages point of view—and I saw from a totally different, modern perspective.

"I don't need a man," I finally said. "I've got you."

That shut him up.

Emily stumbled out of her car and closed the garage door. She didn't know what to do with all those bags they'd given her. She'd left them in the trunk. That way she wouldn't have to think about them for a while. Mark's "personal effects." That was what they'd called them. They made her sign something to say she'd received them all. One of the officers had strapped Mark's skis to the roof rack on the car and had loaded everything else in the car for her. That was after they'd opened every bag and checked off the contents on some sort of master list.

His food, his cooking pot, his sleeping bag, his green ballpoint pens. His jeans and his underwear. His socks, the ones she'd knitted for him all those years ago, only the police officers didn't know that. They didn't know any of her and Mark's story. All they knew was that interminable list. It went on and on. Backpack, collapsible cup, three candy wrappers, but no Tootsie Rolls. Mark never went anywhere without his Tootsie Rolls. He must have eaten all the ones she was sure he would have taken with him. But if that was the case, why hadn't they found more than just three wrappers?

She'd been calm through the entire process until that horrible moment when they'd opened the bag with his brown flannel shirt. The collar was dark and stiff with dried blood. Mark's blood.

Why hadn't they warned her before they opened it?

"This isn't fair," she said, pushing open the door into the kitchen. The house felt empty. It *was* empty. They didn't even have a dog. And Mark was gone. He'd asked once, years ago, about getting a puppy, but Emily hadn't wanted the mess, the bother. Now Mark wouldn't be coming home to this empty dogless house ever again. "I hate this place," she said, plopping her purse on the granite countertop.

She wandered into the living room and reached for her knitting bag, but it wasn't there. She always left it beside her chair. She thought back over the past few days. She hadn't done any knitting since they'd arrived here last Saturday. The last time she could remember picking up that brown sweater she'd just recently started knitting for Mark was . . . Was it back in Burlington? Had she left her knitting there? No. Now that she thought about it, she could remember tossing it into the backseat of the car on top of Mark's green binder just before they left Burlington, and she'd forgotten all about it until now.

She trudged back out to the garage and opened the rear door on the driver's side. Yes. There it was. She closed the door, knitting bag in hand, but something seemed wrong. She looked back at the empty seat. Mark's binder wasn't there. Of course it wasn't. He would have brought it inside. But if he had, why hadn't he brought in her knitting as well? He'd always been thoughtful that way.

Inside, she perched her knitting on the ottoman and peered out at the snow-covered yard. The young couple next door must have shoveled her driveway for her. She hadn't even thought about it when she backed out of the driveway earlier today.

She wondered whether she should call that nice Sergeant Fairing and tell her about the box. And the missing Tootsie Rolls, the scarf, the binder . . . They hadn't been with Mark's— it took her a moment to swallow—*personal effects*. What a cold, clinical term for all that was left of her husband. No, Tootsie Rolls and binders couldn't have anything to do with the reason Marcus had been killed. Some maniac. It had to be that.

She rubbed her hands together and shivered. The thermostat was set on eighty-one degrees, but she felt thoroughly chilled. What good were insulation and comfortable furniture and a kitchen full of food when Marcus was gone? She hadn't called him Marcus in more than twenty years, ever since her surgery. Something had died in her, under the scalpel and during those terrible bouts of nausea. Her dreams. The dreams she'd shared with Marcus. Those dreams had died. So, as he sat with her, held her hand, steadied the bowl, cleaned her face afterward with a warm washcloth, she'd started calling him Mark. How could she have done that to him? How could she have insisted on calling him by a name he hated? Her illness wasn't his fault. How could she have picked away at such a good, good man?

He'd never objected. As if he understood.

She thought about the twice-yearly faculty dinners she had to attend in the autumn and spring. She'd never have to attend another one. The last one, just three weeks ago, had been sheer torture. There had been a string quartet playing in the background. Marcus had taken her arm firmly, as if he could lend her his strength through his strong hand. But when two young women from the university choir came onto the little stage and began to sing "The Flower Duet," Emily had stood so suddenly she'd knocked over her wineglass. She could still feel her panic as she'd run from the room. She collided with one of the numerous graduate assistants—they were the ones who served the senior faculty. The impact had knocked the tray out of the girl's hands, but Emily had run on without apologizing. Mark . . . Marcus had caught up with her on the front steps. He'd taken her home without a word of regret for the missed dinner. She was sure everyone there thought she was crazy. Why hadn't they listed the song in the little program they'd handed everyone? That way, she could have been prepared.

Saturday night I'd already given up on the day and changed into my flannel pajamas. With a ghost in the house—a very masculine ghost unrelated to me—I'd been a bit reticent the first couple of months about walking around in my pajamas, but first of all, he was dead, and secondly, I was more covered up in my heavy pj's than I was in a summer dress, so what could it matter?

The phone rang around ten o'clock. I loved caller ID. "H'lo, Karaline."

"You want to go to the cabin with me tomorrow morning?"

"The cabin? Why?"

"To see what we can find."

"Like I said—why?"

"I've been sitting here thinking. You know how I told you Dr. W always squirreled things away?"

"Yeah. So?"

"I got to thinking about how Murphy said there wasn't anything in the cabin except Dr. W and the clothes he was wearing, you know?"

"I know. So, why would you want to go over a cabin that's already been thoroughly searched?" I saw Dirk perk up his ears.

"That's just it, P. I don't think it *was* searched thoroughly."

"But . . ."

She didn't let me get any further. "They didn't know who he was when they searched. They didn't know about his squirreling habit, so they wouldn't have known to look in unusual places."

I thought about that bare, bleak cabin. "Karaline Logg, there aren't any unusual places in that building. It's not big enough to have any"—I pitched my voice in a low, throaty growl—"*unusual places.*"

"Quit the sarcasm. You don't know what you're talking about. I'll meet you—when?"

I did a quick calculation. The ScotShop was open from noon to five on Sunday. "Let's go early so I can get cleaned up in time to open. No, wait; you have to be at the restaurant for breakfast. Shall we go in the evening, after five?"

"First of all, we don't want to be out on the mountainside that late. Gets dark early this time of year, remember?"

"Yes, ma'am," I said with exaggerated politeness. "What's your second point?"

"Second point is that Dolly and Geraldine are going to handle things tomorrow morning. I have full staff working, and I'll be back well before the lunchtime rush, so I'll be on your front step about seven?"

"Seven? No way. What about nine?"

"Eight," she said and hung up.

*   *   *

I made the mistake of getting up in the middle of the night for a glass of water. Then I got to feeling hungry, so I thought I'd scoot down to the kitchen and make myself some stove toast.

Dirk turned away from the kitchen window when I snapped on the light. "Could ye no sleep?"

"You don't," I said with a blithe disregard of logic, "so why should I?"

"Ye are no dead," he said, which was such an obvious statement I ignored it and headed for the bread box.

"Ye maun go to see Mistress Emily again."

It had taken me a while to learn that "maun" meant "must." He'd been *maun*ing me right and left for most of the past week. Except when he was folded up. "And why would that be?"

"She doesna have visitors."

He folded his arms, changed his mind, and planted one fist on his tartan-clad hip. The other hand drummed against his kilt, setting it to vibrating.

I tried not to look down the length of his leg, but I sort of lost that battle. Before he could notice—at least I hoped he hadn't noticed, but there was an uplift to the side of his mouth that said maybe he had—I averted my eyes and paid attention to the buttered bread in the fry pan.

"The puir woman. She has been widowed for only a short while."

His hand stopped the drumming and went to his other hip. It made his shoulders look extra broad. "Have ye never lost someone dear to ye? Have ye never grieved for a year and a day?"

"A year and a day? What are you talking about?"

"Everyone kens that when ye lose a husband or a child, a parent, brother, or sister, ye maun mourn for one day more than a year."

"Everybody might have known that back when you were alive—although I've never heard of it so maybe it was just a Scottish thing—but we don't do that sort of enforced mourning thing anymore." I turned the toast to brown the other side.

"Why do ye no? How do ye deal wi' the grief or help friends and family to deal with theirs? How would ye honor your dead?"

"Well." I thought about it. I'd never lost a husband—maybe because I'd never *had* a husband—and both my parents were still very much alive. "Maybe it's because we don't deal with death quite so much in this century as you had to do back then." I flipped the toast one more time. "Not on a day-to-day basis."

The line between his heavy eyebrows deepened. "Everyone must die."

"That's true, but I think we generally do it a little later in life than you used to."

He didn't look convinced.

"Look at you," I said and plopped the stove toast out onto a small plate. "You died when you were thirty, right?"

"Aye."

Plate in hand, I headed toward the woodstove. It felt cold in the kitchen. Maybe it was because I hadn't put on my slippers. Maybe it was Dirk's frosty attitude. "And Peigi, your ladylove, you said she was about twenty when she died?"

"Aye."

The grief I heard in that one syllable almost stopped me in my tracks. It was a few seconds before I could follow through on my train of thought. "Nowadays, if you lived now,

I mean, you'd expect to reach seventy-five at least. And Peigi could look forward to reaching eighty."

"Why would she want to live longer than I?"

Men. "It's not a matter of wanting to outlive you. Statistics just say that women live longer than men. Wasn't it like that in your day?"

He worried his lower lip with his very white upper teeth. "Ye mentioned Master Stuhststicks once before, but ye didna explain who he was."

"It means the chances of something happening. Statistics are the numbers of things that some people keep track of, and that gives us an idea of the likelihood . . ." My voice trailed off in the face of Dirk's look of absolute bewilderment. I tried again. "Nowadays people—some people—keep track of how long individuals live. Once you've counted enough people, then you have *statistics* and you begin to see, uh, trends?"

"Did people count these things when I was alive?"

"I doubt it." I opened the damper a bit to rack up the heat. "I think statistics is a fairly modern field."

He seemed to mull this over. "Many women were widowed when I lived. But then again, many of the women died in childbirth. A man who outlived three or four wives was not unusual."

"Childbirth isn't quite so scary nowadays."

He strode to the window and back. My living room wasn't nearly big enough for pacing. At least not for someone with legs as long as Dirk's.

"Ye havena answered me yet."

I took a big bite and asked, with my mouth full, "Answered you about what?"

"About ye going to visit wi' Mistress Emily."

"Oh, all right, I'll go after I close the shop tomorrow— later today—but you have to come along, too, again."

He raised one eyebrow. It wasn't quite a scowl, but it was close to it. I could almost hear him saying, *I could ha' come wi' ye many times to many places if ye didna keep rolling me up in yon wee shawl.*

He had a point. It didn't matter whether or not he said it. I got it.

29

A Wee Ski in the Woods

Sunday morning, Dirk called out to me from the bay window a couple of minutes before eight. "Ye maun be ready to go. Mistress Karaline is close by."

"I'm ready," I said. "All I have to do is finish tying my shoelaces." Of course I also had to pull on a stocking cap and adjust the shawl around my shoulders. I fastened it with a sword-shaped kilt pin, one I'd bought the first time I visited Pitlochry, when I was considering opening the ScotShop. I stuck two big cloth hankies in a zippered pocket on the front of my pants leg and a third one in my parka—much better than paper tissues that came apart after the first two wipes.

Dirk waved out the window. I glanced outside in time to see Karaline wave back from the end of the walkway where she leaned lightly on one of her ski poles. A pair of skiers—people I didn't recognize—glided past, looking up at my house. They couldn't see me, far back in the living room as I was. And they certainly couldn't see Dirk. I could just imagine them wondering why she was waving at an empty house.

"Okay. Let's go." I opened the door, and Dirk glided out onto the porch as smoothly as if he'd been on skis himself.

That first breath of chilled early-morning air over a three-foot-deep covering of snow made my nose hairs crinkle when I stepped outside. Between zero and five degrees, I guessed. Not that it mattered. We were going regardless of the temperature. The blizzard still raged throughout the rest of New England; I was glad I didn't have to deal with zero visibility this morning.

I pulled my skis from the mound of snow I'd stuck them in last night, brushed them off lightly with my glove, and laid them next to each other flat on the snow at the top of the ramp that led down from my deck. My twin brother, Drew, seldom visited me in the wintertime. Dealing with the snow under his wheelchair was just too much hassle. I truly did wish I'd thought to have heating elements installed underneath the ramp, only then the ramp would have had to be metal, and I wasn't sure I liked that idea.

I inserted the metal toe of my right shoe into the front binding until I heard a *click*. Once I was sure that shoe was secure, I did the same with my other foot. "Ready," I called, and followed Karaline down the middle of Hickory Lane. Before we got home in a couple of hours, the snowplow would already have done its damage, so we'd have to take off our skis to cross the street, but for now, life couldn't be better.

Harper, I thought.

Well, all right, it could be better, but in the meantime, what with no vehicle traffic, the heavy blanket of snow that had fallen overnight, and a glorious morning, I wasn't holding off on enjoying any of it. My neighbor had once again shoveled the end of my drive where the snowplow had made one pass, most likely well before dawn. With my bedroom at the back of the house, and with Shorty purring so loudly beside me as I slept, I hadn't heard a thing.

I sped up a little and veered to my right so I was next to Karaline, but I didn't say anything. I wanted to tell her everything I'd learned about Emily, but decided to wait until we were off the lane and onto smooth, unbroken snow. The morning was too splendid for talking, so far, anyway. Even Dirk seemed subdued. Wrong word. He seemed quietly happy. It was a good feeling, knowing he cared for each of us. Why had I ever thought to get rid of him?

"Good morning!" The greeting came from our right, where the street forked. Scamp pranced at the end of a leash. He looked like he was walking Gilda rather than the other way around.

Dirk squatted. I noticed that he took care to drape a fold of his kilt between his legs—a necessary precaution if he had nothing on under there. Why was I thinking of such a thing on a Sunday morning?

Scamp tugged on the leash, slowing when he was within a few feet of Dirk. He stretched his neck, his nose wriggling like crazy.

"What's he doing?" Gilda asked. "Scamp, are you okay?"

Karaline chuckled. "He probably just likes to sniff the air."

And the resident ghost.

"I didna know Mistress Gilda had a wee doggie."

"How long have you had Scamp?" I thought I'd be helpful.

Gilda looked at me funny. "Since the summer."

"That's right. Too bad you didn't start bringing him to the ScotShop until just the last few days."

Dirk peered up at me. "Whan that I was . . . wrapped . . . in the wee shawl? Is that when the doggie appeared? Is that why I havena met him until now?"

Scamp tilted his head from one side to the other, and we all laughed. Thank goodness. It kept me from having to answer my wee ghostie.

Gilda gave the leash a gentle tug. "Come, Scamp. Time to head on home." She raised her chin. "We walk at least three miles every day."

"Good for you. I'll see you at noon." I watched them until they were out of sight. He sure was a cute pup. Maybe I could get a Scottie for myself.

Within a couple of blocks, we came to the place where a public path led between two houses. We had to stop so we could sidestep up the enormous mound of snow piled beside the road from previous snowplow runs. Dirk watched with a growing sense of hilarity. We started, standing sideways next to the four-foot-tall mound, with me about six feet in back of Karaline. We each lifted one foot far enough so the ski was off the ground. Once we'd dug that ski into the side of the piled-up snow about a foot and a half up the pile, we had to haul the other one up beside the first one and slightly downslope from it. Then we had to dig that ski into the snow enough to be sure it was securely anchored; once that was accomplished, we'd lift the first ski higher and repeat the process.

By the time we reached the top of the pile, Dirk was practically rolling on the snow. "Ye look like two mallards," he croaked between guffaws. "Quack, quack."

I didn't think it was nearly that funny. "You'd quack a different tune if you had to try it yourself."

Within moments, Karaline was laughing too hard to pay attention to what she was doing. She slid on her side down the final couple of feet, quacking as she went, skis flailing in the air ahead of her. I'm happy to say I maintained a more dignified demeanor as I descended and helped her brush off the snow—and dig some of it out of the bottom of her jacket.

We glided side by side most of the way across the meadow where the Hamelin Highland Games were held each summer to the edge of the forest, at which point I dropped behind Karaline and let her break the path up the Perth trail. When we came to what I increasingly tended to think of as my Robert Frost spot, we stopped for a moment. We had to keep our feet moving, of course, but we stood there, skis firmly planted, raising one heel as high as we could and then the other. "I visited Emily yesterday," I said.

Karaline just looked at me. I could tell she wasn't particularly interested.

"Remember how we were wondering what Dr. W might have seen in her?"

She perked up her ears—well, they were under a knit cap, but she looked more involved in the conversation than she had been a few seconds earlier. "Did you find out something?" She bounced up on both feet a couple of times. "Something interesting," she added.

"Wait'll you hear this." By the time I was halfway through recounting the story of Emily's career and the throat cancer, Karaline had forgotten to move her feet. So had I, for that matter.

"It was worth putting up with her steam bathhouse," I said.

"What do you mean?"

I explained about the heat. "Such a waste of energy," I said. "And to think she lives in such a well-insulated home. It's not like she has to keep the heat up to compensate for cold air coming in through cracks."

Karaline looked up into the bright sunshine above us, as it danced through the trees, but I had the feeling she wasn't really seeing it. "Of course she's cold all the time," she finally said.

"What do you mean?"

"For why would ye say that?"

Dirk's and my questions came out at the same time.

"I bet her cancer affected her thyroid." She didn't say anything else, almost as if she expected me to know what the heck she was talking about.

I looked at Dirk. He looked at me and made one of those gestures that said, *Beats me*, although I didn't think that phrase was available in the fourteenth century. Karaline must have tuned in to our lack of response. "Thyroid cancer," she said again. "When the thyroid is injured or destroyed, the body can't regulate its temperature—can't heat itself from the inside. Weather that seems moderately balmy to us can feel bitingly cold to someone with low thyroid function. They would have given her a prescription, but I'd be willing to bet the dosage needs to be adjusted."

Things began to make sense. "I don't think I've ever seen her without long sleeves, and some sort of scarf or wrap around her neck, even at the height of the summer."

Karaline began to shuffle her feet again. "Speaking of cold, we'd better hurry if we're going to get back to Hamelin before noon."

"You think we'll really find something?" I asked. "That cabin is truly minuscule. There's nowhere to hide anything the police wouldn't already have found."

"You'd be surprised," she said, and headed up the trail.

Harper sat on the side of his bed Sunday morning, still in his boxers. He was ready to pull his heavy socks on, but unwilling to let go of the thoughts swirling around his brain. First, his dad. Of all the stupid things he could have done, getting thrown in jail in the middle of South America was one of the stupidest. Especially since he'd caught a bug of some sort. A bug that killed him.

By the time he got the body cremated and the ashes home, Harper had been ordered to Poughkeepsie because of a break-through in a case he'd worked on—an identity theft ring. Even with the break, that investigation had gotten nowhere. He'd developed something of a reputation when he worked in Poughkeepsie, what with the first ring he'd busted. But now this new one was better protected, harder to crack.

And then there was the Wantstring death. Harper wasn't ready to quit on this investigation, no matter how frustrating it felt to be so far past the death date and still not have a clue. He wouldn't quit. Not yet. Something was bound to turn up.

Maybe he should ski up to that little cabin where the body had been found. Murphy said he'd checked the place thoroughly, but there was always a chance something minor had been overlooked. Something that seemed minor but might be the key to cracking the case wide-open.

He dressed quickly, threw an insulated bottle of water into a small day pack, stuck the metal-reinforced toes of his ski boots into his cross-country skis, and headed for the Perth.

He'd find some answers there. He was pretty sure of that.

30

Search Party

I couldn't figure out why anyone would build a simple cabin with a door that was easily seven and a half feet tall. In fact, I had no idea who owned the cabin. Maybe he—or she—was a giant. The good thing was that Karaline would never have to duck her six-foot frame. I pushed the door open and took an immediate step backward, inadvertently running into Karaline. I hadn't realized she was practically on my heels.

"What's wrong?" The breath puffing out of her mouth froze in the cold morning air, making her look like a steam engine.

I puffed right back at her. "You may not want to go in there."

"Why not?" She pushed past me and stopped on the threshold. "Oh. Oh my God."

Somebody had done a halfhearted job of trying to clean up a little, but a trail of Dr. Wantstring's blood still stained the floor beside the woodstove. It was too cold for there to be much smell, but I could tell Mac had been lying here for four days. With his broken leg and smashed fingers, the out-house in back of the cabin would have been a pipe dream.

I was suddenly glad it was such a cold winter, and I began to truly feel sorry for Mac.

Without saying anything—what was there to say, after all—Karaline shrugged out of her day pack and pulled out a heavy-duty flashlight. "Let's get this search party going," she said and began to investigate the woodpile. I climbed the ladder to look around the top bunk. What a grandiose term for what was only a platform made of planks of wood. I remembered when I'd first seen the place. I loved the little laminated sign beside the door, but I did recall thinking how uncomfortable it would probably be trying to camp out here.

Dirk thrust his head over the edge of the bunk into the shallow well formed by a one-by-four screwed into place along the front edge of the platform, probably to keep people from rolling out of bed in the middle of the night. "He wouldna try to hide anything here," he said. "Not even a wee youh-ezzbeedrive."

"What are you talking about?"

He repeated the word. Or rather, his idea of the word.

"It's an abbreviation, Dirk." I explained—sort of. My knowledge of the ins and outs of data storage was limited at best, and I had no idea what "USB" stood for, but I'd already told him about computers and had shown him my Mac laptop, so he had a general idea of what I was talking about.

"There's nothing up here," I said. "That's for sure. But I think you're wrong about his not hiding anything here. I think it would make a great hiding place."

"Nay," he said. "Anyone could look into it as I am doing." He bent his head almost into the well, and his chin didn't even graze the top edge.

I studied him a moment. "Maybe anybody as tall as you are, but what if our murderer was short?"

"He wasna," Dirk said with finality, but I wasn't going to let up on this.

"Why are you so sure?"

"Mistress Karaline has said that her Dr. Doubleyou was a tall man, aye?"

"Yep," came Karaline's comment from all the way across the room, which meant less than a dozen feet from us. "He was a few inches taller than I."

Dirk nodded, as if that proved his point.

"I don't get it," I said.

"It's simple logic," Karaline said. "Dr. W was tall enough not to consider this a good hiding place, since he'd be able to look right into it without climbing up the ladder, the way you had to do, so he wouldn't have hidden anything there." She poked around in the ashes of the woodstove. "And the murderer must have been equally tall."

"For heaven's sakes, K, how can you say that?"

"Anyone able to bring an ax down on the head of such a tall man . . ."

". . . maun ha' been a tall man himself." Dirk finished her thought with a distinct flourish in his voice.

"Mawn?" Karaline shut the woodstove door. "What's *mawn*?"

I guessed I hadn't clued her in. I explained while Dirk prowled around the perimeter of the room, looking under the table, and leaning to look behind the woodpile. When he didn't find anything, he asked if he might take the shawl.

"Sure," I said, unhooking my kilt pin and removing the shawl from my shoulders. "Why do you need it?" I tucked the kilt pin into a front zippered pocket.

"I would like to look around outside the wee cabin."

"If I were you I'd walk up the trail a ways," Karaline suggested. "Tell us if you think the snow's been disturbed by anyone in the past week."

"Aye; that I will, but for why?"

"Maybe whoever murdered Dr. W escaped that way. There's a trail. He might have left some kind of sign."

Dirk made a sort of wiggly motion with his hand in the air. Maybe it was a Gaelic blessing of some sort. "God bide," he said, or something like that, as he headed for the door, throwing the shawl casually but lovingly over one shoulder. I opened the door for him, watched him skirt around the skis we'd propped against the side of the cabin, and closed the door behind me.

On second thought, I opened it again. We didn't have a fire going, but we'd been so active, we'd both maintained our body heat. There wasn't any wind, and I thought we could use the extra light from the open door. Also, I'd gotten a little bit used to the stink, but the room could still use some cross ventilation. I crossed to the window on the other side and opened it all the way.

Harper opted to cross people's backyards until he was out of town. The road would have been faster, but then he'd have to get up and over the heap of snow left by the snowplow, unless he was lucky enough to find a house where the people had already shoveled out their driveway. That wasn't too likely this early on a Sunday morning.

He'd lived for a short while in the South, and he could never get over how people there had no concept of what to do in a heavy snow. Heck, they didn't know what to do in a *light* snow. Here in Vermont, over the course of a winter, particularly if there were a lot of heavy snowstorms, the streets would get narrower with each passing month as the mounds of snow built up and up. Harper could remember one year when he was a teenager, when there wasn't the usual January thaw, and the path to each house in his hometown of Arkane was more like a tunnel than a walkway. The streets were barely wide enough to accommodate a single car. That was the year the snow was too heavy and too deep for the plows, and the town had to hire bucket loaders to scoop it up. Luckily, that didn't happen very often.

He saw one couple coming toward him. They looked elderly, maybe because they seemed to be out for a leisurely stroll, hard to do on skis. It was so much easier to ski fast, so the momentum would carry you along. All you had to do was keep your legs moving. Going slowly, though, as these two people were doing, it was more like shuffling than skiing. *They'd be better off on snowshoes*, Harper thought. As he watched, he saw the man begin the distinctive wobbly motion of someone whose skis were sliding backward, out from under him.

Harper stopped to help the man back to his feet. Once he was sure nothing was broken and the fellow had his legs under him where they should be, he waved good-bye and skied on. "Thank you," came the woman's voice, muffled somewhat by the heavy scarf wound around her face and neck.

Harper gauged the look of the sky and the cloud cover, taking into account how cold it was, and what the wind felt like. He'd be okay skiing up the Perth. All he had to do was reach the little cabin. You couldn't get lost on that trail.

He headed for the dark oval at the beginning of the trail, where old-growth trees joined hands high in the air above the path, and skied, fast, into the yawning maw of the path, still heavily shaded from the early-morning light by ancient evergreen trees that stood like sentinels.

Mac Campbell hated breakfast; he hated having to depend on those snotty nurses for everything he needed; most of all he hated not knowing what was going on at the station. He needed his hands in the action. He yanked the rolling table closer. Maybe there was someone he could call. Somebody who needed to hear what had happened to him. Maybe that Andrea woman who worked for the newspaper. She should have come by to interview him. It wasn't every day the Hamelin police chief was incapastiated . . . incaspipitated . . . laid up. As Mac reached for the phone, he knocked that stupid report off his lap. He'd fallen asleep reading it. Boring as heck. Nothing to report. They needed him there directing the operation. The perp would be behind bars already if Mac had been in on the investigation.

Shoving it out of the way, his glance passed over one word. *Insurance.* Mac perked up, pushed the phone away, and started reading. Five-million-dollar insurance policy. Sole beneficiary Emily Fontini Wantstring. What kind of middle name was that? Damn Eyetalian.

He picked up the phone. Harper wasn't there, out investigating something, Moira told him. "Put Murphy on, then."

"Sorry, Chief. He's not available. I can connect you with Fairing."

Mac swore. "Awright, put her on."

When Fairing came on the line, Mac told her to arrest Emily Wantstring for the murder of her husband.

"But we don't have a shred of evidence to implicate her."

"You don't call a five-million-dollar insurance policy evidence?"

"No . . . sir. I'd call that a possible motive, but it's not evidence."

"Quit stalling. I order you to arrest that woman. Now!"

"Have you found anything yet, K?"

She shook her head and kept on dismantling the woodpile, moving the logs one or two at a time from the corner of the room to a place beneath the window closest to the bunk bed.

"What are you doing?"

"Remember how when we came in, this woodpile was disturbed, like some of it had fallen over?"

"Yeah," I said, "and I know why it was." She paused in the process of hefting one particularly large log. Somebody was going to have to split it; it wouldn't fit through the stove's doorway. "When I visited Mac in the hospital—"

"Poor, dumb you," she muttered.

"I know. I have no idea what got into me. Anyway . . ." I took the log from her, like a bucket brigade, and added it to her new pile. "Mac told me he'd pulled the logs over on himself."

"Stupid move, wouldn't you say?"

I tried to be fair. He was a jerk, but his leg had been broken, after all. "He was trying to get just one log off the top of the pile so he could get a fire started, but when he snagged his ski pole on it and tugged, that whole end of the pile collapsed on him. That's what broke his two fingers."

"Serves him right," she muttered.

"So," I said, "why are you moving the woodpile?"

"Because if somebody disturbed it—Mac or anybody else— he may have inadvertently covered up a CD or a USB or something that Dr. W hid. I hope it wasn't a CD—too much danger of breaking. The woodpile would make a perfect hiding place."

I wasn't too sure about that.

She must have noticed my look of disbelief. "Really," she said. "About a third of the way up from the bottom is where I would have put it." She picked up one more log. "And ta-da," she sang out, "here it is."

At first I thought she was teasing, but she lifted a dark blue flash drive and held it high.

We high-fived it. And somehow I ended up with the thing in my grasp.

"I'll be happy to take care of that for you."

Karaline and I spun so fast it was a wonder we didn't fall over. "Who are you?" We both said it. I couldn't tell which one of us had spoken first.

The voice sounded fake, as if it were disguised on purpose. Between the black ski mask and a heavy parka, I couldn't identify either the hair color or weight of whoever it was. Average height. Black gloves—well, glove, singular; one hand was out of sight behind his back.

"Let's just say I'm somebody who should have that thumb drive and leave it at that."

Karaline backed up a step, but I stood my ground. "No."

Black Mask shifted his weight, moving his legs farther apart, with one a little in front of the other. He brought his other hand forward. Why on earth had we let Dirk go wandering off into the woods? I hated guns.

Especially if they were aimed at me.

"I want you to set it down real easy-like," the black-masked guy said. "Then shove it across the floor to me. We wouldn't want it to get hurt in the process, would we?"

I had to disagree. Whatever was on the USB, I didn't want this monster to have the information.

"Wouldn't want either one of you to get hurt, either, but I already killed one person. It wouldn't bother me much to kill two more."

Everything in my heart screamed to fight, not to let this creep get Dr. W's flash drive. At the same time, everything in my head told me to be a good girl and give it to him so he'd leave.

"Give it to him, Peggy," Karaline said. I was surprised her voice sounded so calm.

I thrust my chin forward. "Give me one good reason why I should."

"He's got a gun," she said, and I paused. She had a point.

The more I thought about it, the more it began to sound like a perfectly good reason. If I bent down really slowly, though, I could get my balance arranged so I could throw the thing at him when he least expected it. But I'd have to act fast.

"Don't try anything funny," the guy said from across the room, shifting his shoulders as if the weight of his backpack was bothering him. He was too far away for us to rush him. He could kill at least one of us the moment we started to move. "Like I said," he added, "kill one, kill three. Not much difference."

"He has a point," Karaline said, echoing my sentiments. "Give it to him, Peggy."

"You already said that," I said, stalling for time. Where was Dirk when I needed him? All he had to do was run into the guy from behind and this fellow would pass out faster than he could shake his gun.

And the gun might go off accidentally, a niggling little voice said inside my brain.

"Okay." I knelt as slowly as I could and set the flash drive on the old wooden floorboards. All I had to do was give it such a hard shove, it would spin out of control through the open door. Then Dirk could tackle the guy and . . .

"Very good," El Creepo said. "Now just slide it across the floor, real gently." He held up an admonitory hand—the one without the gun. "If you try anything funny," he warned me, "I'll shoot you for the fun of it."

Nice guy. Too bad he was a mind reader. I sent the little navy blue bit of plastic and metal spinning across the floor. He trapped it under one booted foot—cross-country ski boots, I noted. More like shoes than boots. So that was how he'd gotten here. Out of curiosity, I asked, "How long have you been following us?"

"Following you? Don't be so self-centered. I wasn't following you." He bent so quickly to scoop up the USB that neither Karaline nor I had time to react. "I came this way to be sure I hadn't left anything of our dear doctor's behind." He waved the gun negligently. I sure hoped it wouldn't go off accidentally. On the other hand, if it did, Dirk would be sure to hear and would come running to investigate.

The guy took one step backward, and another one. One more step and he'd be in the doorway. Dirk couldn't help but see him—if that ghost of mine were anywhere close by.

"I saw your skis leaning against the wall outside," Creepo the Malignant said, "so I knew two people were here."

And one ghost, I thought. Where the heck had Dirk disappeared to?

"I just happened to overhear your little discussion about what you were looking for. It was too good an opportunity to pass up."

Stalling for time, I asked, "What opportunity?" Not that I was curious about it. I just wanted the guy out of here, but maybe Dirk would show up any minute now.

"You mean you can't guess?" His voice still sounded like he was disguising it deliberately. "I was letting you do my work for me. And you did a great job. You found the flash drive. I didn't really believe there were only two of them, but that was all I could find. So I'll just say thank you and be on my way."

I expected him to turn and flee. I took a quick glance at Karaline. I could see she was thinking the same thing. *Turn around, buddy. Just turn around once and we'll both tackle you.*

He must have heard us thinking, or maybe it showed on our faces. Karaline certainly looked grim.

A slow smile revealed white teeth through the mouth hole of his mask. "Both of you, sit down and take your shoes off," he said. When we hesitated, he barked, "Now!" His voice sort of squeaked, and I wondered for an insane moment if this was some misbegotten young boy whose voice was in the process of changing, going out of control when he least expected it. I sank onto the floor, took off my gloves, and groped for my shoelaces, all the while studying the little I could see of his face, hoping to identify eye color at the very least.

No such luck. The ski mask was loose on his head, as if he'd bought it—or stolen it, for all I knew—two sizes too large. That meant his eyes were shadowed by the excess fabric; not enough to block his vision, but enough so that all I could tell was that the eyes were too dark for me to see. It would have been easier if he'd had Paul Newman eyes. Robert Redford eyes. Mel Gibson eyes. Donald Sutherland eyes. Eyes so icy blue you got cold looking at them. But no, they were brown or gray or hazel or mud-colored for all I could tell. How could I ever pick him out of a lineup? If I even survived long enough to make it to that point. *Short guy with white teeth and muddy eyes* wasn't much of a description.

He waited for us to comply. "Now, toss them over into that far corner."

If he planned to take our shoes, he wasn't going about it the right way. He'd have to walk over there away from the door in order to pick them up. How could I be thinking so clearly when my heart was racing, my ears were pounding, and I was so close to peeing in my pants I had to cross my legs right there on the floor? Where was Dirk?

"Now, lie all the way down, on your stomach, flat on the floor. Stretch your hands straight up above your heads."

"Why?" I couldn't let him do this to us.

"You really think I'm dumb enough to let you jump me before I can get away from here? Lie down. Now!" Each word got progressively louder, and his voice cracked again as he shouted the last order. Threatened by a beardless teenager? I hadn't noticed any facial hair around the mouth hole. No convenient moles on the upper lip. No jagged scars where his face had been sliced open by a sword in a duel. No black eye patch. No parrot on his shoulder. I was losing my mind.

As I stretched out next to Karaline, I wondered whether boys could grow beards before their voices changed. Maybe not, but they sure could carry guns.

I didn't know what Karaline was thinking, but the look she gave him was thunderous. I couldn't think of any way out of this, other than to hope Dirk would show up. I hated having no options. Or rather, I had options, but the only ones I could think of would get one or both of us killed.

Once we were lying down, I reached for Karaline's hand. I halfway expected him to blow our brains out within the next couple of minutes, and if he did, I'd be darned if I wanted to die alone.

But he didn't. He still had more instructions for us. "Now start counting. Slow and out loud. Count all the way to a thousand before you even think about getting to your feet. You hear me?"

Karaline's fingers tightened around mine.

"I can't hear you," El Creepola growled.

"One," Karaline said. I'd never heard her voice so low, so dangerous-sounding. "Two."

"Louder!"

"Three," I chimed in.

"Four," Karaline said.

Between numbers, we heard his shoes clomp backward out the door, and within seconds we heard those same shoes click into their cross-country toe clamps outside the door. By that time I'd reached eleven. "Twelve," Karaline intoned. Under her breath she said, "Where do you think Dirk is?"

"Thirteen." My voice fairly rang through the little cabin. "I don't know," I said softly, "but I wish he'd hurry up."

"Louder," came the voice from outside. But we both heard the clunk of a ski pole against the wooden step and the unmistakable sound of skis beginning to swish across the snow.

"Fourteen." Karaline let go of my hand and began to gather her knees up under her.

"Fifteen." We must have looked like a couple of shoeless caterpillars, inching our way upright.

"Sixteen," she shouted.

"Seventeen. To heck with this." I stood, bracing myself for a second against the woodpile. My hands shook, but whether with fear or anger, I wasn't quite sure.

I slid across the room and grabbed our shoes, tossed hers to her, and slipped mine on. No time for laces. I tiptoed the few steps over to the front wall, peeked carefully around the window frame at the empty clearing. I could see his fresh ski tracks. "He's gone," I said. "Let's get out of here."

"No way," Karaline said. "He still has that pistol. I don't know about you, but I don't want to run into him halfway down the mountain. Besides, there's one more thing I have to do." She finished tying her shoes and grinned. "You won't believe this."

"Believe what?"

"Remember when he first surprised us and we spun around?"

"Like I could forget something that happened four minutes ago." It seemed like we'd had that gun pointed at us for three hours, but really, it couldn't have taken more than a minute or two before we were down on our bellies.

Karaline was still grinning like a demented monkey. "As we spun around, I saw . . . Never mind. I'll show you."

She strode to the doorway and reached up toward the top of that ridiculously tall door. For some reason, I glanced to my left out the window and saw a puff of smoke spout from the edge of the woods, just to the left of where the path headed sharply up out of the clearing, followed half a heartbeat later by the report of a gunshot. He'd been waiting to see if we tried to follow him, the creep.

Karaline doubled over and staggered back a step, both hands clutching her midriff, her face ashen.

"He shot me." Barely audible, her voice was thick and breathy. She took two faltering steps and sank to her knees, onto a wooden floor worn smooth by decades of passing feet and still stained with the blood of her beloved professor.

31

Encounter in the Woods

Emily Wantstring settled in on her orange chair for a nice cup of hot chocolate, wishing she had Marcus sitting across the table from her in his blue chair. She wondered if he might have enjoyed hot chocolate. She'd never thought to make it for him. Thirty-nine years she'd lived with him—thirty-seven of them married—and she didn't know something as basic as this.

When the phone rang, her first thought was that it must be Mark, and she had to wipe her eyes and take a breath before she answered. "Hello?"

Her brother-in-law, Josie's husband, had a breathy voice, unusual in so large a man. "Em, I'm sorry I didn't call you sooner, but I wanted to let you know what's happened."

"What do you mean? Aren't you calling about Mark?"

"Mark? No, what about him?" Without waiting for her answer, he plowed on. "Josie was attacked on the stairs of the

Capitol on Saturday. I should have called you from the hospital but I just flat forgot. I was so worried about her."

"Josie?" Emily placed her hand over her heart. She couldn't take this. "Josie?"

"She's doing okay. Some guy knifed her. I saw him headed toward her and I tackled him, but he sliced her leg open pretty badly. She had to have a lot of stitches. She just asked me a few minutes ago if I'd remembered to call you, so I thought I'd better."

"Thank you." Emily could tell her voice sounded very weak.

"Now, don't you worry about her. She's going to be fine." He made a few huffing sounds. "I need to get going. You take care, okay?"

Emily sat there, unthinking, for several minutes before she realized she hadn't told him about Mark. Why hadn't she called her sister?

The doorbell surprised her. Deciding it must be Peggy come to visit her again, she opened the door without even looking out first. Sergeant Fairing stood on the porch. She looked . . . What was the word? Rueful?

"Emily Fontini Wantstring?"

"You know that's who I am. I met you when I was at the station giving my statement. Come on in so I can get the door closed."

With my hands shaking harder than I could ever remember, I unzipped Karaline's parka. "We have to see where the blood's coming from, K. Hold on. You'll be fine. We'll get help." I moved her right hand, the one on top, as gently as I could. "You have to let go, K. I've got to get your parka out of the way."

She didn't resist me as I lifted her bloody left hand and pushed the flaps of her parka back away from her body. There was a rush of blood and I pressed the heel of my hand against the center of the place it seemed to be coming from, hoping I wasn't doing any more damage.

By this time, the whole left side of her hip looked like she'd been spangled with splotches of red dye, as if she were being costumed for some sort of bizarre Christmas pageant, with K as a bunch of holly berries.

Even as I pressed, more blood seeped from under my hand. As far as I could tell, it wasn't spurting, and I knew that was a pretty good sign, but I couldn't think what to do from here. The Red Cross first-aid training courses I'd taken might as well have been watercolor classes for all the good they did me here, now. I couldn't recall a single thing except that arteries spurt, veins leak. And something about the pupils. I was supposed to look at them.

"Open your eyes, K. Look at me."

She cracked one eyelid half a slit. Her face looked blotchy. "No," she said. "Hurts," as if even one extra syllable would take too much effort.

I felt her weight shift as she slumped to her left, onto the unforgiving metal of the woodstove. "Don't you die on me! Don't you dare!"

In the movies, people get shot all the time. They just grit their teeth and keep on going. Karaline looked like she might not go anywhere anytime soon. I didn't like whatever scriptwriter had written the current episode. "Dirk," I shouted as loudly as I could, levering myself up so my lungs wouldn't be so compressed. "Dirk!"

Karaline's eyes sprung open. "Ow! Don't . . . push so . . . hard."

At least she could talk.

There had been about half a chapter in my Red Cross manual on gunshot wounds, with a lot of emphasis on *entrance and exit wounds*. Only one shot. Karaline had been facing out the door toward the clearing. This meant that what I was holding, just inside the bump of her left hip bone, had to be the entrance wound.

I could remember the concise voice of my instructor. *The entrance wound is usually considerably smaller than the exit wound. The exit wound is frequently where the greatest blood loss occurs. Always remember to look for an exit wound.* She had droned on and on, and I had never in my wildest imagination believed that I would ever need that information. One thing I did remember was that the instructor stressed the importance of getting the victim to the hospital as soon as possible. And, crapola on toast, here I was on a mountain.

"K," I said as soothingly as I could, "I have to examine your back."

"Shot . . . in . . . front . . ."

I had to strain to hear her. "I know, but I have to see where the bullet came out."

A fleeting expression colored her face for a moment. "I might . . . bleed to death?"

"No! You are NOT going to die." I tried to put as much conviction as I possibly could into my words, but my voice squeaked, just like that stupid, asinine, idiotic, dim-witted, fiendish freak of a maniac who'd shot her. "You are not going to die!"

I had to look at her back. Without my knowing it, she could be bleeding to death back there, her parka soaking up the fluid, the blood, *her blood*, before it could puddle around her. With my free hand, I pulled the two big hankies out of my leg pocket.

I wadded them up, eased the wad into place, and pressed her right hand over the makeshift bandage. "Hold this here." When I was sure she had at least a little bit of pressure on it—she looked so weak—I positioned her left arm. "Push against your right hand with your left elbow," I said. "Hold it tight against you. That way you won't have to do all the pushing with your right hand."

She studied me for a second or two. "Huh?"

"Never mind. Just push as hard as you can. I have to look at your back, and then I've got to find a bandage of some sort, and we need to figure out how we can get you down the mountain, and—"

"P?"

"What?"

"Shut . . . up."

God, she sounded weak.

Harper was pushing as hard as he could. The cold felt good. He heard the sound of a distant gunshot, not a common sound along the trail, but it was so far ahead of him, he didn't worry. He waited to see if there would be another report, but the mountains, the woods, were silent. Some poor rabbit had probably hit the dirt—he chuckled to himself—hit the snow.

He tried to focus on the Wantstring investigation, which had gotten precisely nowhere, but the pull of the exercise, his muscles working harder than they generally got a chance to do, was almost intoxicating. He'd spent so much time doing basically nothing recently, it felt good to push himself to go a little faster, lengthen his stride, swing his arms. He hadn't looked at his watch before he left, but he could tell he was making good time. He forgot about his job, forgot about everything but the swish of his skis across the snow.

Ahead of him, another skier approached, heading downhill a lot faster than Harper was managing uphill. Harper adjusted his weight to carry him about a foot to his right and could see the other skier moving about that far to *his* right, so they could pass with no danger of collision.

"Good day to be out skiing," Harper called out as they drew near to each other. The skier nodded in friendly acknowledgment. At least, Harper assumed it was friendly. It was hard to tell when someone was wrapped up that much against the cold.

As they passed each other, Harper had time to notice the ring of ice fully formed on the fellow's knitted face mask, where the frigid air had frozen the moisture-laden breath coming from the skier's mouth.

Harper shrugged—as much as one *can* shrug on skis. Full face masks were worthless unless you were standing still. Good thing the fellow was moving fast headed back toward town. That much ice would create a problem eventually. Happy to have his face free, he inhaled deeply. By the time that breath reached his lungs, his body had warmed it.

32

Crapola on Toast

I didn't want to risk folding her over, so I reached behind Karaline and felt underneath her parka all the way from her hip to her shoulder blade. All the fabric was intact.

I tugged off my parka and tried to rip it apart. All that happened was I got something approximating rope burns on my fingers. How did women in pioneer days ever manage to rip apart their petticoats for bandages? They were always doing it in books and films. Now, when it was real life and I desperately needed something other than a couple of hankies to stem the flow of my dear friend's lifeblood, I couldn't make a scratch, much less a rip in the fabric. I tried my teeth. The effort left my parka soggy with saliva, but still intact.

I vowed to pull out my old Swiss Army Knife and carry it with me everywhere from now on.

But for right now, what could I do? *Please let her live.*

* * *

Harper paused near a rock wall that towered twenty feet above the trail and unzipped his parka about halfway, releasing a cloud of steam. Cross-country, especially when you were going uphill, could work up a sweat.

He'd always liked this part of the Perth, ever since he'd found it while exploring shortly after he moved to Hamelin. Once these investigations were out of the way, he planned to invite Peggy up here for a picnic. He knew she loved it, too, because of the way her voice had softened when she described it for the police report. For that reason alone, it was doubly precious to him.

The police report. He went over the details in his mind, how Mac had broken his leg—where? He skied a few yards farther up the trail and located the sharp lump of fallen granite and the heavy branch beside it. The first bone Harper had ever broken was his big toe. Dropped a heavy rock on it when he was about eleven or twelve. It probably wouldn't even have made a dent if he'd been wearing shoes. But he'd spent most of his boyhood summers barefoot over in Arkane.

He turned ninety degrees to his left, a maneuver that took a bit of time on skis, moved off the trail a few feet, and stopped, looking straight ahead of him at the curves of two birches leaning in toward a maple. If he squinted his eyes, he could see how they formed almost a heart shape.

He wondered what Peggy had looked like as a little girl.

I'd just leaned Karaline back against the woodstove when Dirk pounded through the door at a dead run. "Wha' would be wrong?" He skidded to a stop—hard to do when you're a ghost who can't touch anything. How had he gotten any traction? "I heard the . . . the cannon," he said for want of a better word. Maybe they didn't have handguns where he was in Scotland when he was alive. "I was atop the wee hill." His motioned toward the top of the steep mountain incline behind the cabin. "Mistress Karaline?" He studied her pale face, the blood on both our hands, and looked over at me. I could see fear, anger, and something approaching dread in his eyes.

"She's going to be okay," I assured him, hoping to convince Karaline and myself, too. "I know people died from wounds like this back in the fourteenth century, but we have surgery and antibiotics nowadays." I'd tried explaining antibiotics to him once, and he'd listened politely to my treatise on germs, but I could tell he didn't really believe me. So much of twenty-first-century life was just a great big fairy tale to Dirk.

"Chirurgery?" He rolled the word around on his tongue.

"It's something that's going to help her. The good news is this is the only place she's bleeding."

"No . . . exit . . . wound," she managed to say between whimpers.

"Right. Isn't that great?" It was hard to sound enthusiastic when deep down inside you had a dark feeling that your dear friend might die after all.

"That means . . . the bullet . . . is . . . stuck inside me?"

"Crapola on toast!"

Years ago my mother had tanned my hide for saying a swearword. I guess the lesson stuck. But there were times I just had to say something more pertinent than *gosh golly darn it*. And saying it at full volume seemed to help somehow. At least it felt good for half a second as my rage reverberated in the cold air.

Ambulance. I whipped out my cell phone. "Crapola! No service." I could have gone on shouting, but it wasn't helping Karaline.

I pulled myself back together and turned to Dirk. "What we need to work on first is to get a bandage put together, and then all we'll have left to do is get her down the mountain."

It took him just a moment to register what I'd said. Then he turned and slammed his fist violently but soundlessly against the wall. "I canna help ye' move her." The anguish in his voice tore into me. "What good is my life here when it isna really a life and I canna aid my friends when they ha' need o' me?"

I'd never in my life heard so much anger followed so quickly by so much sorrow. I didn't know how to answer him, so I busied myself taking off my lightweight sweatshirt, since I didn't happen to have a petticoat to tear apart with my teeth. All I had left on was a silk tee. I didn't even bother with modesty. I'd be clothed in goose bumps soon enough. They'd cover me nicely.

Dirk paid no attention whatsoever. He stationed himself next to Karaline, hand on his dagger, watching her intently, forming a ghostly barrier between her and anything that might come her way. If he'd been between her and the shooter when the shot was fired, I wondered, what would have happened to the bullet?

Harper glanced over his right shoulder. Even with the snows that had fallen since last week and the tracks of two or three other skiers, he could see a wide, depressed swath that led from this spot up to the top of the hill. He never would have thought Mac had it in him. It must have taken an incredible amount of determination to crawl that distance in the shape he was in. Adrenaline would have helped a lot, but surely the adrenaline charge must have worn off after a while. What would have kept him going in the face of all that pain?

Harper pictured the big, burly police chief, always ready with scorn, but powered by a bluff congeniality that usually worked with men. Some men. It had been enough to get him appointed as chief and to keep him in that position for all these years. Harper had seen the covert cringes, though, in the body language of women who'd had official dealings with the man. Political correctness went out the window when Mac walked into a room. If Mac hadn't been related to someone on the Board of Selectmen, he never would have been appointed as chief of police. Harper was half expecting Fairing to enter a charge of harassment any day now. The only woman on the Hamelin force, she'd had to put up with—

"Crapola on toast!"

He heard the voice as clearly as if the speaker stood next to him, even though he could tell it had drifted down to him from over the hill to his right. Even as he executed a jump turn, the fastest way to change direction on a pair of cross-country skis in motion—although he'd never before managed it while he was standing still—he knew it was Peggy. She was the only person he'd ever heard using that particular turn of phrase. He'd know her voice anywhere, anytime.

He topped the rise and, glad there was such a steep slope down into the little clearing where the cabin stood, he crouched and used momentum, ski poles, and gravity to propel him toward where he knew she must be.

33

His Peigi's Shawl

Harper was the last person I expected to see burst through the open doorway, and I couldn't prevent a cry that was 50 percent surprise and about 90 percent delight. Even as he stepped into the room, causing Dirk to jump back out of the way, I could see his eyes swing over the entire space, checking for danger.

He looked me over with a glance that was so all-encompassing, and so . . . so soft, I felt like I'd been touched. I hoped to all get-out it wasn't just my imagination. Then his eyes moved to Karaline, and the blood. After one more quick glance around, he knelt beside her.

"She's been shot."

"Are you hurt?" His nod encompassed my bloody hands.

"No. Just her."

"Bandage?"

"I'm trying." I held up my sweatshirt. "Okay, Karaline, let's move your hand. . . ."

"And . . . elbow," she grunted.

Harper supported her arm, and I could see how white her knuckles had become as I peeled them away and pressed my folded sweatshirt over the hankies against the center of the wound, hoping with every ounce of me that the bullet hadn't torn into anything vital, anything that couldn't be repaired.

Harper zipped his parka the rest of the way open and extracted a long scarf. It looked hand knitted. When I glanced from the scarf up to him, he said, "My mother knitted this for me, but I don't think she'll mind if I put it to a better use than warming my neck." He slid one hand, firmly clutching a scarf end, behind Karaline's back. I grabbed it on my side and worked it underneath her left arm.

Once it was over her tummy, Harper checked the placement of the sweatshirt bandage and tied the scarf tightly in place. "I hope that'll hold," he said, "until we can get her out of here."

By this time I was shivering uncontrollably. I donned my parka and felt the kilt pin in my pocket. I pulled it out and handed it to Harper. He smiled warmly as he pinned the scarf so it would be more secure. Karaline raised one corner of her mouth about a quarter inch. I had the feeling that was about as much of a smile as she could manage.

He nodded and pulled out his cell. "No service." He slipped it back into his pocket. He looked around, muttering under his breath. "Three pairs of skis. We'll need two pairs for us."

"There's no way she can walk," I said.

"We could probably work up some sort of sling to support the upper half of her body, but I'm afraid her legs will have to drag all the way down the mountain."

"I can . . . take it," Karaline said in a voice that was more bravado than certainty.

"We really need three poles," he said, "to make a travois."

"What would be a *travoy*?"

"The Indians used them. Triangular contraptions to haul goods on."

Harper looked at me funny. "I know that."

Karaline chuckled; at least, I thought it was a chuckle, but hardly any air came out. She must have been in incredible pain, and she let out an involuntary moan.

Harper took off his parka.

"What are you doing? It's five degrees out here."

"We need a big block of sturdy material to support her weight. We'll have to attach this to the skis somehow and tie her onto it."

"Stop," Dirk said, and Karaline and I both looked over at him.

Harper noticed the direction of our gaze, and looked around. "What?"

"Nothing." I looked at Dirk and raised an eyebrow.

"Ye need the shawl. Yon man may be gallant, but he would freeze wi'out his coat. His coat isna large enow any the way."

"That's true," I said.

Harper drew back his chin. "What's true?"

"Ye could use my Peigi's shawl." Dirk lifted it from his shoulder where it had been draped over his kilt pin.

"You can use my shawl," I said to Harper.

His eyes swept this way and that, searching for the as-yet-invisible shawl. I pushed myself to my feet. "I left it over by the woodpile." I headed that way, almost tripping on my untied laces. Dirk followed and handed it to me as I bent as if to pick it up from behind the logs. I turned around and held it up for Harper to see.

He looked as if he thought he might have missed something, but couldn't for the life of him figure out what it was.

Boy, was he right. What he'd missed stood right in front of him wearing a kilt. Harper put his parka back on.

The shawl had always been large, warm, and enveloping, but as I held it now, it seemed heavier, denser, longer than I remembered. That was ridiculous. I'd had it on in my living room this morning. I couldn't have forgotten its size in the past few hours. But somehow, it was big enough to tie firmly at the corners so it formed a sling between Karaline's skis.

We set it up so the curved, pointy ends of her two skis would slide along the ground behind us. I picked up the square back end of one of her skis in my left hand and my ski pole in the other. Harper, to my left, took up the other ski.

Poor Karaline was horribly unbalanced, what with Harper's and my disparate heights, but we did the best we could. We couldn't keep her weight from pushing the shawl down to the ground, so it wasn't just her feet that dragged. It was her whole bottom.

We managed to struggle all the way across the clearing and up the tree-topped incline before Karaline's groans became almost more than I could bear. We eased the make-shift arrangement down as gently as we could. I stepped out of my skis and knelt beside her. "I don't know what else to do, K. We have to get you back to town."

Before she could answer, before Harper could say anything, Dirk walked up beside me. "I havena been able to help before this, but I do think I may be of some small service." He laid a cool, transparent hand on Karaline's forehead, and a look of genuine amazement came into her eyes. "Ooooh," she said, and closed her eyes.

Harper looked from Karaline to me, and back again. When his gaze returned to meet mine, he asked, "What just happened?"

She didn't look dead, but I felt for her pulse, just to be sure. "I, uh, I think she fainted."

I had the feeling he wouldn't let this one pass. What on earth could I tell him?

I stood, kicked my toes into the ski bindings once more, and got ready to pick up my side of the load again, but in doing so I looked forward down the hill to where two slender birches bent in solemn promise toward the old maple tree. "Excuse me," I said. "I'll be back in just a moment."

Dirk stayed standing beside Karaline, his hand touching her head and then her waistline, while I retrieved Mac's buried ski and presented it to Harper in triumph.

"Right," Harper said. Karaline stayed blissfully asleep while we repositioned the shawl and added the third ski, creating a stable triangle. It involved a bit of fancy footwork on Dirk's part so he could keep his hand in contact with Karaline's forehead or tummy without letting Harper run into his ghostly presence.

34

Off the Mountain

Pulling a makeshift travois down a mountainside across deep snow is not easy. We hadn't gone much farther than the Robert Frost spot. Harper wasn't breathing as heavily as I was—a northern winter is a dead giveaway. Little puffs of mist came out of his nose or mouth every four or five seconds. I, on the other hand, looked like a steam engine, with an exhalation gushing out in front of me every second or so. I hoped maybe he wouldn't notice.

"Do you have enough breath to tell me what happened? Did you recognize the person who did this?"

"No. He had on a black ski mask."

Harper's stride faltered. Maybe there was a fallen branch under the snow.

"He was short," I said, "and he talked funny, like he was trying to disguise his voice."

Harper took another few steps. This wasn't like cross-country at all. With all this weight behind us digging into the snow, there was no way we could glide, but I knew that if we took off our skis, we'd sink up above our knees. "Do you think he might be someone you'd recognize if you heard his voice?"

"I hadn't thought of that." I ran a brain scan over the citizens of Hamelin, but couldn't think of anyone. "He was about the same height as Mr. Pitcairn." Harper had met my next-door neighbor. "But I know it wasn't him."

Harper didn't ask why; he just waited for me to get my thoughts together. He seemed to be thinking, hard.

"With the mask, I couldn't see much skin, but his lips looked . . . young somehow."

"Young?"

"You know. There weren't any wrinkles."

"Good observation. What about eye color?"

"Dark, not light, but that was about all I could tell. He wasn't wearing glasses."

It kept on this way for quite a while. I managed to tell him most of what had happened, leaving out any mention of Dirk, of course.

He already knew about Karaline's connection with Wantstring, and he seemed to accept without comment my description of Dr. W's squirreling habits.

"He had ballpoint pens—green ones—but nothing to write on," he told me as we took an extremely short rest break. I knelt beside Karaline's left hand, but she seemed to be sleeping still.

Harper moved to Karaline's right side, and Dirk simply stepped across Karaline. I had to move up closer to her head so my busy ghost wouldn't run into me. I pulled off my glove and laid a hand on her forehead. Cool, but then, in this weather everything seemed cool. I hoped her toes weren't freezing.

Harper continued with his thought. "There weren't any writing materials in the cabin, no laptop, nothing like that."

"He had to be using paper. The charge wouldn't last long on a laptop." I told him what Karaline had said about a special project. "Do you think whoever murdered him took something he might have been writing?" It certainly made sense to me. I just wondered what he'd been working on. Whatever it was, it probably held the answer to why Dr. Wantstring was murdered.

"Could be. He was wearing a backpack."

I couldn't remember having mentioned that fact. "How did you know that?"

He moved back up to the front of our rig. "I passed the guy on my way up here."

"And you didn't stop him?"

"He was just a guy skiing." He bent to lift his side of the jury-rigged travois. "Have you caught your breath? We need to press on. I don't want her getting frostbite on our shift."

Dirk stayed beside Karaline the entire time. I glanced back a couple of times, and his hand was either on her forehead or on the bandage at her waist. The third time I looked back, it seemed as if both his hands had disappeared, had merged with her wound. It was a good thing he didn't have to watch where he put his feet; he never would have been able to manage. He didn't even seem to be moving his legs. He just sort of hovered there beside her. I couldn't stare too long, though. I needed to watch where I was skiing. Some of us had legs that had to move.

Not that they were moving very fast. We tried at one point to take off our skis and pull her that way, but we sank so far down into the snow cover with each step it was like slogging through mud two feet deep. "We should have brought snowshoes," I said.

Harper didn't even bother to answer.

Once Harper could get cell service, he called for an

ambulance to meet us on the outskirts of town. The paramedics swooped into action the moment we reached them. Dirk had to back out of the way, but I could see in his eyes how little he wanted to give up his contact with Karaline. I answered their questions as best I could. After only a minute or so, Harper touched my arm. "I'll get my car," he said. "Wait here."

"No. I'm going with Karaline."

"Sorry," said an ambulance attendant. "You can follow later. We're taking her to the Arkane hospital." They hoisted the gurney between the yawning doors, and the bright artificial light inside swallowed my friend. They jumped in after her, and I stood alone, beside the remains of the travois, watching the red taillights of the ambulance as it pulled out of sight. Only I wasn't really alone. Dirk touched my shoulder, and I felt a cool stream of comfort, even through my winter parka.

Before Harper returned with his car, I dismantled the skis, wrapped myself in the shawl—it was really cold with only a silk tee on underneath the parka now that I wasn't working to haul Karaline—and thanked Dirk for his service. "I think you saved her life."

"I didna know what else to do." He shook his head, and the trees I could see behind him seemed to waver a bit. "It felt . . . It seemed . . . right somehow to lay my hands upon her." He raised those hands and stared at them. "I couldna see my own hands when I touched her."

"I know," I said in a dry tone. "That's because they went inside her."

At his look of confusion, I told him what I'd seen on the trail. I didn't really believe it. But then again, I had a ghost attached to a shawl that was woven in the fourteenth century. If I believed that, why not believe anything? Like the fact that the shawl fit my shoulders just fine now, but for the last few hours it had been big enough to support Karaline's six-foot frame when she needed it and the corners had been skinny enough to tie around a ski. It made no sense. But then again, neither did having a ghost.

We asked for Karaline at the emergency room desk and were directed to a small waiting room. I shed my parka, but kept the shawl around me, not because it was cold—it wasn't. The hospital was heated like a Turkish bath. But all I had on was my silk tee. Anyway, I wanted to keep Dirk close by. Awful things happened when he wasn't around. Some time later—I didn't have my watch on and there was no clock on the wall—a doctor in blue scrubs entered. After we identified ourselves, he asked, "Are you a relative of the patient?"

Without a qualm, without a quaver in my voice, I said, "I'm her sister." Well, I almost was. Sort of. Would have been if only we'd had the same mother. Harper's hand twitched slightly where it rested on the small of my back.

"Your sister is already in surgery," the doctor said. "I attended her in the emergency room, but I'm not a surgeon." He bit at his lower lip. "You told the paramedics she'd been shot at least three hours before you finally got her off the mountain. Is that right?"

"Yes," Harper said. "Why?"

"There just seemed to be too little blood loss for that type of injury, and I've never seen so little swelling of tissue in a gunshot wound."

"That's good, though," I said. "Isn't it?"

The doctor's face cleared all of a sudden. "You must have packed it with snow. That's what you did. That could explain it. Good thinking."

Harper looked over at me, and his brow furrowed.

"I wonder why the paramedics didn't mention that," the doctor continued.

"They must have been busy trying to keep her alive," I said.

The doctor rubbed the back of his neck and turned to leave. "That snow saved her life. You did well."

"Thank you," I said, looking as innocent as I possibly could. The doctor probably thought I was talking to him, but I was making eye contact with Dirk, who hovered just to the doctor's left side. "We did the best we could with what was available." Dirk raised his hands again and looked at them in wonder.

"Don't worry too much. One of our best surgeons was on call. Your sister is in good hands."

I wondered what he would have said if the second-best—or seventh-best—had been the one on call.

A nurse in purple scrubs walked into the room. "Are these yours?" She held up my bloodstained sweatshirt and a hand-knitted scarf. My kilt pin caught the light.

I took the sweatshirt. My hankies were stuck to it with dried blood.

Harper accepted his scarf back. There was surprisingly little blood on it. I smiled at Dirk.

35

Ten Hours in Limbo

We thanked the doctor, and the nurse led us to the surgery waiting room. I entered the room, but she detained Harper. "We'll need to have each one of you fill out a Gunshot Wound Report Form."

Funny how you can hear capital letters in people's voices, I thought.

"Come with me, sir." She glanced at me. "Just wait here. Someone will come to get you in a little while."

"I don't want to leave, in case I miss Karaline."

The nurse looked at me, and I thought I saw pity in her eyes. "She'll be in surgery at least eight hours. Maybe ten."

"Ten hours? You have to be kidding."

She started to reply, but Harper held up a hand. "It was an abdominal wound, Peggy, and no telling what else was involved. They'll have a lot of cleanup to do in there."

"Cleanup?" I hated sounding so dense.

"The intestines are in there, stomach, things like that. Anyplace the bullet went through spilled its contents. It'll have to be cleaned and sewn up. Then they'll have to clean out the whole abdominal cavity." And on that happy note, he told me he'd be back as soon as he could.

Like I had anything else to do but wait. And worry. By this time, Karaline must have already been in surgery for an hour. I put in a quick call to Gilda and asked her to let the folks as the Logg Cabin know what was going on. The whole time I was talking I kept hoping the surgeon would come through the door with a report on Karaline's complete recovery. I knew it wasn't going to happen, but I couldn't stop myself from wishing.

I hated to admit it even to myself, but I had a deep-seated fear she wasn't going to make it. About the third time I bounced out of my seat to pace around the otherwise-empty waiting room, Dirk planted himself in front of me.

"Sit. Bide a while," he said. "Ye canna help Mistress Karaline by falling into a hundred pieces yoursel', now, can ye?"

A million pieces, I thought. I'd tried to tell him once about how much a million was, but he hadn't quite grasped the concept of a number that large. *Like sand grains on a beach*, I'd said. But Dirk had never seen the ocean. A hundred was more than enough as far as he was concerned. *We ha' no need for any more of a number*, was his comment, and I hadn't been able to answer him. I didn't have an answer now, either. I leaned my head slowly, tentatively forward until my hairline touched his plaid, right next to the branch of antler that formed his kilt pin. I felt his capable hands flowing gently over my shoulders. "God bide ye," he said. "She will be well," and I felt inestimably comforted.

* * *

Harper returned from the bowels of the hospital maybe half an hour later, accompanied by a woman in a gray suit. She gathered me up and ushered me out into the hall.

At the door I turned back. "Stay here, will you?"

"I canna. Ye have the shawl."

"Don't worry," Harper said. "I'll wait for you."

Something in his tone of voice sounded . . . uh . . . *weighted* somehow, as if there were a meaning I wasn't privy to. I nodded, waited for Dirk to drift through the doorway, and followed the gray suit down the hall. She took me back to the same place Harper had been, or so she said, where I filled out a form as well. They apparently wouldn't take Harper's word for it since all his knowledge was secondhand. He hadn't seen the shot. He hadn't seen the shooter in action. I wondered if they'd ask Karaline to fill out a form once she was back from surgery.

I sure hoped I'd never be called on to testify in a trial. How, with a ghost as an almost constant companion, could I possibly tell the truth, the whole truth, and nothing but the truth? I wrote my highly edited answers, handed the paper to the woman, and we followed her back to the waiting room where I sank onto a hard couch facing Harper, who sat on an equally hard one. He didn't say a word, other than, "Welcome back."

I nodded. A few minutes later, Dirk, his kilt swirling around his legs, stopped at the end of the little table between the two couches. He looked at Harper, whose forehead rested in his hands, and at me. He raised an eyebrow.

What? I mouthed.

He crooked his forefinger and wiggled it at me by way of answer. "Huh," I said without uttering a sound.

Dirk pointed to Harper, pointed to me, and back at Harper.

"Go to him. Let him comfort ye," he said, and his voice was so soft I could almost feel his thoughts about Peigi, his ladylove—so long dead, but never *really* dead since she lived in his heart.

I stood, almost in a daze, bypassed the coffee table, and sat next to Harper. He raised his head from his hands. His charcoal eyes were shadowed, sorrowful. He really had lost a lot of weight recently. He put an arm around me and pulled me closer against his side. I nestled my head against his shoulder, watching as my sweet, gentle, lonely ghost turned his back and walked to the other side of the room.

Harper stepped out of the room and approached the little desk just down the hall. The volunteer behind it looked up expectantly. "We're going to grab a bite to eat. If there's any word about Ms. Logg, would you be able to send word to the cafeteria?"

"Of course. I'll be happy to do that. I'm sure you and your wife must be very worried."

That sounded so good to Harper, he didn't correct her. He just collected Peggy and headed downstairs. They both picked chicken potpie. It was surprisingly good.

After the first few bites, Harper asked, "So, what's been going on for you other than all"—he waved his hand around—"all this?"

Peggy swallowed, wiped her lips, and thought for a moment. "You saw Scamp? The little Scottie dog?"

Harper nodded and relaxed as he listened to the saga—rehab, Sherpa bag, dog on the ottoman in the window.

When she wound down, he asked, "Anything else?"

"No . . . Oh, yeah. Karaline and I went to UVM Monday before we knew Dr. W was dead."

"Why? You plan to enroll?"

She flicked her fingers at him, as if they were dripping with water. "It was a side trip, really. Karaline had to go to Kittredge Foodservice Equipment in Winooski to get a mixer, but Chester Kerr—he's the manager—said they didn't have any and there wouldn't be one for another eight days. Because of the storm."

Harper nodded. Peggy wrinkled her forehead. "I guess I'll have to go back up there Tuesday and pick it up for her. I'll get D—" She looked up over his shoulder at something. "I'll get somebody to go with me."

"Who?"

"Oh, my dad or somebody. So, anyway, we took a side trip to UVM so Karaline could look in on Dr. W, only he wasn't there, of course."

Harper loved watching her face. It was so animated. He only half listened to her until she mentioned a six-foot invisible rabbit. "What did you say?"

She looked at him and took a last bite of her potpie. "I said that PD said they'd almost called her Rabbit instead, because she was always invisible."

"Called who Rabbit?"

"Stripe. Haven't you been listening?"

"Sorry. I got confused there. Why was PD called Stripe?"

"No. PD stands for Polka Dot, and Stripe was a childhood nickname." Peggy bunched up her napkin. "I'm done here. Can we go back upstairs now?"

It took seven more hours. I was pulled out of sleep by Dirk's excited comment. "The chirurgeon is coming!" A woman of medium build appeared, wiping her forehead with a green square of cloth that matched her scrubs. I swung my feet off the highly uncomfortable couch and sat up. As I did so, I had the distinct impression that my head had been pillowed in Harper's lap, but by that time he was already on his feet.

She gave us her name, which I promptly forgot, and motioned to Harper to sit back down. She took a seat herself on the facing couch. "I removed one intact bullet," she told us.

I nodded. "There was only one shot."

She looked at me, registering my comment, but continued with her own train of thought. "From everything I could see, the bullet does not appear to have fragmented inside Ms. Logg's body." I reached for Harper's hand. That possibility had never occurred to me.

She looked at Harper. "Did you fill out the gunshot wound report form yet?"

One-handed, since I was clutching his other hand, he pulled out his ID and showed it to her. "Yes. I'm a police officer. I know the ropes."

"What about you?"

I nodded and raised my spare hand, palm open wide. "I never saw a gunshot wound before today," I said, "except in movies."

I couldn't quite interpret her expression, but I was fairly certain she thought the idea of a *realistic movie* was an oxymoron.

"Have you contacted the rest of your family?"

My family? Why would I do that? Oh, wait. My family. I was her sister.

Harper looked at me. I shook my head, terrified suddenly that she was going to say Karaline was dying.

"They'll take her to the intensive care unit," Dr. Whatever-Her-Name-Was told us. "She can't have visitors yet, but I'm guardedly optimistic."

I pulled away from Harper. "What on earth does that mean?"

The surgeon clasped her hands together in front of her. "It means I'm fairly certain she won't die tonight. I'm sorry I can't predict the future." She gave me a minute to pull my last hankie out of my parka pocket and blow my nose. It was really gross by this point, but I figured the doctor had seen worse. So had Harper, probably, being a cop. "Your sister is healthy, well nourished, and appears to have a strong heart. It may take her a long time to recover completely, but—as I said—I am optimistic."

"Thank you, Dr. Marston." Harper apparently did not have trouble remembering names. "Can you tell us how much internal damage there was?"

"The incision had to be much longer than I ordinarily would like to see, but the bullet did not appear to have impacted any major organs other than the intestines and diaphragm."

"She could hardly breathe," I said.

The doctor nodded. "Was the shooter below her?"

"I . . ." I had to think for a minute. "The cabin is up two steps, and the clearing slopes downward from the cabin before it rises quite a ways up to where the path continues down the mountain. He was at the base of that rise."

The doctor shook her head. "The trajectory went from lower left to upper right."

"She was reaching way up over her head when it happened."

Her face relaxed, as if she just solved a major problem. "That would account for it." She wiped her face again. "Her liver was intact, as I'm sure you know."

Harper nodded. I looked blank. He bent his head a little closer to mine. "If the bullet had hit her liver, she would have bled to death before we got her out of the cabin."

I went a little limp at that. If she'd been standing in a slightly different position, an inch or two to one side . . .

"Spleen, stomach, everything else important was untouched."

"What would be a *spleeeen*?" Dirk's question was only halfhearted. He knew perfectly well I couldn't answer him.

The doctor, unaware of this small interruption, kept talking. "The bullet pierced a number of folds of her intestine and went through the colon multiple times. That was what took most of the time to clean up and repair. It lodged in a rib, resulting in a longitudinal fracture." She drew her finger along her right side in illustration. "I can arrange to have you see the bullet in the X-rays, as long as your sister agrees."

I didn't give a hoot about seeing Karaline's rib. "How soon will I be able to see her?"

She looked at me with great compassion. Or maybe she was just tired after fishing around for a bullet and sewing up my friend's gut for ten hours. "Let's get her through the rest of the night, why don't we? You can call in the morning."

"I don't want to wait that long," I blurted out.

Harper looked at his watch. "Can we call around seven?"

Dr. Whosits nodded.

"Good," Harper said, and squeezed my arm gently. "It's after one in the morning. We can wait a few more hours."

It sounded like an eternity, but I noticed he'd said "we."

Dr. Question Mark seemed to think we'd leave, go home, get a good night's sleep. She had to be out of her mind. I had no intention of leaving the hospital until I could see Karaline, be sure she was alive.

Harper agreed with the doctor, though. He thanked her profusely and turned to me. "Peggy," he said, and my knees went a little wobbly to hear my name on his lips, "whoever that was who shot at you and Karaline, he's—"

"He wasn't shooting at me."

Harper's eyes went sort of pointed-looking, like he was

burrowing into a . . . a cave or something. "I don't know whether he's an experienced sniper or whether he was just lucky, but he could just as easily have hit *you*."

"No, he couldn't. I wasn't by the door. I was looking out the window."

"And what if he'd shot through the glass?"

"Oh." I'd been so worried about Karaline I hadn't thought about much of anything else. I sat down rather quickly.

"Let me take you home," he said.

My heart gave a little leap.

"You can hug your cat and get some rest. If I can, I'll be back over there at seven so we can call the hospital together."

"What do you mean, *if* you can?" Was he trying to give himself an out?

"I'll head to the police station as soon as I drop you off."

"You will? Why?" Hadn't he written all his reports about the gunshot?

"There's a killer out there. It's my job to catch him if I can."

Can't you let Murphy do that? I thought, but I didn't say it.

When Harper opened the car door for me, I waited long enough for Dirk to scoot in and vault over the seat into the back. "Thank you," I said, preparing to slip into the passenger seat. Harper stepped closer to my right shoulder, close enough that I thought he might be leaving the next step up to me.

Dirk cleared his throat, loudly, in the backseat. "Are we no going soon?"

Maybe I didn't want a kiss with an ambivalent ghost making comments. First he practically pushed me into Harper's lap; now he wanted to get me away from Harper as fast as possible.

As close as I'd felt to that ghost of mine all afternoon and evening, maybe I'd wrap him up again in the shawl just for a little peace and quiet.

"I'm glad I could be there for you today, but now I have to go play cop," Harper said as I hesitated, and the magic was broken.

"Me, too." I climbed into the front seat. *What a dumb response.*

Settling behind the wheel, he fastened his seat belt. "I'll need for both you and Karaline to sign witness statements."

"Whenever you need me I'll be available." I hoped that didn't sound like what I thought it might have sounded like. And maybe what I wanted it to sound like.

Harper was surprised to find Fairing at the station.

"I thought you pulled the day watch this week." She rubbed her hands over her face, covering an enormous yawn. "Things went all screwy while you were gone. We have us a prisoner."

Harper's step faltered. "Did you find him?"

"I don't know what you're talking about." Her voice turned to vitriol. "Mac ordered me to arrest Emily Wantstring."

"He what? That son of a . . ."

"My sentiments exactly. Murphy and I both argued with him, but he was absolutely convinced she did it."

"Let me guess—he finally read the report?"

"Yep," she said. "The big fat insurance policy."

"Where is she?"

Fairing nodded toward the day room. "What Mac doesn't know, he can't argue about. I gave her a blanket and told her she could stretch out on the couch in there. Last time I checked she was sound asleep."

"I'm glad you didn't lock her up. She didn't do it."

"I know that. I'm sure there're some white-haired people who commit murder, but I sure don't think this one did."

"You're not listening to me, Fairing. I said she did not do it. About"—he glanced at his watch—"thirteen hours ago, I saw the person who did."

After he explained, Fairing asked, "You want to take her home, since you're the one who cleared her?"

Harper stretched his arms up over his head and groaned as his back popped. "No, you do it. I need to sit here and think."

She stood and walked toward the closed door of the day room. "She kept asking me if we'd found her husband's scarf. You know anything about that, Sherlock?"

"No clue, Watson."

36

Monday Blues

I managed to doze off and on for a few hours, but deep sleep wouldn't come. I kept seeing red blood and Karaline's ashen gray face. At five thirty I sat up in bed and called Harper. I got his voice mail. "I can't wait," I said after the beep. "I'm heading for the hospital. I'll let you know as soon as I learn anything."

It vaguely occurred to me that as a police officer, he might be able to get more information than I could. No. Wait. I was her sister, right? They'd tell me the truth.

When I opened my bedroom door, Shorty materialized and meowed so plaintively at me, I scooped him up for a big, fuzzy, purry hug. I could feel my muscles relax. *Hug your cat,* Harper had said. How had he known I needed to do this? Maybe if I'd picked up Shorty last night, I might have slept better.

Dirk waited at the bottom of the stairs. "Did ye sleep?"

"Not much," I said. "How about you? Were you able to settle, or did you pace all night?"

"I didna pace at all." He nodded his head at Shorty. "Wee Short One laid himself down beside me on the arm of yon chair, and I didna want to stand for fear of waking him."

"Yeah," I said. "Shorty's good at trapping people in one place. I'd better feed him, and then I want us to go to the hospital."

"I didna think ye would wait until seven o' the clock."

Once Shorty had settled into his food bowl, purring contently—how could somebody swallow and purr at the same time?—I walked into the hall and reached for my parka, recoiling at the last moment as the bloodstains came into focus. "I need to get cold water on this." I yanked it off the peg. "Why didn't I do this last night?"

"Mayhap because ye were so exhausted, ye were almost asleep on your feet."

"If I was that pooped, why couldn't I sleep last night?"

"Ye did sleep, but the only thing ye remember is the times ye awoke."

"Quit being so logical. It's too early in the morning."

I started dunking the bloody parts of the parka into cold water in the kitchen sink, scrubbing and squeezing each section before moving on to the next.

Finally I ran fresh water and left it soaking. Why was I even trying this? It would have to go to the cleaners.

"Let's go."

Thank goodness I had a second parka.

Harper stepped out of the station restroom and headed toward his desk. A little red circle winked on his phone. One voice mail. Peggy. What was she doing calling him at—he looked at the time listed beside her name—5:32 in the morning? He played the message, hit *Call Back*, and listened to her phone switch to voice mail. Wasn't it possible to speak with a real person anymore?

He called the hospital, identified himself, and asked to speak with someone in the ICU. When a somewhat harried-sounding voice came on the line, he identified himself again and asked to be notified when Karaline Logg was available. The voice interrupted and told him she'd been moved to third floor.

So he went through the routine again, asking to be contacted when Ms. Logg was available for . . . He didn't want to use the word "interrogation." That made her sound like a suspect. "Can you call me when she's awake? I'm working on tracking down who shot her, and I need her side of the story."

He wondered how long it would be.

The good news was that Karaline had been moved from the ICU to a regular floor. Even so, I was getting sincerely sick and tired of hospital waiting rooms. Dirk had no pity for me, doggone him. "Ye should ha' listened to the constable and waited." He sank down on the chair next to me, but I stood and paced again.

"I want to be here when she wakes up," I said. "The Scot-Shop's closed on Mondays, so I don't have anything else to do."

"Do you always talk out loud to yourself?"

I spun around, uncomfortably aware of what had happened the last time someone walked in on me like that. Dirk had already whipped out his *sgian-dubh* and bounded to my left side. I guessed sitting down like that he couldn't get to his dagger fast enough. "You startled me," I said.

"Sorry." She wore scrubs, but no name tag that I could see. "Do you work here?"

"I dinna trust her."

She nodded, but seemed to be looking around for something. "I start my shift soon. Is there somebody else . . ." She let the sentence hang.

I glanced at Dirk. "Somebody else? What do you mean?"

"It's just that you were talking to someone when I came in. I know you were. It's a man, I'm pretty sure." She scanned the room and her gaze settled, unfocused, near my left shoulder. She tilted her head to one side. If she'd had black hairy ears, she would have looked like Scamp. Her whole body quivered for a moment, like a dog shaking water off its fur. "Sorry," she said again. "Sometimes I *feel* things."

"I can see that."

"It's hard, working in a hospital where so many people . . ." Again, her sentence trailed away to nothing.

"She was about to say, *Where so many people die*, was she no? D'ye think she kens I am here?"

"I know somebody's here," she said, but I couldn't tell whether she was answering him or just continuing her thought from before. And there was no way to find out without clueing her in. I wasn't sure I wanted to do that.

"Dinna tell her," Dirk said.

I didn't dare answer him.

A nearby door opened and a woman wearing the ubiquitous scrubs, these with little purple doggies romping all over them, said, "Hi, Deidre." Without skipping a beat she looked at me. "Are you Ms. Winn?"

When I said yes, she motioned for me to follow her. "Ms. Logg is awake and asking for you."

At the door, I glanced back. Deidre was watching me—only she wasn't looking directly at me. She was looking directly at Dirk. The obvious confusion on her face convinced me she hadn't seen him, but she knew.

* * *

"Harper here." He listened to the voice on the other end of the phone. "Thank you. I'll be there as soon as I can."

"That sounds promising," Fairing said.

"Sure is. Logg is awake and alert."

"Drive safe."

"Always do."

"It's . . . about time . . . you two came to visit." Karaline's voice was weak, but had that old ring of her indomitable spirit.

The nurse pointed a finger at her. "I'm not visiting, as you well know. Now, I'm only going to let your sister stay for about five minutes." Turning to me on her way out, she pushed a blond hair away from her forehead and said, "Don't tire her."

"I wouldn't dream of it."

She closed the door and Karaline smiled. "I wonder what . . . she'd have said . . . if I'd said, *Thank . . . goodness the ghost is here*? . . . And what's . . . this *sister* thing?"

"It was the only way they'd let me in. Family only."

"Yeah, well . . . you both qualify."

Dirk leaned close to her. "I am so pleased ye are well, Mistress Karaline."

I took her hand and stroked across the knuckles. "You had me scared there."

"It wasn't . . . like I planned it." She had to pause. "It hurts . . . to breathe."

"That's because your diaphragm got nicked."

"Dinna try to talk, Mistress Karaline."

"Okay. I'll just sit here . . . while you tell me . . . what you found on it."

"On what for aye?"

"On the USB."

"What are you talking about, K?"

"Didn't you . . . get it? The . . . one over . . . the door?"

I took a step back and studied her for a moment. "I have no earthly idea what you're talking about."

"Dr. W's . . . flash drive. Remember . . . I told you I'd . . . found it, and then I . . . reached for it . . . above the . . . door-frame . . . and then the . . ."

"You didn't tell me it was a USB. You just said you'd show me something and then you got shot and I couldn't think about anything except getting you to safety."

"We maun return to the wee cabin."

"I don't want to leave Karaline."

Dirk skewered me with one of those looks of his. "Do ye want to find our wee murderer?"

Oh. Well, when he put it that way.

"It's tucked . . . on the . . . ledge . . . above . . ." Karaline struggled to breathe, and something beeped beside the bed. A little red light flashed on.

"On the doorframe. I get it."

"On . . . right . . . side."

The door opened. "Time's up. I'll have to ask you to leave."

"It hasn't been five minutes yet."

"I know, but look at those lights."

"Hurry . . . back . . . let me . . . know . . . wh . . ."

The nurse hurried forward. "You've overextended yourself. I was afraid this would happen." She didn't exactly glare at us—at me—but Dirk and I scooted out as quickly as we could.

"We will return, Mistress Karaline," Dirk said as the door closed behind us.

As we pulled out of the parking lot, I saw Harper stride toward the front door. *I really ought to go back in there and tell him what she said about the other USB drive*, I thought.

But, of course, I knew that was nonsense. Karaline would tell him. Anyway, I wanted to get up to that cabin and back again as soon as possible.

Harper took the stairs three at a time. He was slightly out of breath when he approached the nurses' station. That was what happened when he had little or no sleep. He pulled out his badge and showed it to the dark-haired woman behind the desk. "Harper, Hamelin Police. Someone called me. I'm here to speak with Karaline Logg."

A blonde in purple scrubs with a busy pattern looked up from a cabinet against the wall. She adjusted the stethoscope around her neck. "She can't talk. She's been sedated."

"I was told she was awake."

"She was, about ten minutes ago, but she had a bit of excitement and needs to rest now."

"Could I just have a word with her?"

The nurse lowered her head so her eyes focused on him above the steel rims of her glasses. "She's asleep. You can try again this evening."

The dark-haired woman spoke up. "I'm sorry you came all this way for nothing."

37

Hearts Carved on a Tree

Fairing pushed her chair back from her desk. "Come look at this map, Harper." She walked to the far side of the room and he joined her. "You saw the guy in the face mask here, right?" She pointed.

He moved her finger up a quarter of an inch. "About there," he said.

She stuck a small yellow adhesive dot to the spot. "He'd have to have come out here." She indicated the bottom of the trail. "We combed the whole area. No sightings of anybody matching what little description you could give us."

"Short guy unknown race on cross-country skis unknown make in a black ski mask with ice around the mouth hole; medium gray parka of unknown brand; maroon ski shoes ditto," Harper recited. "You don't think that was enough?"

She snorted and pointed back to the map. "Motels here, here, here, and here. No overnight guests except for couples

the motel owners knew, two or three women, and one man—
don't get excited. The guy was six and a half feet tall."

"Couldn't be the one on skis."

"I didn't think so."

"Did you check the bed-and-breakfast places?"

She raised one expressive eyebrow. "You think we have
the staff for that? Do you know how many there are?" She
didn't expect an answer. "I didn't think somebody bent on
murder would stay in a B and B. Too much chance of being
identified. Motels are more anonymous."

Harper nodded. "What about somebody who lives here
in Hamelin?"

"A local," Fairing said. "That should narrow it down. I
doubt there's more than ninety or a hundred gray parkas in
town. Maybe a hundred and fifty with maroon ski shoes."

Harper raised his eyebrows.

"Dawson Mercantile had a sale on the things last summer, remember? He said he must have sold a hundred pairs.
Maroon was the only color he'd put on sale."

"That's a big help."

It didn't take Dirk and me long to get to the cabin. Well,
almost an hour, but that was so much faster than the last
time we'd been on this trail.

I had to drag one of the chairs over to the door so I could
reach the ledge, but there it was, a little gray USB. Hard to
believe such a minuscule thing had caused such a major uproar.

We made it down the trail in less than half an hour—that
had to be some kind of a record.

As soon as I reached home, I rushed toward my office.
"Come on, Dirk. We need to see what's on here."

A minute or two later he asked, "What does the wee box mean?"

"Crapola on toast. It means this file is password protected."

"*Pass word p'teckted*. What would that mean?"

I double-clicked on the other three files; two of them opened, but they didn't seem too promising. Just a bunch of jumble about protozoa and such. The final file needed a password, too. I was in no mood for either biology or a computer lesson. "It means we can't see what's on here. Dr. Wantstring locked the important files."

"How do ye know 'tis important?"

"Because he wouldn't have locked them otherwise."

Dirk craned to look behind my iMac where I'd inserted the thumb drive. "Where did he hide the wee key?"

I clicked on the little *eject* symbol. "Hopefully in Karaline's head. She might be able to figure this out." I slid my laptop out of the deep drawer where I usually stowed it and checked the charge. 89 percent. Good enough.

Karaline was waiting for lunch.

"Aren't they feeding you intravenously? I wouldn't think your intestines would work after being shot like that."

She patted her abdomen. "I'm on liquids only. It's tender, but the doctors are amazed at my recovery so far. I should be out of here by Thursday or Friday."

"You're kidding."

"Nope." She pointed at Dirk. "We have a built-in, invisible healer here. And he does a great job. Too bad we can't patent him."

"What would be . . ."

She laughed. "Never mind, Dirk. It just means I'm eternally grateful to you for saving my life."

"Enough syrup. Your breathing sounds a whole lot better, so if you're up to it"—I held up the USB and slung my laptop bag off my shoulder—"let's get busy. I tried to open it, but three of the five files need passwords."

I positioned the computer and moved the adjustable table so she could reach it, but so it wouldn't press against her tummy. She studied the file listing, glanced through the two open files, and said, "Very interesting."

"What?"

"The test results on this microbe—it's the one PD said he was working on—show a high degree of . . ."

"Speak English, please."

"It killed his lab rats, and it looks like it would kill people, too."

"He was going to kill people?"

"Don't be ridiculous, P. Anyway, he said it was easy to neutralize." She clicked on one of the three locked files and got the warning box. "I know what Dr. W's password probably is."

"You do?"

"Yep." She smiled a crooked little grin. "He always used the same one. *EF&MW*, all capital letters."

"What did it mean?"

She shrugged and winced just a little. I thought there might not be quite as much healing as she'd claimed. "It's like what he'd do for a girlfriend, or in this case, his wife. See—MW, his initials. And EF. I thought it was kind of like somebody carving his and his girl's initials on a tree trunk inside a great big heart."

"Mistress Emily," Dirk said.

Karaline nodded as she typed in the password. The file opened.

"Oh my God," she said after reading for only a few seconds. "It's the third jungle book."

"What?" I moved the laptop slightly so I could focus on the screen. "Jungle Passion," I read, "by Denbi Marcas. Who's Denbi Marcas?"

"Denbi Marcas!" Why did Karaline sound excited?

"What," Dirk asked, "would be a *jungle*?"

"You don't know about jungles?"

He shook his head.

"You know Latin and Greek, but you never heard of a jungle?"

"Leave him alone, P. He grew up in Scotland. They don't have jungles. Is the whole book there?"

I looked at the bar along the bottom of the document. "It says it has 79,254 words. Does that sound like a complete book?"

She nodded. "That's about right."

I scrolled down a page and read aloud. "*Chapter 1. July 23rd, 1782. I honestly don't think I would have fallen for him so hard if he'd kept his shirt on. Those abs of his, sweat-drenched as they were in the steamy rainforest, shone in the light of the full moon.* What on earth is this drivel?"

"Drivel? It isn't drivel," Karaline said. "Do you have any idea who Denbi Marcas is?"

I looked at her blankly.

"You don't read romance novels, right? Otherwise you'd know. Denbi Marcas is only the best-selling author of dozens of romances. She's a prolific writer. She turns out maybe three books a year."

"You read romance? I didn't know that. You never told me."

"You never asked me."

"What would be *romance*," Dirk asked, and then corrected himself. "That is to say, I ken weel enow what r-r-romance is"—the *r*'s fairly rolled off his tongue—"but I didna think it was something to read. Read *about*, mayhap."

I stopped scrolling to answer him. "It's a type of novel. Book. Story."

Karaline turned my laptop back and kept reading. "She writes historical romance," she said.

"Like that makes it better?"

"Quit being such a snob. You can learn a lot about history reading these. Denbi Marcas always researches her books."

I looked over her shoulder. "How would you know?"

"I've read her interviews. And book jackets."

"What would be—"

"She writes history? In a steamy jungle?"

Karaline scrolled back to the top. "It's set in the 1700s."

"I don't think 'abs' was a term they used in the 1700s, K."

"What would be—"

"And why would Marcus Wantstring have a file with a Denbi Marcas book in it?"

I reached across her as a flash of color on the screen caught my eye. A comment. I let the cursor hover over it. *Abs?* it said. *In 1782? Where on earth did you come up with that one, Denby? Can we change it to shoulders?* The author of the comment was listed as *MW*.

"Denby? What kind of name would that be?"

"Good question, Dirk. Wish I knew the answer."

"The only Denby I know of—with a *Y* at the end," Karaline said, "is Denby Harper, that other UVM professor I mentioned. Dr. H, but he died recently. I read about it in an alumni bulletin."

I looked at Karaline. She looked at me. "Pen name," we said at the same time.

Dirk looked blank. "What," he asked, "would be a *pin name*, and what is in the ither wee boxes with a lock?"

"Good question. I'll tell you in a second." She fiddled with a few keys, and a second file popped open. The lurid book cover featured DENBI MARCAS in caps and the title in bright red letters.

"Where do you suppose they came up with a model with pecs like that?"

"What would be *pec*—"

"It's photoshopped," Karaline assured me.

"What would be *foto*—"

I had to agree. The polish on the red-lacquered nails on the hand that clung to his biceps never would have lasted in any jungle I'd ever heard about. "Did they even have nail polish in the 1700s?"

Karaline ignored my question. "It's a very good pen name."

"Yeah, but what do you think they do if they have to sign books at a bookstore? Two middle-aged men show up?"

"No wonder they were keeping it a secret," Karaline said.

But then we both seemed to remember at the same time that neither of these men would ever sign another book.

"What," Dirk sounded aggrieved, "would be in the ither box?"

But the password wouldn't work on this one.

"Wait," I said. "What on earth could this novel have to do with that other file about the lab rats?"

"Maybe it was research. Some sort of jungle parasite that takes over the world."

"In a romance novel?"

"Yeah. You're right. They're not connected."

Dirk made one of those growly sounds deep in his throat. "Ye twa have caprine minds."

"Kapreenuh? What's that?"

He muttered something. It sounded like "goat brain."

Harper picked up on the first ring. All this time and he still had no leads. Gray parka, black ski mask, short guy with maroon ski shoes. That was it.

The voice on the other end, female and no-nonsense, identified herself. "Tolly Smith, lieutenant, Burlington Police. You the one who called our station about the murder of Marcus Wantstring?"

"Right. I did."

"His house in Burlington was broken into sometime late last Saturday or early Sunday." She gave the dates. "A neighbor found it when she went in to water the plants. She finally got around to reporting it this morning. Said she thought we ought to know about it. Name's unusual—I recognized it and put it together with the homicide. The neighbor said the windowpane on the back door was broken. With this being glove weather, I doubt there'll be any fingerprints, particularly since the neighbor's husband nailed a plywood panel over the door."

"Why?"

"Good Samaritan, I guess. Didn't want anybody else walking in."

"You think it's connected to the murder." Harper wasn't asking a question. That was the way any cop worth his— her—badge would think.

Smith didn't even bother to answer. "Could you connect with the wife on that end? If she needs to come up here— and that's your call—your job is to convince her."

"Convince her? Why would I need to do that?" Harper

pulled out the combined Hamelin and Arkane phone book, all 126 pages of it, including the business listings at the back, and thumbed to the Ws.

"Get this. The neighbor said Mrs. Wantstring hadn't washed her dishes before she left. Didn't want us seeing the mess, so she told the neighbor not to call us."

"So why did the neighbor call today?" He dropped the phone book back in the drawer. He could get the number from the police report.

"Neighbor said she got to thinking about it and wondered if it had anything to do with Mark Wantstring's death. You think? So she called. It's only been a week since she discovered something had happened."

"Does Mrs. Wantstring know she called you?"

"No idea. Can you imagine a woman afraid we'd think less of her if she hadn't washed her china?"

A blur of images crossed Harper's mind, the hundreds of crime scenes he'd visited, mostly when he was on the force in Poughkeepsie. He'd seen so much devastation. And Emily Wantstring was embarrassed about dirty dishes? "I'll talk to her and get back to you. Did the neighbor know if anything was taken?"

"Laptop, she was sure about, but didn't know of anything else."

Why hadn't Emily Wantstring called the Hamelin Police to report that there'd been a break-in at her house in the city? Did she really think it had no bearing on the murder of her husband? Why hadn't she mentioned it while she was here at the station for hours on Thursday?

He knew she wasn't the one with the gray parka, but was there a possibility she'd hired gray parka to murder her husband and steal his laptop? Then she might not want anyone to know about the break-in, although he couldn't for the life of him imagine why she'd think that way. The Vermont estate tax didn't apply unless the estate was valued at 2.75 million dollars, and from what he'd seen, the Wantstrings didn't look like they had that kind of money. Of course, she'd have five million soon enough, but not if she'd murdered her husband for it.

Had he been wrong about her, or could it really have been something as stupid as embarrassment over dirty dishes? Good thing the neighbor was a little more civic-minded.

He wrapped up the conversation with Smith and checked the address in the file. He picked up his parka. Something like this was better done in person.

The phone rang as he reached the door, but Moira routed it to Murphy, so he kept going.

Emily peeked out the window beside her front door. It was that nice policeman. She couldn't remember his name. *Pianist* or something like that. She knew it was something having to do with music. Somebody who played an instrument. Her throat tightened, and she had to make a conscious effort to breathe.

"Come in, Officer. Did you find the scarf?" She didn't want to admit she couldn't remember his name. The other one, the one who had talked to her last week at the station, had a very Irish name. Sergeant Patrick. Was that right? And Miss Fairing. She remembered that one.

"Scarf? No. I . . . I'm Captain Harper."

Harper, not Pianist. She showed him into the living room and motioned to the blue couch. She sat on the yellow one. "What can I help you with?"

He unzipped his parka but didn't take it off. "I understand someone broke into your house in Burlington."

"How did you . . . That is, I mean . . . yes. My neighbor said she thought someone had taken my husband's laptop."

"Was there anything else missing that you're aware of?"

"No, there wasn't. I drove up on Monday as soon as Sandra called me. All the china and silver was where it was supposed to be."

"I'm sure you know . . ." He seemed to take a very deep breath.

She admired the smooth flow of air into his lungs. Baritone? No, she decided. He'd be a bass. She loved the way those low notes vibrated. For a moment she wished he would sing her a happy birthday song. Still, it didn't seem right to think about her birthday now that Mark . . . Marcus was gone.

". . . that there's a chance this break-in could be connected to your husband's murder."

"I don't see . . . There's no reason for anyone to kill Mark . . . Marcus. He worked with bacteria, microscopic bugs, silly things like that." Emily couldn't imagine that anyone on earth would find that even interesting except another microbiologist, and there were precious few of those here in Hamelin.

"Is there a chance someone might have felt threatened by something he was working on?"

"Threatened by bug studies? You have to be joking."

"No. I'm afraid there's no joke. Somebody wanted him dead."

"But there's nothing we can do now, is there?"

"There's quite a bit we can do." She could tell he was trying to make his voice as soothing as possible. "The investigation is proceeding, but the break-in at your other house might have given us some clues if you'd let us know right away."

"Are you here to arrest me again?"

Emily thought he looked a little embarrassed, as well he should.

"Mrs. Wantstring?"

"Yes?"

"Is there anything else you haven't told us?"

She looked down at the small wooden puzzle box on the coffee table. "Well . . ."

38

Password Protected

Back at the station, Harper shuffled through a stack of reports. Very few people in Hamelin had known Dr. Wantstring, but those who'd known him had liked him. More people knew his wife, but most of those didn't particularly like her; he could understand why. If somebody from here was the murderer and the motive was personal, why hadn't they killed Emily? And what could the Burlington break-in have to do with this?

He scanned down a few lines on the report. Murphy had checked phone records again to see whether Wantstring's cell had been used in the past two weeks. Nothing since the Saturday when his wife had last seen him. He made a note in the margin and turned to consider the wooden puzzle box sitting in the center of his desk. He'd never had any luck opening those things, and this one had proved just as insoluble.

He picked it up and tried it again, twisting, pushing, rotating. Nothing.

Harper was only vaguely aware of Murphy hanging up the phone, and he sucked in his breath when Murphy materialized beside him. Had he been so engrossed in this box that he'd tuned everything out?

"Fender Lady just called, but that's not what you need to know. Mrs. Wantstring called while you were gone."

"I was just there talking with her."

"You were? She called only a minute or two after you left."

"What did she want?"

"She said she couldn't find her husband's three-ring binder, green. Asked me to look for it."

"Did she say what was in it?"

"She didn't know, but she thought it was important because he always kept it with him."

Harper couldn't recall anything like that on the personal effects list. "Did we have it?"

"No. There weren't any books or writing materials in the cabin. Except for a couple of ballpoint pens he had in his shirt pocket."

"I noticed that."

"They were green. You think he color-coded his pens and binders?"

Harper ignored that one.

"And she says she's missing a scarf, too. Brown."

"I heard about the scarf. We don't have it. But why did she wait all this time to mention the binder?"

"Maybe she really is the murderer. But we haven't found a motive yet. Other than the five million dollars." Murphy laid on the Irish brogue. "And wouldn't I hate to ask Fairing to arrest the poor woman one more time. We can't arrest her without due cause, can we?"

"Why not? We already did once." Harper twirled his blue

pen around on the desk. "Why would he have pens in that cabin if he didn't have anything to write on?"

"I wondered that, too, so I thought—"

"You thought right. Our murderer took any books or papers he found, and maybe that green binder, too, and then broke into the Burlington house to steal a laptop. So, the question is—"

"What was in the binder?" Murphy finished Harper's sentence with what looked to Harper like satisfaction.

"Okay. So what can you deduce from that?" *Good grief,* Harper thought, *I do sound like Sherlock Holmes talking to Dr. Watson.*

"I'd say murder with malice aforethought." Harper raised his eyebrow and Murphy hastened to explain. "That means murder in the first degree, like she planned it ahead of time."

"I know what 'malice aforethought' means, Murphy, but we don't usually hear that term within these hallowed walls. What are you doing, studying to be a lawyer?"

Murphy reddened. "I'm taking some courses online during my off time."

"You want to be an attorney?"

Murphy looked around. Moira was on the phone. Sergeant Fairing looked like she was texting somebody. Murphy straightened his back. "I plan to be chief someday."

Mac'll have to die first, Harper thought.

I could hear Harper's phone switching over to voice-mail mode. "Grrr! Why isn't he available when I need him?" Dirk made a placating sound, but it didn't calm me down. I disconnected. "I'm going to drive over to the police station. He'll have to show up eventually."

"Why do ye not leave him a wee message?"

Dirk had been fascinated by voice mails ever since I'd first introduced him to the concept. Crazy thing was, he was right. I called back, getting my message composed in my mind as the phone rang once, twice.

"Harper here."

"Why did you answer your phone?"

"Because . . . it rang? Is this some sort of trick question?" The undercurrent in his voice made me think maybe he was laughing at me. "I was expecting voice mail."

"I know. I saw that you called."

"I have something I have to show you. It's what Karaline and I were looking for at the cabin."

"I thought you said the gray parka guy took it."

"There was another USB. She was reaching up to pull it off the top of the doorframe when she was shot." I paused. "I don't know if it has any bearing whatsoever on his death, but I thought you ought to know."

"Where are you?"

"In the hospital parking lot."

"Headed in or out?"

"Out. Karaline knew the password to open two of the locked files. We can't get the other one unlocked, so I'm headed to your office."

"Drive safely, but get here as fast as you can."

I started the car, turned to look at Dirk in the passenger seat. "We're going to the police station. Please, please, don't make a single comment while we're there."

I'd halfway expected a smart rejoinder, but Dirk's face was entirely serious. "We maun stop this nathaira. I willna slow ye."

"What's a nathayra?"

"A snake." The *S* came out like a hiss.

* * *

Harper scoffed when I told him Wantstring had kept the same password for twenty years, but eventually he asked, "What was in the files?"

"We could only open two of the locked files. One was a romance novel. The other was the cover art."

He cocked his head to one side.

"The constable looks like the wee black dog when he does that."

"You look like Scamp," I told Harper.

"I appreciate the compliment."

"No, really. He cocks his head like that when he's thinking."

"You can tell when a dog is thinking?"

I pushed my chair back a few inches. "You've never had a dog, have you?"

"I sure did." Harper sounded indignant. "I had a GBBD when I was a kid."

"Gee what? I've never heard of that breed."

"Stands for Great Big Brown Dog. Best kind ever built."

I scoffed. "Not as smart as a Scottie."

He must not have had an answer to that one, or maybe he decided it was time to get back to the subject at hand. "What does a romance novel have to do with Wantstring's murder?"

"He wrote it. With another professor. Somebody named Denby Harper. Same last name as yours. They used a pen name. Denbi Marcas."

Harper got a really funny look on his face. I had no idea what was wrong, but he swallowed, hard, a couple of times. "Romance novel? They wrote a romance novel?"

"This was number twenty-four or twenty-five," I explained. "Karaline wasn't sure how many, but they're a very successful writing team, apparently. If you like that sort of thing." What was wrong with him? He looked like he'd swallowed a black fly. "Anyway, there's another locked file on the thumb drive, and we thought maybe it—and maybe the novel, too—had something to do with why he was killed?" I couldn't keep the question mark out of my voice. The whole idea sounded inane.

Harper shuddered. What on earth was wrong with him? "My . . . Denby . . . Denby Harper was my dad."

"Oh, Harper." I reached for his arm. "I'm so sorry. I had no idea."

"And I"—his mouth took on a stern cast—"had no idea my father wrote novels."

I didn't know what to say. My dad was a woodworker. I knew everything there was to know about him.

"I thought I knew him," Harper said. It made me wonder whether my own dad had any secrets.

After a few moments, during which I traced the blue veins on the back of Harper's hand, he pulled his hand away from me and asked, "Do you know what's in the other file?"

"No. The usual password didn't work, and Karaline couldn't think of another one."

"Fairing's good with computers. Maybe she can crack it." He picked up a small wooden cube and spun it around on his palm.

I reached for it. "I used to love these puzzle boxes when I was a kid."

"You did?"

"Yeah. Where'd you get it?"

"Emily Wantstring found it hidden in a boot."

I looked at him, and I could feel my eyes go out of focus.

"My dad's a woodworker," I said. "He showed me a lot of tricks." I studied the box carefully, touched a finger to it here and there. Twisted something. Applied pressure. Twisted again. Yes.

Inside was a little piece of paper.

M W < 3 E F

Marcus Wantstring loves Emily Fontini. He'd finally changed his password. The one to the final file.

I'm going to marry this woman someday, Harper thought, but he knew better than to say anything too soon. She was a woman who needed time. Time to get used to him. Time to get to know him. Marriage would have to wait.

But the file had nothing to do with the romance novel. It was a draft of a letter to someone named John Nhat Copley, reprimanding him for—Harper sucked in his breath—for complicity in a scheme to promote identity theft, and informing him that he was henceforth—what an old-fashioned word—barred from classes not only in the microbiology program, but the entire biology curriculum.

Harper leaned back in his chair. Identity theft. Was this the answer? Or the key to how to find the answer, how to crack the ring?

Peggy interrupted his thought process. "I need to let Karaline know what's happened, and I have to pick up that SRM20 tomorrow at Kittredge." She laid a hand on his arm. Harper felt it all the way to his toes. "Be careful, will you?"

He touched the tip of her nose with his index finger. "You, too."

I couldn't leave like this. It felt like there was too much still hanging. "Senator Calais," I said. Something niggled in the back of my mind, but I couldn't call it forward.

Harper's gaze sharpened. "She's the one who got knifed."

"That's right. She's recovering slowly . . ." *She needs a ghost*, I thought, and smiled at Dirk, who hovered nearby listening.

That *something* that had been bothering me clicked. "You don't suppose . . ."

"What?"

"I was just thinking. Somebody tried to assassinate her shortly after Dr. W was killed."

"And?" Harper sounded guardedly optimistic, I thought, borrowing Dr. Marston's phrase.

"Maybe Dr. W had already tried to call her about this identity theft thing. If her name registered in the *recently called* section of his cell phone, maybe they were afraid to let her live."

"Maybe," Harper said, but he didn't sound convinced.

"I have to drive up to Kittredge in Winooski tomorrow to pick up that mixer for Karaline," I reminded him. "The manager—Chester Kerr is his name. Did I tell you he wears red suspenders all the time? Anyway, he absolutely promised it would be there."

"It might be a good idea for you to call him before you leave."

"I was planning on leaving about six so I don't miss too much ScotShop time."

"He might not open until ten. Call first; then you won't make the trip for nothing."

"You're probably right."

"Get a good night's sleep, Peggy."

Naturally, Dirk was full of questions.

I was almost asleep when I remembered that Emily had told me she'd called UVM on Wednesday, and one of the grad students had told her Dr. W's car was parked there. My last thought before I drifted off was, *I ought to tell Harper about it.*

39

Anyone for Martial Arts?

Tuesday morning, I woke up with a crick in my neck. I must have slept with my head at a funny angle. My stiff neck didn't stop me from eating, though. I shoveled in a huge breakfast and called Kittredge at seven thirty, hoping to hear a voice mail informing me how soon they'd open. Chester answered, and I could imagine his suspenders bursting with pride. "It's here. We had a sewage line get stuck late yesterday, and nobody can get here to fix it and clean up until sometime this morning, so we're closed, but I had to be here for that, and I thought I'd stick around until you got here. Be sure you use the facilities somewhere else, because you won't be able to do it here."

I was pretty sure Chester had a wife. Or sisters.

"Somebody else called a few minutes ago to ask if you were going to pick it up today."

"Really? Do you know who it was?"

"She didn't leave a name."

Karaline. She'd probably called from the hospital. But why hadn't she called me directly? "Well, if she calls back, tell her I'll be there by ten thirty at the latest, probably more like ten."

He said something else. It sounded like, *She called yesterday, too*, but his words sounded choppy. I looked at my phone. Two percent. Phooey. I said good-bye, hoping he'd hear me, and plugged it in. If I dressed fast, I could make it.

I wouldn't say I set a world record, but I was at my front door in only a few minutes. "Come on, Dirk. Let's leave."

"Will ye call the constable to let him know ye are leaving?"

"No, he may still be asleep. Here, you carry the shawl while we drive over to Karaline's to pick up her SUV."

Emily woke early. She'd been doing that ever since Marcus died, almost as if she were taking on his habits. He was always up early. He always ate an enormous breakfast—which he cooked himself. He always walked to work. Emily's breath caught.

He always walked to work. Always. So why had that grad student said his car was there? She hadn't questioned it at the time, but they only had one car, and Emily had used it to drive to Burlington after the break-in. So Marcus couldn't have driven it to UVM. He couldn't have, anyway, because that was Wednesday, three days after he was already . . .

She reached for the phone. *He won't be up this early*, she thought, *but I'll leave him a voice mail*.

When Harper's phone rang, it took him a moment to bring his thoughts back to the present. "Harper here."

"Oh."

The voice sounded flustered. "Can I help you?"

"I thought I'd get your voice mail. This is Emily."

Harper listened to what she said, but he didn't see any problem. People mistook one car for another all the time. "Thanks for letting me know," he finally said. "I'll look into it."

He wrote himself a little note, knowing all along he'd never do anything with it. He pulled his in-box toward him and lifted the stack of three or four items, most of which he knew had been there for days. He slid the note underneath. The papers right above it were fastened with one of those round, curly paper clips. He never used those. Give him a jumbo gem clip any day.

He pulled the clipped items out, saw it was Fairing's fender file, and laughed. The young officer reminded him of Sarah, his little sister. Not so little, he reminded himself, and started to jot a note to call Sarah tomorrow on her twenty-ninth birthday, but the driver's license photo of a guy in suspenders caught his eye and stopped him in mid-phrase. Peggy had been talking about suspenders. Some guy at the food equipment place.

He looked through the item. Owner of possible dent-and-run. Cessford Kerr. Home address in Winooski. Two other possibles, guy named Featherstone lived in Bennington, and woman named Harvey was from Burlington.

Winooski. The equipment place was in Winooski. What had Peggy called the manager? Chester Kerr. Cessford Kerr? Blazing badges, was she driving right into the clutches of the gray parka guy? He checked weight and height on the license and compared them to his memory of the gray parka on skis. Could be.

He stood and walked to the wall map. It wasn't far from the bottom of the Perth trail to where the fender bender happened. They could be connected.

He called Peggy, but her phone rang five times before it went to voice mail.

He looked up the Kittredge address and plugged it into his GPS.

"The sun, 'tis well above the horizon. Should ye not stop and call the constable?"

We'd made good time. I'd probably be there by ten thirty. "Why are you so anxious to have me call him?"

"I dinna like ye being out here wi' no one knowing where ye are."

"You know where I am. That's good enough for me. With your magic hands, I couldn't be safer."

"Mistress Peggy . . ."

He sounded so serious I glanced over at him.

"Keep your eyn on the road," he ordered. "But ye need to know this: I dinna understand what I did, why my hands . . . I dinna ken if I could do it again."

"Don't worry about it," I told him. "Something in you responded to the need. Karaline is your friend. We both did what we could."

He didn't look pacified, but I didn't know what else to say. I didn't understand it, either.

"All right. You win," I said, pulling into the next scenic overview. "I'll call."

But when I reached for my phone, that pocket on my purse was empty. "Crapola on toast! I left it charging at home."

I pulled back onto the road. "Dirk, I need to talk something through. Are you willing to be a sounding board?"

"I am nae bored."

Once we got that straightened out I said, "I've been thinking."

"Usually a good idea," he said. "One maun think."

"Hush! And quit laughing at me. You remember having lunch with the grad students? Am I crazy or did PD have a brown scarf around his neck?"

"Aye. That he did."

"I think it's the one Emily was telling me about. The one she gave her husband."

"He gave away a wee gift from his wife?"

"No. No, I think . . . This is nuts, but I saw a stain on that scarf."

Out of the corner of my eye I could see him lean forward and look at me. "What are ye saying?"

"I think PD is the killer." Before Dirk could object, I pressed on. "He's short. He would have had to disguise his voice because we'd already talked with him."

"Aye."

"And he has the scarf he stole from Dr. W. Can't you see it all fits together? What do you think?"

"Since my dagger doesna appear to work so weel now that I am deid, I think we maun stay well awa' from the wee bug building."

Harper wanted a perfectly clean, dry road; there was no way he could make any time on a snowy road with icy patches where trees shadowed the asphalt. Maybe she'd have a flat tire. Maybe she'd get hungry and stop for a bite to eat. Just in case, he examined the parked cars in the few towns he went through; he'd recognize her brown Volvo anywhere.

He kept trying her phone. He kept getting voice mail.

He had to stop her before she got to Kittredge.

Between towns, he broke the speed limit by a wide margin.

He was almost there before he thought that he should have called Tolly Smith. She could have had a SWAT team there on a moment's notice.

I pulled into an empty parking lot at Kittredge. I'd probably have to go around back somewhere to get the thing loaded, but for now I wasn't sure just where, so I settled Karaline's SUV fairly close to the front door.

Dirk preceded me into the showroom. I saw—or thought I saw—someone bending over behind the counter, but I was still blinded by the bright sunlight outside. As my eyes adjusted I walked forward calling out, "Chester? Is that you?"

He rose, and everything seemed to happen at once.

It wasn't Chester. Dirk jumped in front of me. Through him, I could see PD in his black ski mask. "You're . . . I recognize you."

"This is for John Knot," he cried—at least that was what it sounded like, and his voice sounded high-pitched with fear, excitement, anger? I couldn't tell and didn't care, because as he shouted, he flung a spray of liquid at me. I could barely see the test tube in his hand—with Dirk in front of me, everything looked hazy.

He whipped off his ski mask, and I gasped, inhaling some of the horrible-tasting liquid. "That's enough microbes to kill a dozen people. You're dead already," said Stripe, "only you can't feel it yet."

By the time Harper made it to Kittredge, his hands were so tight on the steering wheel, he thought he'd have to peel them off, but her car wasn't in the parking lot. He drove past a big white SUV and circled the building just to be sure. In back he saw two cars. One was a gray Ford with a smashed right rear taillight. It had to be Chester's car.

He called Tolly Smith, asked for backup, and reached for his Glock. He knew it was stupid not to wait, but there was no time to delay. Not if Peggy's life was on the line.

Somehow I found my voice. "Wait! Don't do anything." I was talking to Dirk, but Stripe didn't know that. I reached out and touched Dirk's arm. The cool water-like feeling was calming.

"How d'ye know she isna hiding one of those wee cannons?"

He had a point, but I thought maybe Stripe would have used it already if she'd had it with her. After all, she'd shot Karaline without a second thought. "I have to find out what's going on."

"You're going to die—that's what's going on."

I rubbed my other sleeve across my face to get the liquid out of my eyes. "You probably got some on yourself."

I heard tears in her voice. "That doesn't matter. Without John Nhat, nothing isn't worth it anymore."

Poor grammar, a piece of my mind said. "Who the heck is John Knot?"

"Not Knot. His name was John Nhat Copley."

"Was? What happened to him?"

"Wantstring found out what he was doing, and he had to leave. He didn't even answer my last e-mail about the senator. It doesn't matter if I die." There was so much venom in Stripe's voice, every *S* sounded like a hiss.

"The senator? Is John the one who knifed Senator Calais?"

"He . . ." Stripe's voice wavered. "He succeeded?"

"Don't you listen to the news? Of course he didn't succeed. He was arrested."

She snarled and took a step forward.

Dirk must have felt the threat, as well. "Ye wee nathaira. Ye willna last a heartbeat once I get my hands on ye."

I hung on to Dirk. If I had to die, I wanted him nearby to ease the pain. Of course, the one I really wanted at the moment was Harper. Why hadn't I called to say good-bye?

Stripe edged closer. I backed up and pulled Dirk with me.

Harper tried three back doors off the loading platforms. All were locked. The fourth one opened without a squeak. He ducked inside. He wanted to shout her name, but Chester was probably desperate. Harper was bitingly aware that Chester could be hiding in here anywhere, tucked behind any one of these enormous shelves.

The moment he heard voices, though, he moved as quickly and quietly as he could. The door to the showroom was ajar. He listened just long enough to hear what was happening. He stepped into the room.

"Police! Put your hands in the air."

Chester—*wait a minute—how could Chester be a woman?*— raised her hands, but Peggy cried out, "Don't come in here! Don't! She's the one who shot Karaline. She doused me with something deadly. Get away while you can."

That was all Harper needed to hear. He strode toward the woman. He'd find out her name later. "You are under arrest for the murder of Marcus Wantstring. You have the right to remain silent. . . ." The words rolled out without his even having to think of them.

* * *

"Don't come in here," I said, but he didn't pay any attention to me. He started that Miranda thing and stopped only when a voice from the front door said, "I wouldn't worry about it if I were you."

Harper shifted to his left, swinging his gun between both of them. "Hit the floor, Peggy."

Even as I dropped, I had time to register that I'd been wrong about the scarf.

"Like I said," came PD's voice from behind me, "nothing to worry about. I incinerated all your little microbes, Zebra, and substituted an ascosporogenous yeast."

I lifted my head. "A what?"

PD ignored me. "Rather stupid of you not to notice the different color gradation."

Harper didn't know whom to trust.

Not until the woman flung herself forward. "You bastard! I'll kill you!"

Harper couldn't fire, not without the possibility of hitting the wrong person. But he needn't have worried. The woman obviously didn't know karate.

The other one did.

40

Time to Tell

Harper asked me to call an ambulance for the man behind the counter. He didn't have time to say much more, though. I wondered vaguely if I'd be able to get Karaline's SRM20, but Chester still looked in pretty bad shape when the ambulance crew took him away. There was a fair amount of blood where Stripe must have clonked him on the head. Poor guy. I hoped he'd be okay.

Wednesday morning, Harper picked me up early.

I let Dirk slip out the front door before I locked it behind me. But when Harper held his car door for me, he was standing so close I couldn't figure out a way to let Dirk climb in.

Dirk held up the shawl. "Dinna fash. So long as I have my Peigi's shawl, I will be content."

I looked a question mark at him. I could tell Harper was

wondering what the delay was. Dirk swept his hand around, narrowly missing Harper's shoulder, and said, "The snow doesna bother me. I canna get cold. I will take a wee walk while ye are wi' the constable."

"Okay," I said. "I guess we can go. Bye."

Harper looked at me, looked behind him. "Do you always talk to your house?"

"Only when it behaves itself. Otherwise I just fold it up."

Dirk laughed and walked away.

Harper gave me one of those looks I was getting used to. I was going to have to tell him sometime, but I sure didn't know how to begin.

Karaline had already pushed her hospital breakfast out of the way. "Tell me everything," she said before we could even draw chairs close to her bed. "What happened, what did you find out, how did it turn out?"

"Well," I said, "I had a lovely trip up to Winooski."

"Margaret Walter Winn, if you don't tell me right now . . ."

"Your middle name is Walter?" Harper sounded aghast.

"It's Waltera; I was named for my dad. Karaline can't remember the last syllable 'cause she's senile."

She threw a spoon at me.

"Okay. It started when I walked into Kittredge."

"Having forgotten to take your cell phone with you," Harper added. "I was worried about her because I'd figured out that Chester was the ringleader."

"Chester?" Karaline put her thumbs up at her collarbones. "Suspenders?"

"Yep. Chester with suspenders."

"Only *I'd* already figured out that *PD* was our murderer," I said.

"Why?"

"Well, mainly because of the brown scarf he was wearing when we had lunch that day. It was Dr. W's—Emily had given it to him years ago. I saw the brown stain on it, only I didn't register the connection at the time."

"He took Dr. W's scarf?"

"No, Zebra took it and gave it to him to make him look guilty."

"Who's Zebra?" Karaline looked thoroughly confused.

"That's why her nickname was Stripe."

"Are you pulling my leg?"

"No, really," I said. "The best we can figure out is that Zebra—Stripe—was in love with another grad student—his name was John Nhat Copley—and he recruited her into the ID theft ring. When John got caught by Wantstring and thrown out of the graduate program, she tried to track down any other documentation Dr. W might have made about the ring, but the real reason she killed him was as revenge for what he did to John."

Harper patted his hands on his knees, as if underlining my words. "The funniest thing is that she was really upset when she found out the three-ring binder had a novel manuscript in it. She thought she should take it in case it contained some sort of code."

Karaline sank back against the pillow. "Why did they do this whole ID theft thing to begin with?"

Harper leaned forward. "They were making a lot more money at it. That's what it came down to."

Karaline snorted, one of her less-endearing sounds. "Lots of good that'll do them in prison."

I thought Harper might agree wholeheartedly. Instead he just sighed and said, "What a waste."

*   *   *

Two hours later Harper knocked on Mac's door.

"It's about time somebody came. I could have been rotting for all anybody cares. What have you found out?"

Harper closed the door and drew up a chair, one of those stiff, uncomfortable plastic ones—maybe they didn't want visitors to linger—beside the bed, near Mac's right shoulder. Of course, this put Mac in the position of having to turn his head at a sharp angle to look at Harper. Not that Harper was being vindictive.

"We have clear evidence that Wantstring—"

"Who?"

"The victim, remember? We've found evidence that shows he was aware of an identity theft ring."

"What?"

"Identity theft. Credit cards and drivers' licenses. There's a group that's bigger and better organized than most of the penny-ante groups we've come up against in the past. And Zebra Harvey killed Wantstring."

"Killing somebody over credit cards? Zebra? What kind of name is that? You expect me to believe that garbage? Get out of here, Harper. Quit pulling my leg and do some serious work for a change."

Pulling Mac's leg? Great idea. Harper eyed the pulley that held the heavy cast up in the air. Sighing, he restrained himself. Probably not the best move, even though Peggy would think it was funny.

The thought of Peggy made him smile. He put both hands on his knees and pushed himself up to stand. God, he needed a good night's sleep.

Mac would find out soon enough what had happened.

*   *   *

I thought I'd have to wait an hour. Luckily there was a chair in the corridor and I commandeered it. But it was only a couple of minutes before Harper came back out of Mac's room.

He reached for my hand before I stood, and it felt good to have him help me to my feet. "Let's go to the Logg Cabin for breakfast," he said. "There's something important I have to tell you."

I looked into his charcoal eyes. "There's something important I need to tell you, too."

"Good," he said. "We'll trade stories."

"Pancakes first."

"Whatever you want."